Lucas seemed to recognize Kathleen's confusion and his penetrating gaze intensified. He took a step toward her, his nearness causing her heart to pound painfully against her ribcage. It was as if he commanded the air around them, making it impossible for her to breathe in enough oxygen.

"It's not important whether you believe me. It *is* important for you to understand that your daughter is in tremendous danger. She's traveling into dimensions she's unprepared to handle."

His features were taut with suppressed emotion and his eyes burned with an infernal flame. "She must be trained. Right now another force is attempting to control her. She has to be taught to channel her energy, master her talent."

He stepped closer still, his breath warm on her face as heat from his body pressed in around her. "We must act quickly if we are to save Gina. I will need to spend time with her, teach her. I'll need to be near her day and night."

A quick protest rose to Kathleen's lips. Open her home to this man? Impossible. She knew nothing about him. What if he was just another nut?

Still, even as this thought arose, a vision of Gina filled her mind. She closed her eyes, knowing she would do anything, risk everything to find her daughter some peace, to keep her safe from harm. She opened her eyes and looked at Lucas Connelly . . . afraid to give in to him, afraid not to. "Okay."

THE
MAGICIAN

CARLA COOK

LOVE SPELL NEW YORK CITY

To my agent, Laura Peterson.
Thanks for everything.

LOVE SPELL®

June 2002

Published by

Dorchester Publishing Co., Inc.
276 Fifth Avenue
New York, NY 10001

ISBN 0-505-52490-2

The name "Love Spell" and its logo are trademarks of Dorchester
Publishing Co., Inc.

Printed in the United States of America.

Visit us on the web at www.dorchesterpub.com.

THE
MAGICIAN

Chapter One

Gina Marlowe fought sleep. She was afraid to go to sleep. She wasn't scared of bad dreams about monsters that ate little girls, or the spooky shadows that danced on her bedroom wall right before she closed her eyes. She was afraid of flying.

She lay in bed on her back, staring up at the ceiling, fighting sleep, terrified of where it might take her. She said her ABCs softly, over and over again in the singsong fashion her mother had taught her.

Turning over on her side, she heard voices drifting up the stairs from the living room where her mom and Bill were watching television.

Forgetting all about the alphabet, Gina frowned as she thought of Bill. She didn't like him much, although she liked that her mommy was finally smiling again. Mommy hadn't smiled much since Daddy had died.

Bill had helped her laugh again. Gina supposed she should like him for that reason alone. Still, she knew Bill was one of those grown-ups who smiled too much and laughed too hard and always said what a cute little girl she was, but Gina knew deep down he only did those things because he liked her mom, not because he liked her.

Pulling her favorite stuffed rabbit closer against her, she rubbed the furry softness against her cheek and thought about the first time she had flown.

It had been the night of her sixth birthday party. The party had been fun. She'd invited her whole class from school, and almost everyone had come. She hadn't even minded when Kevin Richards showed up. He was the yuckiest boy in the whole school. He'd spent the afternoon making fart noises with his hand under his armpit, then had pretended to throw up as he was eating birthday cake, but she'd refused to let him ruin her special day.

That night she'd gone to bed happy but tired, and she'd fallen asleep almost immediately. That's when it happened. She'd flown out of her body and into a dark, scary tunnel, and there was somebody . . . or something in the tunnel with her, calling to her, forcing her on through the black emptiness.

Gina shivered and hugged Reggie Rabbit tighter. Somehow she'd come back to her body on the bed. She didn't want to go back in that tunnel again. There was something bad in there.

She didn't want to fly again. She was afraid that she'd fly into that tunnel and never, ever find her way back to her bed again. She'd be lost forever.

In the darkness of her bedroom, Gina repeated her alphabet again and again. Fighting sleep. Afraid . . . so afraid.

* * *

Kathleen Marlowe punched the mute button on the remote, silencing the newscaster detailing the tragic aftermath of yet another earthquake in California.

"God, it seems like there's just one natural disaster after another anymore," Bill Abrahms observed as she walked with him to her front door.

"Hmm, it's getting so I hate to turn on the news each night." She smiled self-consciously as he reached out and pushed a strand of her hair away from her forehead.

In the last couple of months there had been more of that . . . the casual touching, the seemingly inadvertent brush of hands, all the signs that usually preceded a deeper intimacy between a man and a woman. It was something Kathleen wasn't ready for, not at this point in her life.

"Bill . . . it's late." She stepped away from him and opened the door. He smiled, the gesture transforming his face from slightly homely to almost attractive.

"Okay, doll. I'm going." He leaned over and kissed her on the forehead, his lips lingering for a fraction too long. Then he turned and left. "I'll call you tomorrow."

She watched as he walked down the sidewalk. Then she closed the door and leaned heavily against it. She was going to have to do something about Bill. The problem was she wasn't sure exactly what she wanted to do.

She knew he was more than a little in love with her, always had been despite his friendship and professional relationship with Sutton. Now that Sutton was gone, Bill's feelings for her were much more blatant, and she knew she would have to deal with them sooner or later.

She locked the door, then went back into the living room and turned off the muted television. At the built-in mahogany bar she splashed a bit of brandy into the bottom of a glass. She curled up on the sofa and waited for the phone to ring.

Theresa called every night between ten and eleven. It had become a nightly ritual since Sutton's death ten months ago. It was as if Theresa, who never spent less than a moment alone, worried about Kathleen in her tragedy-created aloneness.

She also suspected that Theresa had a horrible fear that Kathleen would fall into a relationship with Bill, who Theresa thought was exceedingly dull and uptight. Kathleen smiled. But then Theresa found almost everyone exceedingly dull and uptight.

She leaned her head back on the throw pillows and sipped the brandy. The alcohol deliciously warmed the pit of her stomach.

The familiar sounds of the house comforted her . . . the rhythmic ticking of the grandfather clock in the corner, the hum of the refrigerator from the kitchen, the metallic popping as vents filled with cooled air from the air conditioner.

And yet, she was aware of the absence of sounds as well. No crackle as Sutton turned the pages of the evening newspaper. No *click . . . click . . . click* of his lighter as he lit his pipe. Odd, how she should miss the presence of a man she'd grown so apart from during the course of their eight-year marriage. Odd that the absence of his sounds should fill her with such yawning loneliness.

She jumped as the phone rang. She grabbed the receiver, at the same time spilling a few drops of her drink, then sputtered an unintelligible hello.

"Kath? You okay?"

"Fine. I just spilled some brandy." She grabbed a napkin and dabbed at the spots.

"Ah, you're having your nightcap. That means Dudley Do Right must have gone home."

"Theresa," Kathleen admonished with a smile. "Bill has been very good to Gina and me since . . . since the accident."

"I don't trust a man who has no obvious vices. Bill Abrahms is too good to be true. He probably cross dresses in the privacy of his own home."

Kathleen laughed at the vision Theresa's words suddenly evoked of Bill in black-hued pantyhose and a curly wig. "Theresa, you're horrible."

"I am, and that's why you love me. I gotta go, I've still got a dozen essays to grade before tomorrow. I just wanted to check in with you. I'll see you in the morning in the teacher's lounge."

Kathleen remained on the sofa long after she'd hung up. She and Theresa Langdon had been best friends since the sixth grade. It had been a friendship that had survived different dreams and different lifestyles.

Kathleen had come to Long Island because of the man she had married. Theresa had moved to the same town to start fresh after her third divorce. The friendship that had waned because of distance and the difference in life choices suddenly flourished once again when the two found themselves teaching in the same high school.

Thinking of her job, she finished the last of her brandy and stood. She'd better get to bed if she was going to make the staff meeting early in the morning.

As she went around the downstairs, turning off lights and checking to make certain the doors were locked, she considered selling the big house and moving into a more manageable-sized apartment.

"You could make a small fortune if you sold," Bill had told her again and again.

But she already had a small fortune. Sutton had left her and Gina well provided for, so the promise of easy cash didn't tempt Kathleen. What did tempt her was that the house was huge and drafty and had never really felt like a home to Kathleen despite the ten years she'd lived here.

The house had been Sutton's ancestral home, owned by Marlowes since it had been built in the early 1900s. It seemed almost sacrilegious to sell it to strangers after so many years of it being in one family.

Maybe it was time to redecorate, exchange the heavy, gothic furnishings that Sutton had loved with something up-to-date, airy and light.

She climbed the wide staircase, suddenly exhausted. There were days she wondered why she'd ever decided to try to teach literature to high school freshmen. It had to be some latent streak of masochism.

She stepped into Gina's room, all other thoughts falling away as she smelled the sweet scent of strawberry bubble bath, the subtle fragrance of innocence and childhood.

Ah, sweet Gina. She was the one thing Kathleen and Sutton had managed to get absolutely right. Stepping closer to the bed, Kathleen smiled at the little face illuminated by the Barney night-light.

Gina had gotten the best of Kathleen and Sutton. She had Kathleen's thick, dark hair, Sutton's piercing green eyes, Kathleen's sense of humor and Sutton's keen intelligence. She was Kathleen's heart, her soul, her life.

Kathleen leaned over and gently pressed her lips on the sleeping child's forehead. She frowned as she felt the unnatural coolness of her skin. "Gina?" she whispered.

Her heart thudded in an unnaturally fast rhythm as she watched the little chest beneath the thin pale pink cotton nightgown.

Was it moving with breaths? No. No, it wasn't.

"Gina?" she said loudly. She gently shook one of Gina's shoulders.

The little girl didn't move. No sleep sigh escaped her lips. She didn't protest as Kathleen shook her again, this time more forcefully. Gina's head lolled forward as if her spine was nothing more than a cooked strand of spaghetti. "Gina, wake up for Mommy."

Gina didn't stir. Panic crawled up the back of Kathleen's throat. She yanked Gina into her arms. The child was as unresponsive as a rag doll. "Gina! Oh God."

Something was wrong . . . horribly wrong. Gina wasn't breathing.

Without rational thought, knowing only that her baby was in trouble, Kathleen jerked her out of the bed. The panic that had moments before crawled up her throat exploded throughout her entire body.

Call 911. Call for an ambulance. No, no time. There was no way she could wait for an ambulance. Day after day the papers were full of stories about dying people waiting in vain for the ambulance service that had one of the longest response times in the state.

She raced down the stairs, Gina's weight cumbersome but not slowing her down. She grabbed her purse from the hall tree in the entry, then hurried out to the car.

Her mind shut down, knowing only the need to get help. Hurry. Hurry. Her head screamed as she placed Gina in the passenger seat. She buckled her in, then quickly got behind the wheel and started the engine with a roar.

Driving like a woman possessed, she kept one hand on the wheel and the other stroked Gina's face. Cold . . . so cold. The child's skin radiated a deathlike temperature.

"It's okay, baby," Kathleen repeated over and over again, but it wasn't okay. Why was she so cold? Why was she so unresponsive?

It took her only minutes to reach the emergency entrance of the Suffolk Memorial Hospital. She jumped out of the car and quickly lifted Gina into her arms.

She ran in through the emergency room doors. "Help me." Her voice was strident, gaining her immediate attention. "Please, help me. My daughter . . . she's not breathing."

As if in a haze, Kathleen allowed Gina to be taken from her by an orderly, who hurried her to a nearby examination room. She lingered just outside the door, frightened by the flurry of activity taking place around her.

Maybe I overreacted, she thought with desperation. Maybe Gina was just so soundly asleep she couldn't wake up. But, even as she thought it, she knew it wasn't true. Gina had never been a particularly sound sleeper.

She moved aside as a nurse ran toward her, pushing a cart with a machine on top.

"No," Kathleen whispered as the nurse brushed past her and into the room with Gina. A doctor followed, moving brusquely past Kathleen and into the room.

Kathleen sank down onto a plastic molded chair, her trembling legs unable to hold her any longer. Although she couldn't hear what was going on in the room, she knew what was happening. She'd recognized the machine the nurse had rushed into the room. It had been a defibrillator.

That meant Gina's heart wasn't beating.

That meant Gina was dead.

* * *

Lucas Connelly sat straight up in bed, his heart slowing to a more normal pace as the nightmare fell away. He threw the sheets off, sweat glistening on his nakedness as he padded to the window of his Manhattan penthouse.

He drew a deep breath and released it on a sigh as he gazed out at the streets below. Sunday night and still the city found no rest. Like him, it seemed haunted by night terrors.

The concrete and steel of the buildings across the street appeared to undulate and shimmer amid the unnatural heat wave that had gripped New York for the past month.

He swiped a hand through his hair, trying to shrug off the lingering effects of his dream. He walked over to the thermostat on the wall and turned it down, grateful for the immediate hum of the air conditioner coming to life. He returned to the window and stared out blankly with a deep frown.

It wasn't the first time the visions of the little girl had haunted his sleep. However, it was the first time he'd recognized her for what she was—a very old soul whose future was intrinsically bound to his.

The recognition of the dark-haired child with the piercing green eyes caused dread to twist in Lucas's gut. He didn't know what caused the dread, only that her presence in his dreams portended ill.

He had to find her. He had to find the child with the long, dark hair and eyes that spoke of ancient torments. She was to be the ultimate sacrifice.

He frowned and rubbed his forehead with the tips of his fingers. The strangeness of his thoughts confused him. What had seemed so clear only a moment ago was once again merely a nebulous aura of dread.

9

A storm was coming. A storm of massive proportions, and at the moment the little girl stood in the eye of that storm. But, soon, soon she would be cast into the tumultuous winds of chaos.

He had to find her . . . before the madness began.

"Kathleen."

Kathleen looked up at the sound of her name and saw Theresa hurrying down the hospital corridor toward her. She promptly burst into tears at the sight of her friend.

Theresa's short blond hair stood on end and beads of perspiration had melted off the last of her morning makeup. Her features radiated worry as she sat in the chair next to Kathleen and immediately took her hand.

"What's happening? What's wrong with Gina?" she asked. "I wondered when you didn't show up at school this morning. Then at lunch somebody told me you'd called and Gina was here. What on earth is going on? You didn't mention her being sick when I talked to you last night."

Kathleen squeezed Theresa's hand tightly and quickly related the events of the night. When she had finished, Theresa gasped.

Kathleen released her hand and stood. Her stomach convulsed as she thought of that single moment when she'd realized Gina wasn't breathing. "It was the oddest thing," she said. "They were just about to defibrillate her when she sat up and asked for me. The doctor and nurses almost had heart attacks themselves."

She sat back down. "They've been running tests on her since then. They won't let me see her."

"Have you eaten at all today?" Theresa asked.

Kathleen hesitated, then shook her head.

10

"Come on, let's go down to the cafeteria and grab a sandwich and some coffee."

"No . . . I shouldn't. . . ."

"Yes, you should," Theresa interrupted, tugging Kathleen up from her chair. "You won't be any good to Gina if you don't eat. Besides, everything always looks brighter on a full stomach." Theresa paused, a horrified look on her face. "My God, it's finally happened. I'm turning into my mother."

Despite her worry, Kathleen laughed. "That's okay. I like your mother." They headed for the cafeteria, stopping only to tell the nurse at the station where they would be if needed.

"Do you want me to call Bill for you?" Theresa asked once they were seated at a table. Her distaste for the task was obvious in her wrinkled nose. Kathleen shook her head and picked a piece of brown, wilted lettuce off her tuna sandwich. "Are you sure you should eat that?" Theresa asked, gesturing to the soggy sandwich.

Kathleen shrugged. "If it makes me sick, at least I'm in the right place." She forced a smile that quickly fell away as a deep, hollow ache rose up inside her. "I can't believe this, Theresa. What could possibly be wrong with Gina?"

"Shhh." Theresa reached across the table and took Kathleen's hand. "Eat," she urged. "As soon as the doctors know something they'll tell you."

Kathleen nodded, then stared down at her sandwich. Her eyes felt gritty from lack of sleep and her heart pumped the unnatural rhythm of fear. She had somehow managed to survive Sutton's death, but she couldn't begin to contemplate anything happening to Gina.

She didn't taste the tuna, but ate it to quiet Theresa's uncharacteristic maternal nagging. Then she stood, immediately ready to go back up to where Gina was enduring test after test as the doctors searched for whatever was wrong with her.

"Are you sure you don't want me to give Bill a call? I mean, I think the man is a useless prig, but I know you like him and if you'd feel better with him here . . . " Theresa said as they once again seated themselves in the tiny waiting room.

At that moment a doctor entered and Kathleen stood, eyeing him anxiously.

"Mrs. Marlowe, I'm Dr. Shaye." He shook her hand with a smile. "I've been an admirer of your late husband and his research work. I've read every paper he ever published. He was a wonderful doctor."

Kathleen nodded impatiently. She didn't want to talk about Sutton's glowing attributes and esteemed career. "About Gina?"

He raked a hand through his thin gray hair. "Yes, about Gina. I'm afraid, Mrs. Marlowe, that I don't have much of anything to tell you."

"What do you mean?"

He gestured for them to reseat themselves, then pulled up a chair in front of Kathleen. "We've run a battery of tests, and all we've learned is that Gina seems to be a healthy, perfectly normal six-year-old."

"Healthy, normal six-year-olds don't stop breathing in the middle of the night," Kathleen exclaimed.

"Yes, well, perhaps we all overreacted a bit." Dr. Shaye's face colored slightly, and he looked down at his carefully manicured nails.

"What does that mean?" Theresa asked. "Who over-reacted?"

Dr. Shaye shrugged. "The orderly who took the child from you and perhaps the nurse who did the initial examination.

I don't believe Gina ever stopped breathing. Her respiration slowed to a level that made it difficult to discern a heartbeat. It's like what happens when somebody suffers hypothermia. The body slows to protect itself. In this case, it's most unusual, but what I believe is that Gina was simply in a very deep state of sleep. The tests we've run have yielded nothing to contradict that assessment."

"I'm contradicting that assessment," Kathleen protested. "Dr. Shaye, she wasn't deeply asleep. She wasn't breathing." Kathleen's breath caught in her throat. "She was . . ." She allowed the sentence to drop into nothing, unable to say the dreadful word that filled her mind.

"There's nothing more we can do, Mrs. Marlowe. We've checked her for all the conditions that would cause a cessation of respiration. There is no indication of seizures, nothing to warrant further testing. In fact, I've already signed release papers. She's free to go home."

He gave her a smile of condescension. "I know your husband died in a tragic car accident not too long ago. I'm sure losing him has placed you under an enormous strain, and perhaps Gina is having trouble with the adjustment."

Kathleen's fear momentarily disappeared beneath a wave of ripe anger. What was he trying to imply? That because she had lost her husband she'd panicked and brought a sleeping child into the emergency room?

"Come on, Kathleen, let's get Gina," Theresa said, firmly taking Kathleen's arm. "This hospital is known for its incompetence. The papers have been filled with the stories for months. I know a specialist who can handle this quite efficiently."

The doctor gazed at Theresa as if she were a distasteful

urine specimen, then nodded curtly to Kathleen and whirled around and left.

"Self-righteous asshole," Theresa said.

"Dammit, I didn't overreact," Kathleen said tersely. "I know what happened, and Gina wasn't just in a state of deep sleep." She looked at Theresa. "So, who is this specialist you know?"

Theresa shrugged. "That was just a line of bull. Don't worry, we'll find a specialist. Let's go get your kid and get the hell out of here."

Minutes later Gina sat next to Kathleen in their car and Theresa followed behind them as they drove home. Kathleen leaned over and patted Gina's leg. "You okay?"

Gina nodded, her face wan in the dusk of twilight. "I don't want to go to sleep anymore." She looked at Kathleen, her green eyes fearful.

"Honey, everybody needs to sleep. It's how our bodies rest."

Gina shook her head. "I don't rest when I sleep. I fly."

Kathleen divided her attention between the road and her daughter. "What do you mean you fly?"

Gina pulled herself into a little ball against the passenger door. "First I see eyes over my bed. Then I know I am the eyes and I can see me in bed sleeping, but I'm not asleep. I'm flying above the bed." She plucked at her bottom lip in concentration. "Then I go into a long tunnel. It's dark and scary and I can't find my way out." Gina's bottom lip trembled visibly. "And there's something in the tunnel with me . . . something bad . . . really bad."

Kathleen pulled Gina against her side, needing her warmth, needing her very aliveness to chase away the inner chill that gripped Kathleen's insides. "It's all right, baby," she murmured softly, appalled as her daughter stuck her thumb in her mouth. Gina hadn't sucked her thumb in over three years.

Had it been a childish dream? The flying, the tunnel, the monster, surely a dream was the only rational explanation. Still, according to the doctor and the tests there was no rational explanation for what had happened.

She pulled into the driveway, exhaustion suddenly weighing heavily on her shoulders. Damn you, Sutton, she thought angrily. He'd rarely been here for her when he was alive, and she resented the fact that he wasn't here now. Sutton had been a brilliant doctor. He would have known what to do, how to help Gina.

"Mommy?"

Kathleen shut the engine off and turned to her daughter. "What, honey?"

Gina clutched at her, trying to curl her body into the softer curves of her mother. "Mommy, don't let me go to sleep. Please don't let me go to sleep."

"Shh, it's all right." Kathleen turned in the seat to embrace the little girl who was her heart. "It's all right. I won't let anything bad happen to you."

Gina shook her head, sobs choking in her throat. "I'm scared," she cried. "I'm scared that I'm gonna go into that black tunnel and I'll never, ever find my way back to you."

"I won't let that happen," Kathleen answered vehemently, holding Gina tight enough to hear the frantic pounding of her heartbeat. "If you can't find your way back to me, then I'll come and get you."

"But I think there's a monster in the tunnel," Gina replied, her voice soft with childish horror.

"No matter how dark the tunnel, no matter how big the monster, I'll come and get you."

Gina looked at Kathleen, tears sparkling in her bright green eyes. "You promise?"

"Oh baby, I promise," Kathleen replied. "I'll never let anything or anyone hurt you." She closed her eyes and held her daughter, fighting against a sudden, inexplicable wave of the deepest, darkest terror she'd ever felt.

"Lucas?"

The deep, sultry voice broke his concentration, but he ignored it and remained at the window, watching as twilight claimed the city below. It had always fascinated him, how this huge metropolis appeared to embrace the darkness rather than fight against it.

"Lucas, come back to bed. We still have an hour before we have to get ready to go to the club." He heard her stretch languidly against the sheets. She had a thing for making love in the purple shadows of dusk, had told him there was something sinfully decadent in acting like horny teenagers unable to wait for the cover of night.

He turned and looked at her. Her red hair spilled like rich burgundy wine across the white of the pillowcase. She was as sleek as a serpent and a thousand times more tempting.

Her name was Belinda Samuels and she was a waitress at the nightclub where he performed six nights a week. Two weeks before she had become his lover.

She stretched again, the sheet falling away to expose her full breasts and a length of her tanned, shapely leg. "Come on, Mr. Magic, come show me the charms of your magic wand."

Lucas joined her on the bed, immediately surrounded by

her warmth, the musk of her scent, the heat of her insatiable desire.

She was the most uninhibited, accomplished lover he'd ever had, and without his mind being involved, his body responded to hers.

He moved on top of her to possess her, driving deep within her as she hissed her pleasure and arched up to meet his frenzied thrusts. Their coupling was intense, primal and it took only minutes for him to reach his climax.

He remained on top of her, released and relieved. His head suddenly filled with a pair of piercing green eyes. He was suffused with the deepest, darkest fear he'd ever known. It swelled inside him, a fear with no source and raging out of control. He began to tremble.

Belinda raked her fingernails down the length of his back. "So good, that was so good," she moaned. Someplace in the far recesses of his mind, he realized she mistook his tremors for pleasure. She didn't recognize them for what they were . . . the involuntary shivers of unspeakable terror.

Chapter Two

"I'm sorry, I have no comment." Kathleen slammed down the phone, hoping she'd caused at least a little discomfort to the person on the other end of the line.

"Was that the same reporter?" Bill asked.

Kathleen nodded. "He's called several times since Gina was in the hospital. I'd like to know where the hell he got our names. No other reporters have called." She sat on the sofa with a sigh. She was tired, so very tired.

It had been almost a month since Gina had been admitted and summarily released from the hospital. Since then she had seen a dozen more doctors for dozens more tests, but the results had all been the same.

Gina was healthy. Gina was normal. Yet, Gina was still terrified of going to sleep.

"Maybe you should talk to him," Bill suggested. "He's certainly been persistent."

She shook her head. "I don't want Gina as part of a believe-it-or-not headline in the local tabloid. I can see it now, GIRL ARRIVES DOA AT HOSPITAL AND STUNS DOCTORS BY MIRACLE RECOVERY."

Bill leaned over and gently stroked a strand of her hair. She wanted to lean into him, allow his strength to buoy her. It would be easy now, while she was vulnerable and frightened, to give in to Bill, allow him a more intimate role in her life.

"You can't keep up this pace," he said, his broad forehead wrinkling with concern. "You can't sit up and watch Gina sleep every night, then function at school every day."

"I know," she agreed. "That's why last Friday I asked for a leave of absence."

One of his thick sandy eyebrows danced upward. "Is that wise?"

"There's only a couple more weeks of school left. All I know is that in the last month Gina has had four more episodes, and the doctors can't tell me what's going on." She stood and walked to the bar.

Bill frowned in faint disapproval as she fixed herself a drink. "I know, I know. I'm drinking too much and not sleeping enough. My nerves are shot, and I don't see an end to this craziness."

"What about the monitor? I thought that last specialist had her hooked up to some sort of a machine while she slept."

Kathleen nodded and rejoined him on the sofa. "I took the monitor back to the doctor." She rubbed the cool of the glass against her forehead, then took a sip.

"The last doctor finally managed to convince me that Gina's heart doesn't really stop during these episodes. The monitor confirmed that fact. What frightens me is that no matter what I do, I can't wake her up when she's having one of the attacks. It's such an unnatural sleep."

"So, what's the next step?" Bill asked.

"I've got an appointment tomorrow for us to see a psychiatrist. Several doctors have said that maybe these attacks are somehow self-induced, a delayed reaction of some sort to Sutton's death."

"Oh babe, I just hate to see you going through this." Bill placed an arm around her shoulders, and for a moment Kathleen allowed herself to sag against him.

"Kath, why not let me move in here for a little while?" He stroked his hand down her back, as if seeking the special place that, when caressed, would evoke instant acquiescence.

She moved out of his embrace, irritated with her momentary weakness, and annoyed by his attempt to take advantage of it. "I don't think that's a good idea. It would only confuse Gina."

Bill hesitated, then nodded. He knew better than to push her. Kathleen was one of those women who, when pushed, shoved back rather than gave in.

He could wait. Hell, he'd already waited ten years for her. Another month or two wouldn't hurt.

Once this mess with Gina was straightened out he could step up his campaign, convince her that they belonged together. He was tired of being good old Bill, trusted lawyer and family friend. He wanted more from Kathleen . . . much more.

He watched her get up and splash another jigger of brandy into her glass. Strain showed on her face, tensing the delicate line of her jaw, tightly compressing her sensual lips. Her eyes, usually cornflower blue and dancing with laughter, were darker, more somber, with bruised-looking circles beneath.

He felt helpless, impotent to help her in this particular matter. He'd given her the names of half a dozen doctors, specialists with credentials stringing a mile after their names, and none of them had been able to help.

Perhaps a psychiatrist would have the answers. Sutton's death had been abrupt, and Gina had been unusually close to her father. At that moment Gina walked into the living room.

"Mommy, I can't get this open." She handed Kathleen a small hot pink suitcase. As Kathleen worked to open the latches, Bill studied the little girl.

Gina, too, had suffered over the last month. Poor little thing. She looked like a Holocaust survivor, tired and thin . . . as if consumed by something that ate her from the inside out.

At that moment she turned and her green eyes locked with his. Fear gripped him. It rattled cold in the pit of his stomach. He tried to look away, but couldn't. His breath caught as the fear in his chest grew more oppressive, suffocating him beneath a weight too intense to bear.

He stood, swaying slightly beneath the bleak despair and the inexplicable terror that surged inside him. He finally managed to break the eye contact with the little girl.

"Bill?" Kathleen looked at him curiously. "Are you all right?"

He shook his head, unable to explain, incapable of putting into words the sweeping terror that had pierced through him as he'd looked into her daughter's eyes.

He only knew he had to escape. He had to get out of here immediately.

"I . . . I'm not feeling well." He stumbled toward the front door, vaguely aware of Kathleen setting down the suitcase and following after him. "Maybe it was the chili dog I had for lunch," he said faintly.

"You know what greasy food does to your ulcers," Kathleen chided gently. "Call me later," she said, watching as he walked out into the Sunday evening shadows. He raised a hand in her direction to acknowledge her request.

He got into his car and rolled down the window, gulping deeply of the stifling humid air. As quickly as it had overtaken him, the dreadful feeling of fear dissipated. A shudder worked its way through him.

He reached into the glove box and withdrew a plastic bottle of Tums, hoping the chalky, cherry-flavored tablets would ease the residual burning in the pit of his stomach. He popped two in his mouth, then leaned his head against the steering wheel.

What had happened? What had he seen in the depths of Gina's eyes that had caused such horror, such gut-twisting terror? That moment of gazing into her eyes now seemed merely the aftermath of a particularly bad dream.

He chewed the last of the Tums and started the car engine. Maybe it really was just the hot dog. Kathleen was right, he shouldn't eat junk food with his ulcer.

As he headed down Sunrise Highway toward his Long Island town of Babylon, he noticed the heat lightning that lit the distant horizon.

Damn, he wished this heat wave would break. There was something unholy about it, as if the earth's crust had split open and spewed sulfurous stench and heat upward. Unholy. He shivered again and stepped on the gas, suddenly eager to get home before night fell and darkness reigned.

*   *   *

Kathleen had finally managed to open the suitcase, which held an array of Barbie dolls and clothes when the doorbell rang. Handing the case to Gina, she hurried to the door.

"Mrs. Marlowe, could I please have a moment of your time?"

She frowned at the short, slender man. He stood on the porch, nervously shifting from foot to foot. His hair was a dark brown, his eyes the same color. He was clad in a rumpled suit, also brown, with a tan tie, the knot showing the signs of having been tugged at more than once during the day.

She took the business card he held out, read it, then thrust it back to him irritably. "Mr. Kelly, I've already told you a half a dozen times on the phone, I do not wish to discuss my experience with the Suffolk Memorial Hospital with you or any other person from the press." She started to close the door.

"Please . . . this isn't just about the hospital."

Kathleen hesitated, captured by the humble plea in his soft voice. "I shouldn't have initially introduced myself as a reporter. I don't want a story on the hospital." He held out a photograph. "This is my daughter."

The photo was a studio portrait, the subject a little girl with a sweet smile and a freckle-splattered complexion. Her shoulder-length hair was pulled back with barrettes that matched her red dress.

"This photo of Sharon was taken four months ago. Here's our most recent picture." He held up another one, and Kathleen gasped. Unconsciously she stumbled back a step, as if to escape the image he now held before her.

"Wha—what happened to her?" Despite her reluctance, her gaze was drawn back to the picture of the little girl. She looked as if she'd been nearly swallowed by the hospital bed

23

where she rested. Tubes snaked into her nose, down her throat and her freckles stood out in bas-relief against the starkness of her pale skin.

Kathleen looked back at Keith Kelly, noting in some part of her mind that his daughter had his soft, brown eyes. "What happened to her?" she asked again, not wanting to know and yet unable to stop the question.

"It began with her having horrible nightmares. About a dark tunnel."

Despite the warmth of the evening air, Kathleen shivered as a bone-chilling dread coursed through her. "A dark tunnel?" She repeated the all-too-familiar words in horror.

"Please, Mrs. Marlowe. Will you talk to me now?"

She held on to the door, torn between wanting to know about his little girl and fear. She had the crazy notion that to invite him inside was tantamount to welcoming in a germ, a bacteria . . . a deadly illness that would destroy both herself and her daughter.

"No . . . no we can't talk here. My daughter is already frightened enough." She frowned, thinking. "Do you know where Maggie's Diner is?" He nodded. "I'll meet you there in . . ." she looked at her watch. "Two hours." That would give her time to find somebody to stay with Gina.

He nodded and as he turned away, Kathleen saw the expression in his eyes and was gripped once again by frigid fingers of fear.

What she'd seen there in his soft brown eyes had been pity. That, more than anything else scared the hell out of her.

Two hours later Kathleen walked into Maggie's Diner, the scent of cholesterol-laden food oddly comforting. Not seeing Keith, she took a seat in a booth in the back.

She faced the doorway so she'd notice when he arrived. She ordered coffee from the waitress, then sat back and for the first time in the past two hours allowed her mind to play over her conversation with Keith Kelly.

Surely there was no correlation between his daughter and Gina. It was simply coincidence that his daughter suffered bad dreams about dark tunnels . . . the same thing Gina described from her own night terrors. Sheer coincidence—one of those oddities that life often offered that had no meaning, no rhyme.

He was probably just another nut, and she'd talked to more than her share of nuts in the past several weeks. Theresa, in a misguided effort to help, had contacted a psychic friend she knew who had decided that Gina could benefit from some of her healer friends.

Kathleen had been inundated with calls from people selling everything from magic crystals to furry talismans.

"Crazy, I must be crazy." She finished her coffee and grabbed her purse, realizing she'd been a fool to meet a man she didn't know, a man who had been annoying her with phone calls and messages since the night Gina had been hospitalized.

As she stood to leave, the reporter walked through the door. He hurried toward her, a briefcase tucked firmly beneath one arm. "Mr. Kelly, I've changed my mind," she began, a stain of embarrassment warming her cheeks. "I—I don't know why I agreed to meet you here."

"You agreed because you are frightened for your daughter, as you should be." He slid into the booth and gestured her to sit back down.

"What do you know about my daughter?" Despite her

reluctance, she sank into the cracked plastic booth once again.

"I know she was brought into the hospital supposedly not breathing. I know both the orderly and the nurse assessed her as dead. I know that just before they attempted to shock her heart, she sat up and appeared fine. I also know she told the doctor that she had been flying in a dark tunnel and she was afraid."

"How do you know all that?"

He smiled without pleasure. "As a reporter I have sources, one of whom works at the hospital." He paused as the waitress appeared at their booth. Like Kathleen, he ordered only coffee.

Once the waitress was gone he wrapped his hands around the coffee cup, as if seeking the warmth to assuage a chill. "Mrs. Marlowe, I made a mistake when I originally introduced myself as a reporter. My interest has nothing to do with a story. I have a personal interest in Gina."

His gaze held hers for a long moment, and in his eyes she saw the bleak winds of despair, a sadness beyond her comprehension. "My Sharon had nightmares of a tunnel, and we had her in the emergency room a dozen times because it appeared she had stopped breathing while she slept."

He closed his eyes for a moment and when he opened them again they were liquid with emotion. "We took her to every specialist we could think of. She even spent a couple of days and nights in a sleep clinic. But nobody had any answers. Nobody could help us at all. Sharon was afraid to sleep, afraid of that tunnel. She said she flew, and she was scared of getting trapped in the darkness forever."

"And what happened?" Kathleen's mouth was so dry the words came out as more of a croak.

"She went to sleep one night and never woke up. She flew into that tunnel and got lost."

Kathleen took a sip of her coffee in an attempt to ease the ache in the back of her throat. Her hand tightened convulsively around the cup as he continued. "The doctors have diagnosed Sharon as being in a coma, the cause unknown. She isn't alone." Keith placed his briefcase on the table and clicked it open. "In the last three months I've found two other children who are now in unexplained comas."

He withdrew two more pictures from his briefcase. One was of a boy about ten years old, and the other another little girl who looked to be seven or eight. "I've interviewed both sets of parents, and they tell the same story. Both children had the tunnel nightmares. They feared going to sleep. They spoke of flying. They had episodes where their parents thought they'd stopped breathing, and eventually they went to sleep and didn't wake up."

He placed the photos on the table before her, but she didn't pick them up. She didn't touch them. She was afraid of the obvious insinuation. She was afraid the images were a portent of Gina's future . . . or lack of one.

"What's happening?" she asked in a hoarse whisper. "Is it some kind of a disease? A birth defect? What's happening to these children?"

"I don't know." His voice held the despair that echoed in Kathleen's heart. "The doctors haven't been able to offer any answers or any hope." He put the photos back in his briefcase and snapped it shut again.

"Why are you telling me this? What do you want from me?" Kathleen asked. Her fingers worked to shred a paper napkin, as if she could pull apart the fabric of his story so it would no longer resemble in any way what Gina was going through.

He stared at her helplessly. "I don't know. I guess I wanted to warn you. And if somehow we can figure out what's going on with Gina, then maybe we'll know what's wrong with Sharon." He shrugged and looked down at the scarred table-top. "I'm a reporter. I gather facts and try to explain things. I'm just attempting to help in any way I can, to put my training to use. I don't know what else to do."

He gazed back up at her, looking as fragile as a slender reed in the relentless winds of a tornado. "I just feel like if we can save Gina, then maybe we can help Sharon."

Kathleen's heart and mind rebelled. Gina was not going to lapse into an unexplained coma. She was not going to end up like this man's daughter. Gina was having problems that the psychiatrist should be able to fix.

She wadded up what was left of her napkin and stood, needing to be away from here, away from this man and his tragedy. "Mr. Kelly, I'm sorry. I don't know how I can help you."

She had enough problems of her own. She couldn't take on this man's problems as well, couldn't shoulder his grief along with her own fear.

He looked up at her again, his eyes dulled with grief. "Are you a religious woman, Mrs. Marlowe?"

Kathleen hesitated, unsure how to answer. "I don't go to church very often, but I believe in a higher power. I suppose I'm more spiritual than religious. Why?"

He held her gaze with an intensity that stole her breath. "Pray for your daughter," he said softly, then added, "and please . . . please pray for mine."

She nodded, then ran for the door and burst out into the

night. She gulped deeply of the humid, fetid air.

He's just a desperate father looking for answers, she told herself over and over again as she drove home. His story had nothing to do with Gina, nothing whatsoever. Gina was not going to end up like his daughter Sharon.

She pulled into her driveway, eager to get inside and hug Gina. She needed to feel her daughter's warm little body against hers. Wearily, feeling far older than her twenty-nine years, she climbed out of the car and headed inside.

"Hey, that didn't take long," Theresa greeted Kathleen when she walked into the living room where her best friend and her daughter were playing a game of Old Maid. "Gina's only had time to make me the stinking old maid three times." Gina giggled, a sound that filled Kathleen's heart.

"I guess there are some people just destined to be old maids," Kathleen teased with a forced lightness. Gina giggled again as Theresa picked up a round decorative pillow and threw it at Kathleen.

Theresa stood. "Guess I'm out of here." She handed Gina her cards. "Here, Gina, why don't you pick up while your mom walks with me to the door." As they left the living room Theresa threw an arm around Kathleen's shoulders. "You okay?"

Kathleen hesitated, then nodded. "Yeah, I'm fine. Thanks for coming over to watch Gina on such short notice."

"No problem. You know I love that kid." Theresa leaned over and gave Kathleen a quick kiss on the cheek. "Try to get some sleep. You look like hell."

"Go on, get out of here." She watched as Theresa disappeared down the sidewalk and a moment later heard the backfire of her ancient Volkswagen as it pulled away from the curb.

It was nearly an hour later when Kathleen realized bedtime couldn't be put off any longer. It was eleven and although Gina pretended not to be tired, her face reflected exhaustion. "Bedtime, Gina."

Gina nodded, grim resignation tightening her features. It took only a few minutes for her to change into her pajamas and get into bed. Kathleen pulled a rocking chair up against the side of her bed and eased into it.

"You'll be right here all night?" Gina asked. It was the same question she'd asked every night for the past month.

"All night," Kathleen assured her. Within minutes Gina was asleep. She slept on her back, her cheeks puffing out with each breath she expelled. Her long dark lashes cast shadows on her delicate skin and Kathleen leaned over and lightly touched her hand, reassured by the warmth of the little fingers.

As long as she could see Gina's chest moving up and down . . . as long as her skin was warm with natural sleep, there was nothing to worry about. It was when her breathing slowed and became imperceptible, when her skin grew cool to the touch that Kathleen knew another of the frightening episodes was about to take place.

Assured that Gina slept peacefully, she leaned back in the chair and released a weary sigh. A picture of Keith Kelly unfolded in her head.

What torment he must be in. How horrible to lose a child to some mysterious illness. For surely that's what had happened to his little girl. She'd been the victim of a rare and mysterious condition that had nothing to do with Gina.

She sat up straight as she heard her daughter sigh. It was a small sound, like that of a kitten's mewl, but it was a sound that over the last month Kathleen had come to dread.

Gina's eyelashes fluttered rapidly. Then all movement ceased. "Gina?" Kathleen grabbed her daughter's hand.

Cold. It was as chilled as if she held hands with death itself. "Gina . . . wake up." Tears of frustration and fear burned at Kathleen's eyes.

Even though she knew from past experience that it was futile, she shook Gina's shoulders, trying to rouse her.

Too late. She was too late to stop it from happening. Gina's body was limp, her face as pale as the white sheets. The room around her was flat, without energy, as if the life force had completely left it.

Fighting back a sob, Kathleen left the chair and got onto the bed next to her daughter. She pulled her tight against her, knowing there was nothing to do but wait. The seconds ticked by . . . endless minutes of torture.

It was nearly an hour later that Gina's body convulsed, shaking the entire bed. "Mommy," she cried out, gasping for air.

"I'm here, honey." Kathleen clutched the trembling little girl close. "It's okay, love. I'm right here." She caressed Gina's hair and kissed her brow.

"Mommy. . . ." Gina pushed herself out of Kathleen's embrace and looked at her with widened eyes. "Do something . . . you have to help me. I'm scared that I'm gonna fly into that black tunnel and I'm never going to find my way back home."

The plea ripped at Kathleen's insides. There was nothing more she wanted to do than help Gina. But she didn't know how.

It took Gina a few minutes to fall back asleep. It was as if whatever she endured when she was in one of the frightening states completely sucked the last of her energy away, leaving her exhausted and drained.

Kathleen knew from past experience that Gina would sleep peacefully for the remainder of the night. She'd never had more than one episode in a single night.

Kathleen got up from the bed and moved to the bedroom window. She pulled aside the pale pink curtains and stared out into the darkness.

She could feel the heat from the night air seeping in around the windowpane and wondered vaguely when this latest, hellish heat streak would snap.

Keith Kelly's taut face imposed itself inside her head. His daughter had been scared of flying into the dark tunnel. Kathleen shivered.

Pray. That's what Keith Kelly had told her to do. And for the first time in years, that's exactly what Kathleen did.

Chapter Three

Lucas was almost finished with his magic act when he felt the odd sensation, as if spectral fingers from another dimension probed the inner recesses of his mind.

Normally graceful as a cat while on stage, he stumbled awkwardly. He quickly recovered and shrugged at Amy, his assistant, who grinned at his unusual clumsiness as she moved into position for the finale.

The last trick always brought down the house. It was a simple illusion where Amy appeared to levitate at Lucas's silent command. As she lay down on the table, again he felt the strange sensation, this time not just in his head, but throughout his entire body. He tingled, as if electric currents sizzled through him.

A trickle of sweat trekked down his neck and disappeared into his shirt collar. He was aware of Amy casting him furtive looks, letting him know she was ready to begin.

He raised his hand with a flourish, trying to ignore the

buzz that had begun to resound in the base of his skull. Amy began to rise, aided by an invisible wire around her waist and a dramatic light show that diminished visibility.

She floated twelve inches above the table when the buzzing in Lucas's head reached screeching proportions. He raised his hand to his head and at the same time Amy shot up in the air.

As Lucas watched, she began to tumble head over feet, end over end up . . . up . . . up toward the cavernous ceiling. He was vaguely aware of her screams and the collective gasp from the audience. He lowered his hand and as if in slow motion, she began to descend. Down . . . down . . . down until she was once again lying on her back on the table.

The curtain fell to thunderous applause and shouts of approval. Instantly the buzzing in his head stopped. Amy climbed off the table and stalked over to him. "Thanks for telling me you changed the act, Lucas," she said angrily. "You just scared the hell out of me."

He'd just scared the hell out of himself. As Amy headed for her dressing room, he leaned heavily against a wall. Although the buzzing was gone, he felt the strange tickling sensation in the base of his skull. Like the strains of a melancholy tune, the invasion evoked a deep anguish, an overwhelming sense of loss.

Drawing in a deep breath, he closed his eyes. What was happening? What the hell was happening to him? Against the backdrop of the blackness of his eyelids, he saw a pair of green eyes . . . eyes that glittered with an inhuman rage.

"Lucas?"

He snapped his eyes back open at the sound of Belinda's voice and instantly the image vanished, but not before leaving behind a name that reverberated in his head.

"Are you all right?" she asked. She sidled up beside him, her musk perfume enveloping him in its pungency. The scent filled his head, effectively banishing the last of the strange sensation. She slid a silky arm around his neck.

"I'm fine. Just a little dizzy." It was true. He was dizzied by the pounding of that single name through his mind.

Belinda smiled and leaned against him. "You make me dizzy," she replied. "Dizzy with desire." She reached up and ran a finger down the taut line of his jaw.

For the first time since they had become lovers, Lucas didn't feel a tremor of response to her touch. He felt absolutely nothing. He forced a smile and removed her finger from his cheek. Belinda's smile wavered slightly. "Are you sure you're all right?"

He nodded. "I just have some things on my mind." How could he explain to her the odd sensation he'd just experienced, the power that had momentarily surged through him, and the strange name that echoed within his head like the pounding of a drum?

How could he explain the vision of those eyes . . . eyes that caused a strong, visceral fear? The dreams, the strange sensations assaulted him at odd moments of the day and night.

"George told me to clock out for the night. He's got too many waitresses working." She hesitated a moment, a seductive smile curving her lips. "Do you want me to hang around here or go on over to your place?"

"There's no point in you waiting around here." He handed her the key to his apartment. "I'll see you there after the final show."

She reached up and kissed him on the cheek, then disappeared out the curtain that separated the backstage area from the audience section.

Lucas walked down the long hallway that led to his dressing room. All thoughts of Belinda were immediately buried beneath more weighty concerns.

Once inside, he closed the door and sank down in the chair before the large dressing room table and mirror. What was wrong with him? He stared into the mirror. Instead of seeing his own reflection, he saw the eyes . . . those same haunting green eyes that filled his nightmares.

He averted his gaze, focusing instead on a benign jar of cold cream. What was happening to him? Why were the visions from his nightmares now haunting his waking hours? And who was Gina Marlowe? Why had the name come to him with such violent intensity? Who was she and why did he feel such a consuming need to find her?

Belinda Samuels had long ago learned that it was far easier to embrace the darkness than to hug the light. She learned this simple fact of life the first time her stepfather raped her.

George Randolf Samuels was a pious man, spouting his version and interpretation of Christian values. During the hours of light he was an upstanding participant of their local church, a member of the Chamber of Commerce in their small community, a respected banker who was known for his charitable gifts of time and money to worthy causes.

Only Belinda knew that in the hours of darkness the night contained, George shed his outer skin and surrendered his soul to the pleasures of evil.

She'd been thirteen when he'd come to her the first time, sobbing his apologies as he penetrated her innocence. On that night her hatred was born. He had disgusted her, not so much with his vile acts, but with his guilty sobs of weakness.

Belinda's mother had known. The knowledge had shone

in her eyes each time she had looked at Belinda. And there were times Belinda hated her mother far more than her stepfather, for her failure to protect her daughter was an even bigger flaw than her husband's vile acts.

Belinda's hatred spawned an incredible rage . . . a rage that led her steadily away from the light and into the seductive darkness.

In high school she realized God had never done anything for her and so instead she looked to the Master of Darkness to reward her, embrace her. One only had to look around to realize that evil wielded the power of the world.

She joined a group of Satan worshippers, and when she was seventeen moved in with one of the members, an older man who was thoroughly besotted with her.

He'd served her well, teaching her all she needed to know about seduction and physical pleasure. Belinda had been an eager student, knowing her power would come through her beauty. She had the kind of physical presence that made men think of sin.

Eventually she had left the old man, ready to move on and fully taste her freedom and potential.

She now stood before a floor-length mirror in Lucas's apartment, eager for the night to grow old and Lucas to come home from the club.

Lucas . . . he was a hunger in her soul, an obsession like no other. Now there was power. An innate power thrummed in Lucas's veins. It was made more appealing because he seemed unaware of it.

She moved away from the mirror, a frown furrowing her forehead. Lucas. He was an enigma, a complex puzzle she wanted to own forever. She walked around the bedroom, touching his cologne bottles on the dresser, running her hand across a T-shirt she knew would retain the scent of him.

She wanted to solve his mysteries, indulge in the peeling back of layers, work out the intricacies of his soul.

Initially, he'd seemed as obsessed with her as she was with him, but lately she'd sensed distance. There were moments when he was physically with her, but she knew his thoughts, his emotions had fled to a place where she couldn't follow.

It angered her, frightened her. He was her soul mate, the one she was destined to be with forever and ever. She couldn't lose him. She would do anything to keep him.

Looking at her wristwatch, she quickly grabbed her purse from the table next to the sofa. Lucas wouldn't be home for another hour. She had plenty of time. She pulled a squat, fat black candle from her purse and set it on the coffee table.

At the next meeting of her fellow worshippers she intended to ask Thanatos to give her Lucas for all eternity. Although the thought of asking a favor from the man who was reported to be the right hand of Satan was daunting.

Her hand trembled slightly as she withdrew a packet of matches from her purse. She had only seen Thanatos once, at a meeting six months before.

Belinda had always rejoiced at the evil inside her, but as she'd faced Thanatos, she'd realized her depravity was insipid, her debauchery feeble. She was like a child just learning the rules of the game . . . and he was the Game Master.

He was like a vial of poison . . . as puissant as the stench of death on a hot summer day. Merely being in his presence had imbibed her with a renewed desire to obtain more power . . . the power that only Lucifer offered.

She lit the fat candle and turned out the overhead light. For a moment she was content to watch the flickering flame cast dancing shadows on the walls, shadows in the shape of demons writhing in hell's glory.

Yes, on the night of the next full moon she would ask Thanatos to give her Lucas's soul. In the meantime it didn't hurt to remind the ruler of the underworld that she was a good servant and deserved his unholy blessing. Bowing her head, she began her prayer of blasphemy.

Keith Kelly entered the hospital room as he always did, with his heart heavy and his feet dragging with dread. His wife was there, as she always was, her grief a living, breathing entity in the air.

Before this had happened to Sharon, Keith had never known that grief had a distinctive smell . . . like the biting scent of a strong antiseptic mixed with the dank odor of freshly turned earth.

Grief wreaked of loss, and loneliness and death. The smell emanated from his wife, from his child. And there were moments when he caught it wafting from himself.

Rosalyn lifted hollow eyes to acknowledge his presence in the room.

"Any change?" he asked, keeping his gaze averted from the lifeless hull in the bed. A hull, that's all that was left of his baby girl . . . an empty shell that held no life, no spirit, no soul.

Rosalyn shook her head and he noticed the gray strands that streaked her dark hair, the deep lines that furrowed her forehead. When had that happened? When had his lovely wife grown old? Even as the questions filtered through his mind, he knew the answer. She'd aged since Sharon had disappeared into the deathlike sleep.

He moved across the room to sit next to her and caught

his reflection in the shiny surface of the metal slats of the bed. He paused for a moment, stunned as he saw stooped shoulders, the hesitant half-steps of an old man. He averted his head from the reflection of reality and sat down next to Rosalyn.

As always her hand immediately found his, seeking comfort, requesting solace. And as always, he knew he had none to give. He couldn't comfort her, not when his anger was so rich, so full inside him.

What had happened to Sharon? The doctors had no answers. Nobody had any answers. He was filled with an undirected anger and an aching helplessness.

In truth, Keith was beginning to believe that it wasn't a medical problem at all. Three children . . . and another in danger of becoming the fourth. There was no scientific explanation for their comas, yet each had experienced the same nightmares before lapsing into the deathlike sleep.

Keith had always prided himself on the three major roles he played as an adult: first and foremost a husband and father, then a damned good reporter. The first two had been stolen from him.

He couldn't be a true husband to the woman who sat next to him. Her hollow eyes haunted him, evoked in him an impotent helplessness that ripped his insides. He couldn't be a father to the child on the bed.

The only thing left for him was to do his job as a reporter. And as a reporter he smelled a story. Three children living within a hundred-mile radius had shared the exact same nightmare and had eventually come to share the same fate.

There had to be a common characteristic, something to explain why this had happened to the three. He knew that to find the cure, he had to find the cause. The key rested in the children themselves. Somehow these children were connected. Now, all he had to do was find that connection and see where it led.

The storm came, but it brought no relief from the heat. Thunder rumbled, lightning flashed, and the rain pattered against Gina's windowpane in a sporadic rhythm.

Kathleen was grateful that the turbulent weather didn't awaken Gina. She slept peacefully, a childish snore escaping her puckered lips. Kathleen leaned back in the rocking chair, her thoughts carrying her to the distant past.

How many nights had she sat right here, with Gina a sweet-smelling bundle in her arms? Gina had been a fussy baby, crying often and loudly for no apparent reason. Only the tranquilizing rhythm of the rocker and the warmth of Kathleen's arms soothed her cries.

Kathleen had often wondered if those nights of rocking had created an unnatural bond between herself and her child. She and Gina had always mirrored each other's moods, shared emotions as if their spirits were woven from the same fabric, the same shiny threads of life.

Kathleen stood and moved to the window. She pushed aside the curtain and stared outside. The storm had passed. Faint intermittent lightning disturbed the distant skies. The street below her two-story vantage point gleamed wetly in the illumination of the street lamps. Fog hung close to the ground, giving the illusion of an eerie landscape from another world. She let the curtain fall back into place.

School had ended the week before. Gina's teacher had allowed her to be passed to the second grade despite the numerous days she'd missed over the last two months.

The psychiatrist appointments had yielded nothing new.

After several sessions with Gina, Dr. Pippinfield had proclaimed Gina a relatively well-adjusted little girl who seemed to have a normal view of death and the loss of her father from her life.

No answers . . . and still the episodes continued. A rapid knocking on the front door pierced the quiet of the night. Kathleen jumped and looked at her watch. After midnight. Who on earth could be at her door? She checked on Gina, who hadn't stirred at the noise, then turned on the hall light and crept down the massive staircase toward the front door.

She started to unlock the door, then hesitated, reality jarring her. She was a widow alone with a young child and Long Island was not the kind of place where you opened the door to a knock at this hour.

She stood on her toes and peered out the spy hole, seeing the shape of a dark figure. She knew it was useless to turn on the outside light. It had burned out a week before and she hadn't replaced the bulb. "Who's there?" she called through the door.

A thick silence answered her words. She waited. A loud booming noise filled the silence and she realized it was the sound of her heartbeat thudding a frantic rhythm. "Who is it?" she asked again.

"Mrs. Marlowe. My name is Lucas Connelly. I'd like to speak with you."

She frowned. She didn't know a Lucas Connelly. "Do you have any idea what time it is?"

"Yes. I'm sorry about the lateness of the hour. I work nights and . . . and this couldn't wait."

"What couldn't wait?"

His voice was deep and pleasant, but for some reason it caused a chill of apprehension to dance up her spine.

42

"We need to talk about what's happening with your daughter."

She gasped. Her hand shook as she reached out and tentatively touched the dead bolt on the door. "What do you mean? What do you know about my daughter?"

"Open the door, Mrs. Marlowe. I know what's wrong with Gina." A quiet authority radiated in his voice, a command she found difficult to ignore.

Her heartbeat roared in her ears. Common sense dictated she not touch the door, that she keep this stranger locked out. But, two months of seeking answers, two months of fear, made common sense easy to ignore.

Realizing it might be foolish but unable to stop herself, she reached out and turned the dead bolt, the resulting click exploding in the silence of the foyer. She opened the door and faced the stranger on her doorstep.

He wore black slacks that hugged his slender legs and a black shirt with a deep v-neck and billowing sleeves. His hair was the color of a raven's wings. He seemed to be cloaked in darkness.

Kathleen held the door firmly. "Exactly what do you know about my daughter, Mr. Connelly?" She frowned, wishing she could see his facial features better.

She'd always believed you could tell a person's character from his eyes. Unfortunately, Lucas Connelly's eyes were hidden by the deep shadows of night.

"Your daughter is in danger . . . terrible danger."

"I . . . I don't know what you're talking about." She wasn't about to admit anything to him. But, he'd said the words with dreadful certainty, as if he knew exactly what was going on.

Without warning his hand reached out and grabbed her,

43

capturing her wrist in his hot, firm grasp. "We don't have a lot of time for games, Mrs. Marlowe." He stepped closer and a thin shaft of light from the foyer fell on his features.

His face was thin, aristocratically defined by sharp cheekbones and a straight Roman nose. But it was his eyes that captured her attention and for a moment made it impossible for her to speak.

Beneath thick, dark eyebrows, his eyes were black wells of secrets, haunted depths of mystery. They held the weariness of unforgotten lifetimes, the intensity of a soul not at peace.

Something more than fear raced through her veins . . . an electric charge so intense she jerked her wrist from his grasp and stepped back, her skin burning with the heated imprint of his fingers. "What do you know about Gina?"

"I know the doctors can't help her. There's nothing medically wrong with her, and she can't be cured through conventional means."

Conventional means. Something clicked in her head and she eyed him wearily. "So what's your game, Mr. Connelly? Healing herbs? The magic of crystals? An exorcism?" She tamped down her rising anger. "Go away. Find another sucker to con." She began to close the door but he stiff-armed it, making it impossible for her to shut it.

"I'm not a con man. I'm not trying to sell you anything. I am here to save your daughter's soul."

"If you aren't off my porch in exactly one second, I'm going to call the police and you can explain it all to them."

He sighed. Like the chill winter winds blowing across a desolate plain. The sigh reached inside and plucked at Kathleen's helplessness, her despair. "She's a night traveler. Your daughter is a night traveler."

"Yes, and I'm the tooth fairy. Your second is up, Mr. Connelly."

"If you won't talk to me now, then at least take this." He held out a business card. "She'll start to slip away more easily, for longer periods of time. It's going to get worse. Much worse. When you run out of options, when you're completely out of hope, call me. I just pray it won't be too late."

Before Kathleen could say another word, he dropped his arm from the door, turned, and walked away. She held the card up to the light, squinting her eyes to make out what it said: Lucas Connelly. Master Magician. There was a phone number printed across the bottom.

She stepped out on the porch, looking first in one direction, then in the other. He was nowhere to be seen. Errant leaves displaced by the storm skittered across the cracked sidewalks, like nocturnal creatures with long, scratchy toenails. Where had he gone? It was as if the blackness of the night had swallowed him whole.

The scent of ozone was stronger, burning her nose unpleasantly. Lightning slashed the distant sky. She shivered, a cold chill crawling up her spine. Looking around a final time, she went back inside and carefully rebolted the door.

She gazed down at the business card again, remembering the burning intensity of his dark eyes, the fanatic conviction in his voice. A nut. Surely he was a nut who'd somehow heard about Gina's mysterious affliction. Probably one of Theresa's psychic buddy's friends.

If Kathleen thought healing crystals would help, she'd buy a thousand. If she discovered herbs in India would fix Gina, she'd be on the next plane. If she thought an exorcism would solve the problem, she'd kidnap a Catholic priest and demand he perform the ceremony immediately.

Carla Cook

A magician. She didn't want help from a magic man with a bag of tricks. She dropped the business card into the mouth of the large vase that sat on the marble-top table just inside the front door.

No, she didn't need a magician pulling rabbits out of hats. She needed a miracle.

Chapter Four

Gina peeked out her bedroom window. She saw the man who stood just outside the glow of the street lamp. A man dressed all in black. Only the paleness of his face was visible as he stared up at her bedroom window.

"The dark man," she whispered. The voice inside her head had told her about him, had warned her about him.

She hadn't told her mommy that the voice that called to her through the tunnel now spoke to her throughout the day. It had only started talking to her a couple of days before.

It whispered to her in the night, tickled in her ears during the day. It scared her. Why was the man standing outside and staring up at her window? Had the voice in her head sent him?

She let the curtain drop over the window and got back into bed. Squeezing her eyes tightly closed, her thumb sought the comfort of her mouth as her body curled into a fetal ball.

Gina willed the voice in her head and the dark man away and waited for morning to come.

He'd blown it. Dammit. He should have never come here at this hour of the night. He should have known better. Lucas stood across the street from the Marlowes' two-story home and stared. Patches of fog shrouded the residence and vapors of steam from the earlier rain rose up from the street like restless ghostly wraiths.

He had to make Kathleen Marlowe understand. But how? How did he make her comprehend what remained elusive to him? His life was suddenly out of control.

His thoughts, his impulses, his emotions were being ruled by something he couldn't explain and couldn't fight.

At first he'd thought he was losing his mind. The strange dreams, the disturbing visions all pointed to insanity reaching out an insidious hand to clutch him.

He remembered his father in the last days of his life when he'd babbled gibberish and slobbered sobs of despair. He'd prattled of dragons and demons, devils and saints. Delusion, melancholia, schizophrenia . . . the doctors had spewed diagnoses like whales spouting water.

Lucas only knew that insanity was ugly and cruel, and he feared a dreadful end like his father's, a prisoner of his own dementia.

When the name Gina Marlowe had exploded in his head, he'd feared his own grasp on sanity. Along with the name had come a mental picture of this house, complete with its stone façade and large lot.

He'd immediately known where it was even though he had never been to the Long Island Hamptons. He had no idea what it meant, but he had been compelled to find this house and seek out the child.

Kathleen Marlowe. She'd been a shock as well. He'd known her the moment she'd opened her door. He hadn't recognized the wavy dark hair that fell like heavy silk around her shoulders. Nor had he identified the blue eyes that had gazed at him first hesitantly, then fearfully.

He'd recognized nothing about her physical being . . . but he'd known her with his heart. He'd known her with his soul. He somehow knew that their entwined souls had tumbled through time and once again, in this latest lifetime, had found each other.

He had never thought about reincarnation before, had never considered the possibilities of past lives. But in the instant of gazing into Kathleen's blue eyes, he'd believed.

He'd known they had shared a life that had nothing to do with this one . . . a life filled with pain, with betrayal, with death.

He leaned against the lamppost and continued to stare at the imposing two-story house. The Marlowes' house. He had hoped he wouldn't find it, that it was all just an odd vision that meant nothing.

He hadn't really expected to find a family named Marlowe, and he hadn't envisioned he'd discover a little girl named Gina. But he had, and that meant he wasn't crazy. That meant that all the dreams, the visions, the odd bits and pieces of strange information were real and not just figments of his imagination.

As much as he'd always feared insanity, he'd rather be mad than face what the visions hinted would follow.

*   *   *

"This was a terrific idea," Kathleen said as she sat down on the blanket in the shade of an oak tree. That morning Theresa had suggested a picnic in the nearby community park.

"You and the kid have been cooped up long enough in that house. You both need a day of sunshine and fresh air." Theresa kicked off her sandals and joined Kathleen on the blanket.

Kathleen looked over to where Gina sat on one of the swings, her little legs pumping to and fro. Usually within two weeks of summer, Gina's skin was bronzed from days spent playing outside. Not this year. She was as pale as a ghost. "Remind me in an hour or so to put more sunscreen on Gina."

Theresa nodded and stretched out on her back. "I'm so glad school is over for the year."

"What are your plans for this summer? Anything exciting?" Kathleen leaned back against the thick tree truck, more relaxed than she'd been in months.

"My only plan is to find Mr. Right, marry him and live happily ever after . . . again." She opened one eye and grinned at Kathleen. "In fact, I think I've already found him. His name is John Riley, and he's an investment banker. I met him last weekend at a bar and we spent a heavenly, passionate night together."

"Oh Theresa," Kathleen said with a sigh.

"I know, I know. I'm nothing but a slut. But how will I know if he's Mr. Right unless I sleep with him?"

Kathleen sighed. "I just worry about you," she finally said.

Theresa laughed. "I'm a big girl. I'm not about to be murdered by some Mr. Good Bar."

"In this day and age, there are other things to worry about besides that," Kathleen reminded her.

"You don't understand what it's like to be alone," Theresa said softly. "You had ten years with a man who adored you. You'll find out now how difficult it is to find a meaningful relationship at our age."

"I don't want a relationship of any kind right now," Kathleen replied. All she wanted was for Gina to be safe and happy. She looked over to where Gina played with another child in the sandbox. Her giggles rode the breeze, a little girl sound that invaded Kathleen's heart with warmth. Gina's laughter was rarely heard these days.

"You know I used to be horribly jealous of you and Sutton," Theresa said, capturing Kathleen's attention once again.

Kathleen looked at her friend in surprise. "Why?"

"I always thought *I'd* be the one to find a rich, successful man who loved me madly and passionately. You had such a perfect life with Sutton."

A perfect life. Yes, that's probably how it had looked to the rest of the world. Nobody had known the loneliness, the isolation that Kathleen had felt in her own home, in her marriage.

She'd been an innocent nineteen-year-old when the handsome, successful thirty-year-old Dr. Sutton Marlowe had swept her off her feet.

Initially, the marriage had been everything Kathleen had ever dreamed of. Sutton was passionate and loving, and seemed eager to please his young bride. But the birth of Gina changed all that.

While Sutton was a devoted father, he spent more and more of his free time downstairs in his study, and he rarely sought out Kathleen for anything.

A million times she'd thought of leaving him. But ultimately a streak of cowardice and Gina had kept her in the marriage. She'd traded passion for security, uncertainty for a life without choices.

Then Sutton was gone, taken by a tragic car accident and she didn't have to summon the courage to finally leave her empty marriage behind.

She leaned her head back against the rough bark of the tree, noting that Theresa had dozed off.

She smiled as Gina ran toward her, then flopped down on the blanket next to Kathleen. "When do we get to eat? I'm starving," Gina exclaimed.

"We'll have to wait a few minutes. Theresa is snoozing." She grabbed a tube of sunscreen from her purse. "Here, let me put some of this on your shoulders and face. I don't want you to get a sunburn." She inhaled deeply, relishing the scent of sunshine, of innocence, the sweetness of girlhood that wafted from Gina.

"I hope Theresa made something good for lunch," Gina said. "Sometimes she makes yucky stuff."

"Yucky stuff?" Theresa sat up and glared at Gina in mock outrage. "What yucky stuff?"

Gina giggled. "That fishy stuff."

"That fishy stuff was sushi, and a lot of people like it very much." Theresa ran a hand through her spiky blond hair, then reached for the picnic basket. "But you'll be happy to know that I brought no sushi today."

"Good," Gina and Kathleen replied in unison, then laughed.

They gorged themselves on fried chicken, chunks of sharp cheddar cheese and slices of fresh fruit. Worry slipped away in the bright sunshine and amid the laughter that bubbled easily and frequently from Gina.

After lunch Theresa and Kathleen once again stretched out

on the blanket and Gina returned to the swing set. "I wonder if this heat will ever break." Theresa plucked irritably at the risqué neckline of her blouse. "I was hoping the rain the other night would cool things off, but it just made it worse."

Kathleen grabbed an orange from the basket and peeled it with her thumbnail. Her thoughts drifted back to the night of the storm, and the man who had shown up on her doorstep in the middle of the night.

She hadn't told Theresa about Lucas Connelly. Nor had she told Bill. What could she tell? That a nut had appeared on her doorstep spouting craziness? He'd been a nutcase, albeit a handsome one.

He'd been so strange, so intense. His eyes had been powerful in their burning turbulence. *She's a night traveler.* He'd said the words firmly, without doubt. As if he had secret knowledge that nobody else had.

Who was he? Where had he come from? And how had he learned about Gina? As much as she wanted to dismiss him from her mind, thoughts of him kept returning.

"If you wanted orange juice, you should have just used a juicer," Theresa observed.

"What?" Kathleen looked at her blankly, then gazed down at the orange in her hands. She had kneaded it into a messy pulp and sticky juice ran between her fingers. "Hand me a couple of those napkins, please?"

She quickly cleaned up the mess, then grabbed a cold can of soda from the cooler. "After I finish this, we probably should head back home." She looked over to where Gina was once again playing in the sand. "She's going to need an hour-long bath just to soak the sand out of her skin."

Theresa followed her gaze and smiled longingly. "If I don't

find Mr. Right in the next two years, then I'm going to find Mr. Stud and make a baby."

Kathleen looked at her friend in surprise. "You've never mentioned wanting children before."

"I never thought about it much until lately, but I love Gina and if I had a baby, I'd never be alone again. Besides, suddenly the old biological clock is ticking loudly in my ear."

"Theresa, you just turned thirty. You've still got plenty of time. For God's sake don't do anything impulsive."

"When have you ever known me to do anything impulsive?"

Kathleen grinned. "How about last year when you decided to fly to Las Vegas and marry Roger, whom you'd only known for two days. Or when you and what's-his-name decided to get matching tattoos on your . . ."

"Enough," Theresa protested with a laugh. "Okay, so there have been times in my life when I've been a bit impulsive. It's just another reason why you love me since you never take risks, never do anything before obsessing over it for at least a week."

Kathleen finished her soda, crushed the can, then stood. "A little obsessing is good for the soul. On that note, I think it's time to call it a day."

"Yeah, I should go home, too. I'm meeting John for dinner tonight." Theresa packed up the remains of their picnic as Kathleen folded the blanket.

"This was fun. I'm really glad you suggested it," Kathleen said as her gaze sought her daughter. Gina had left the sandbox and was once again on the swing, although she just sat, her slender legs barely touching the ground.

"She looks like she's ready to call it a day, too," Theresa observed as her gaze followed Kathleen's to Gina.

"Gina. Come on, time to head home." Kathleen turned to Theresa and gave her friend a quick hug. "Thanks for lunch." She grinned. "And thanks for not bringing sushi."

Theresa laughed and grabbed the picnic basket. "I'll call you tomorrow and give you all the juicy details of my dinner date tonight."

Kathleen winced. "If you're dessert, I don't want to hear the details."

"It's a deal." Theresa waved a goodbye, then headed toward the parking area. Kathleen watched her until she was out of sight.

She worried about Theresa, who lived from moment to moment with no thought for yesterday or tomorrow. She also worried about Theresa's penchant for choosing men not only wrong for her, but wrong for the human race.

She looked back over at her daughter, who hadn't moved from the swing. "Gina, time to go home." Kathleen tossed her soda can into a nearby trash barrel and frowned at Gina, who still had not moved.

"Gina?" The little girl's face held no expression. There was only an utter blankness that caused a cold weight of dread to thunk into the pit of Kathleen's stomach.

Never had the little park seemed so vast as when Kathleen raced across the burnt, browned grass to reach her daughter. When she finally got to Gina the frigid anxiety in her stomach expanded, rushing through her veins with icy fingers of alarm.

"Gina!" She yelled again even though she knew it was too late, hopeless. Gina was gone. She'd disappeared into the dark tunnel that, up until now, had only threatened her when she slept.

Kathleen stared at her child, who looked like a malleable

doll who'd been positioned on the swing, but whose face and blank eyes reflected the emptiness within.

"No." The word escaped Kathleen on a desperate sigh as she fought back tears. It had been bad enough when she'd had to be afraid for Gina to sleep. But now, her fear knew no boundaries. It raged through her like a virulent bacteria, twisting in her stomach and rising up the back of her throat.

The sunshine heating her back seemed to mock her, taunt her. This wasn't supposed to happen in the daylight. Gina wasn't supposed to be taken from her when the sun was shining.

She's a night traveler. Lucas Connelly's words came back to her, a haunting whisper in her ear. She'd dismissed him as a nut. But what if he wasn't? What had he meant when he'd said Gina was a traveler? Why had she dismissed him so easily?

Dammit, why hadn't she asked him more questions? And if he knew so much, why hadn't he warned her that this could happen during the day?

With the taste of utter despair in her mouth, Kathleen sank to her knees, wrapped her arms around her child and prayed that once again Gina would find her way out of the dark, dangerous tunnel.

Thanatos stood at the window, peering out into the deepening shadows of the approaching night. How sweet the night. The shadowed mists were a balm to his spirit, a fever in his blood. The night belonged to Satan, as did Thanatos.

He couldn't remember a time when he hadn't known that he was the chosen one, destined to bring the Lord of Darkness back to his rightful place as king of the world.

It was a goal he'd attempted in lifetime after lifetime, in

battle after battle. But this fight, in this lifetime, was the one that would ultimately succeed. He'd won the small battles in other lifetimes, but now it was time to win the war.

He smelled the winds of the storm that approached, felt the power growing, swelling inside him. So good . . . to know that the power would continue to grow and eventually he would rule the earth as the right hand of Satan.

He frowned, knowing that someplace another's power grew as well. And only that somebody stood between Thanatos and his destiny.

A smile curved his lips as he anticipated the battle to come. He would win and consign his miserable adversary to a torturous and painful death.

It was all coming together so effortlessly. So much had already been accomplished. So many lifetimes culminating in this, the final apocalypse. Excitement surged through him, rich and potent as sexual desire.

He craved the chaos to come. He hungered for the anarchy that would follow. He reveled in the power that had been promised to him as the right hand of the Dark Lord.

Soon the final pieces would fall into place. The children came to him, following the sound of his voice as he beckoned them through the passageway that led to hell.

Their souls twinkled like fireflies in the darkness, illuminated by innocence and purity. It was an innocence and purity he would taint, would destroy. There were only a few left to garner before the pieces would finally be in place. The last to be taken would be the girl.

Gina.

She would be given to Satan, the ultimate sacrifice completed.

He threw back his head and laughed, then pointed to the

darkening sky. A spider web of lightning instantly crackled across the horizon, followed seconds later by a deafening boom of thunder that echoed the sound of his laughter.

In a park a hundred miles away, Gina Marlowe opened her eyes and screamed. And screamed . . . and screamed.

Chapter Five

"Keith!"

Rosalyn's voice pierced the veil of sleep. He came awake with a gasp and sat straight up in bed. Rosalyn reached over and turned on the lamp on the bedside stand, the muted light casting shadows on the bedroom walls. "You were screaming," she said.

He nodded, unsurprised. He could still taste the horror in his mouth, feel the pressure of a scream trapped deep inside his chest.

He swung his legs over the side of the bed and slumped over, head in hands. "I . . . I had a nightmare."

"The same one?" He felt Rosalyn's warmth as she moved closer to him, smelled the scent of the hand lotion she put on every night before going to bed. He nodded.

A yawning hollowness filled him as he thought of the nightmare that had plagued his sleep for the last week. It was always the same. Sharon in a long, dark passageway, lost in the swirling mists of a thick fog.

He hunted for her. He couldn't see her, but he could hear her, crying out for him. Her pitiful cries were knives thrown into his heart, piercing through to the most vulnerable areas.

Down the dark corridor he ran, his gasps aching in his chest as he followed the sounds of her cries. He needed to find her, to guide her out of the dank labyrinth that threatened to swallow her. But no matter how fast he ran, no matter how far he raced, he couldn't reach her. She remained just out of sight, just out of reach.

The scream of horror trapped in the pit of his stomach transformed into a sob of despair. He swallowed hard against it. He had to be strong . . . for Rosalyn . . . for Sharon. "I'm all right." He turned to his wife and offered her a forced smile. "Go back to sleep. I'm going to get up and do a little work in the office."

She looked at him for a long moment, a silent appeal in her eyes. He knew what she wanted. She wanted him to hold her, to momentarily banish her heartache with his lovemaking. But he couldn't. They'd tried twice since Sharon had gone to the hospital, but it was impossible. Keith couldn't.

He got out of bed, turning his back on his wife, unable to look in her eyes any longer. He went out into the hallway and hesitated outside Sharon's bedroom. Rosalyn kept a small light burning in Sharon's room, as if it was a promise that Sharon would return to her own bed, return to life.

It had become an obsession with his wife. She checked the bulb first thing in the morning and the last thing before she went to bed. She'd replaced it three times in the last week, afraid somehow that if the bulb burned out, Sharon would never return to them.

He walked into the bedroom, comforted by the surroundings that contained the essence of his daughter's spirit. Ceramic bears in frilly tu-tus danced across the top of her dresser. Posters of famous ballet dancers decorated the walls: Pavlova, Nureyev, Fonteyn and Nijinsky, the greats, the role models of a little girl who'd dreamed of being a ballerina.

"Daddy's little dancer," Keith said softly, reaching down to pick up one of Sharon's tiny ballet slippers. It was worn on the bottom, darkened from use. Would she still be able to fit in them when she woke up?

His heartache grew in his chest, pressing tightly and making it difficult for him to draw in a full breath.

What had been oddly comforting moments before now tormented him. The little girl smell that permeated the room, the storybook opened to a tale of Swan Lake . . . pieces of a little girl now lost. He stumbled out of the room, unable to stay another moment.

Keith's office was the spare bedroom, a tiny room with a desk, shelves of reference books and his computer. He sank down at the desk and buried his head in his hands.

He punched on his computer, waiting for it to load up, then opened the file that was designated with the label: Sharon.

It contained all the material he'd gathered on the other children he'd found suffering the same fate as Sharon. Since speaking with Kathleen Marlowe about her daughter, he'd discovered two more children in hospitals who also were in inexplicable comas.

Like the others, these newest victims had told their parents about tunnel nightmares, flying through the dark and the fear that they would leave their bodies behind and never return.

Still, there seemed to be no discernible link between the victims. The only common denominator was the fact that they all lived within a two hundred-mile area of each other.

He'd read and reread the file, analyzed each and every detail and still the answers remained elusive.

Damn, there had to be something he was missing . . . some key to what was happening. What were these children experiencing? Once again he focused on the facts, seeking a clue, any idea that might provide an explanation.

"Keith, I've put the coffee on," Rosalyn spoke from the doorway, pulling him from his work. Dawn streaked in through the windows, pronouncing the start of a new day. He rubbed his eyes, vaguely surprised by the passing of time.

He followed Rosalyn into the kitchen and sank down tiredly at the breakfast table. She poured their coffee, then sat across from him. "I thought maybe we could take turns reading to Sharon today," she said, breaking the silence that had settled like a suffocating blanket around them. "I checked out some books from the library that I think she will like."

"I'm not going to the hospital today." He didn't look up from his coffee cup, didn't want to see the censure in her eyes. "I'm going into the newspaper office. I . . . I need to get back to work."

He jumped, startled as her hand reached out and encircled his. He looked up, into her beautiful but tormented eyes, eyes that understood his pain and his need to escape back into the orderly, manageable world of his work.

"Yes, you need to get back to work," she agreed softly. He realized then that she found his grief, his anger as big a burden as Sharon's illness, and it would almost be a relief for him to return to his job.

At eight o'clock Keith left the house and took the train

into Manhattan, where he worked for an alternative newspaper called *The Varsity*. The paper focused on tabloid-type stories mixed with good, hard news reports and enjoyed a relatively large readership. Keith had worked for the paper for the past thirteen years, and there was a sense of coming home when he walked into the building.

"Keith!" Myra, the receptionist half rose in greeting. "How's Sharon?" She sank back down into the chair, which groaned beneath her abundant weight.

"No change." Keith thrust a thumb toward the door behind her desk. "Is he in?"

Myra's moon-shaped face darkened. "He's in, and he's been a bear since you've been gone."

Keith nodded, a burst of adrenaline filling him as he pushed open the door that led into his editor's office. Burt Rainwright was a stereotype of the crusty, curmudgeonly newspaper man. He lived on black coffee, cheap cigars, and news.

When Keith entered the room Burt was on the phone, growling into the receiver like a grizzly bear just awakened. "I don't give a damn what your personal problems are, just get me that story by noon today." He slammed down the phone and glared at Keith. "You back here to work?"

Keith nodded and sat in the chair across from Burt's desk. Burt withdrew from the desk drawer one of his infernal cigars and clipped the end, his narrow eyes studying Keith. "How's your kid?"

"No change."

"Tough break," Burt said, and Keith knew it was the last time Burt would mention Keith's personal life. "As a matter of fact, your timing in coming back is perfect. I've got some notes here. . . ." He sorted through the papers and files on top of the desk, moving the unlit cigar like a toothpick from one side of his mouth to the other between his teeth.

"Here it is." He grabbed a small notepad, ripped off the top page and handed it to Keith. "Church desecration. There seems to be a rash of them in the last six weeks or so." He reared back in his chair and removed the cigar from his mouth. "I want you to follow up, find out if the cops think it's gang-related or cult activity."

Keith looked down at the sheet of paper where there was a name written along with two addresses. "Who's this Roger Boyle?"

"That's the cop who investigated the last incident, which was at a church over on the West Side. It happened last night. I've got the priest's name here someplace." Once again Burt dug around in the mountain of papers on his desk and found a scrap of paper, which he handed to Keith. "Well, what are you doing still sitting here? You've got a story to cover." Burt dismissed him with a wave of his hand.

Keith left the office building and walked out into the oppressive heat, the notes clutched tightly in his hand. It felt good to be on a story again. He needed this desperately. He couldn't help Sharon. He couldn't help Rosalyn, but he could get back to work and he hoped the work would help him hang on to whatever was left of his own sanity.

Kathleen sat in the back of the cab, knowing she was crazy. She'd lost her mind. And yet strangely enough there was a certain modicum of peace in her lunacy. Gina disappearing into the darkness in the middle of the day in the park had finally shoved Kathleen over the edge and into insanity.

When Gina had finally regained consciousness and stopped screaming, Kathleen had taken her home and held her for the remainder of the day and long into the night.

Finally, in the middle of the night, with Gina sleeping peacefully, Kathleen had crept downstairs and stared at the vase that rested on the table just inside the front door. She knew it contained, amid other scraps of paper, the spare house keys, the button from her blue suit jacket, the business card from Lucas Connelly.

It taunted her . . . holding out the promise of false hope. Foolish, she scoffed. Utter nonsense, she thought . . . still before she knew her own intent her hand reached inside the vase and plucked the card from the other items.

She'd called the number on the business card throughout the next day, always getting an answering machine. The prerecorded message had been a computerized voice stating that Lucas Connelly couldn't come to the phone but could be reached every night at the Club Diablo where he performed between the hours of ten and two.

It had taken her all evening to make up her mind. Finally at nine that night she'd called Bill to sit with Gina while she went in search of the man with the dark eyes who had spoken the only words that made any kind of sense at all.

Someplace deep inside she knew it was crazy, that she was probably pinning her hopes on a madman. But, she was desperate, and at this point she would sell her soul to the devil himself if he'd promised to make Gina well.

"Hot night," the cabby said, breaking through her thoughts. "I'm beginning to wonder if this heat wave will ever break."

"Yes, it is hot," Kathleen answered absently.

"Before long winter will be here and the snow will fly," he observed.

Winter. It seemed an endless night away. Would Gina still

be sick? Would they still be living in this nightmare? The thoughts brought winter to Kathleen's heart, filled her with an arctic chill that terrified her.

She stared out the cab window. Saturday night in Manhattan was like an evening at the zoo. Any and all creatures were present, walking the streets, hanging out in the clubs, drifting in and out of the theaters.

It had been years since Kathleen had been out on a Saturday night. Sutton hadn't been the sociable type, and most of their Saturday nights had been spent with him shut up in his office.

"Here we are." The driver brought the cab to a halt.

Kathleen looked out the window, hesitating before getting out. The warehouse that held the Club Diablo was painted black except for the bright red front door. What would she find beyond the door? Could Lucas offer them the help they so desperately needed?

"In or out, lady. If this doesn't look like your thing, I can take you someplace else."

"Out." Kathleen shoved her disquiet aside. She got out, paid the fare, and then fought the impulse to run after him as he pulled away from the curb.

She turned and faced the doorway of the club, her mouth dry and her palms damp. She raced a hand nervously down the length of her chic black dress, unsure whether she was overdressed or underdressed for what was inside the club.

A low thrum pulsed in the air, like a gigantic heartbeat . . . bass coming from inside the club, she realized. Steeling herself, she opened the door and went inside.

It took a moment for her eyes to adjust to the semi-darkness of the club. Ahead of the dance floor was lit with colored lights, their blinking colors emphasizing the well-dressed couples who moved to the pop music created by the five-piece band in one corner.

She breathed a sigh of relief as a well-dressed host led her to a table in the shadows near the small stage. She looked around with interest. The place was packed. Most of the tables were occupied, and people crowded around the long bar that stretched the length of one wall.

It was definitely an uptown crowd, not a pair of jeans in the place. Designer clothes, expensive jewelry and subdued elegance surrounded her. The fear that had gripped her from the moment she'd stepped out of the cab subsided.

"Hi, how you doing this evening?"

She looked up to see a waitress standing next to her table. Her cheerful, open face held a friendly smile that soothed away the last of Kathleen's unease. The waitress was clad in a spandex leotard with a plunging neckline. A pair of ridiculous-looking stuffed red horns popped up atop her head. "What can I get for you?"

"Just a club soda." There was no way Kathleen wanted anything alcoholic in her system to cloud her judgment.

"Gotcha. Be right back." The waitress turned and left, showing off a swinging red stuffed devil's tail.

"Could you tell me when the magician performs?" Kathleen asked moments later when the waitress returned with her drink.

"Lucas? He should be on in about . . ." she looked at her watch. "Ten minutes. He does his thing at the top of every hour." She set Kathleen's drink before her. "Have you seen him perform before?"

Kathleen shook her head.

"Oh, you're in for a real treat. He's always been good, but in the last couple of weeks or so, he's become phenomenal.

He's packing the place every night. Enjoy the show."

The next ten minutes were the longest Kathleen ever spent in her life. A shiver walked up her spine as the light on the dance floor blinked off and the club was plunged into absolute blackness.

A flash of fire exploded in the center of the stage and suddenly he was there, in the single glow of a spotlight.

He was clad much like he had been on the night he'd shown up on her front porch. Dark slacks hugged his long legs and the white shirt with its billowing sleeves emphasized his slender waist and broad shoulders. He appeared slight in build, more grace than granite, yet with a masculine sensuality that was mesmerizing.

As he began his performance, Kathleen found herself not watching his feats of magic, but rather focused on the man himself. He moved with the sleek elegance of a panther stalking prey, yet with the precision and efficiency of a trained athlete.

He owned the stage and the audience, wearing his intensity like a shield around him. The crowd was utterly silent . . . spellbound as they watched him perform illusions and sleight-of-hand tricks with apparent ease.

Kathleen brought her glass to her lips, then paused as his gaze seemed to connect with hers. She felt an immediate electric shock explode in the pit of her stomach.

His black eyes held her. She felt him probing . . . assessing . . . dissecting her insides, reaching to delve into her very soul.

But that's ridiculous, she thought. He can't see me. He's on a brilliantly lit stage and I'm in the darkness. There's no way he can see me.

Yet she knew he did. She felt his gaze as potently as if he'd reached out from the stage and stroked the length of her hair, caressed the side of her face. As their gazes remained locked, she fell into the dark depths of his eyes.

The crowd and their surroundings disappeared, evaporated as reality shifted and his hypnotic eyes consumed her. Deeper and deeper she was drawn into the abyss. She felt him inside her, as if he were having sex with her . . . an intimacy, a violation, a connection so intense it frightened her.

With a small cry, she tore her gaze from his. Her drink splashed over the top of her glass, and she slammed it down on the table.

She looked around, wondering whether anyone else had experienced what she just had, but she knew no one had. The people around her looked fascinated, awed, intrigued, and she knew she alone had felt that moment of complete submission of spirit and soul.

Who was this man? And why did she feel as if she somehow knew him? For the remainder of his show, she kept her focus on his trickery, not daring to look into his face again, afraid of the power of his dark, compelling eyes.

Chapter Six

The minute the show ended and the red velvet curtain crashed down to hide the stage, Kathleen got up from her table and sought a doorway that would lead her to the back-stage area. She spied one at the left of the stage and hurried toward it, hoping, praying that nobody stopped her.

Nobody did.

She followed the passageway as it cut to the right and found herself in a dark, narrow hallway with Lucas Connelly walking just ahead of her.

"Mr. Connelly . . . Lucas," she called after him.

He stopped and turned around, his features lit only by the red glow of a nearby EXIT sign. Kathleen approached him hesitantly. His energy pulsated in the narrow confines of the hall and panic pressed heavily against her chest.

The flashing red of the sign reflected in the blackness of his eyes, made them look the way she always imagined the flames of hell might look.

He remained motionless, not speaking, his handsome features not telling her if he remembered her or not.

"Mr. Connelly. I'm Kathleen Marlowe. You came to my house about a month ago?"

"I know."

She'd forgotten the sound of his voice, like the low moan of the wind across a desolate, wintry plain. It chilled her, yet drew her closer to him at the same time. "That night you seemed to know something about my daughter . . . what was wrong with her . . . how to help her?" She held her breath.

"It's gotten worse." It wasn't a question. It was a statement of fact, as if he already knew the answer.

She nodded, her breath expelling on a hopeless sigh. "It's happening during the day now. I've taken her to every kind of doctor I can think of, but nobody seems to be able to help us."

He nodded. "They can't help you. Your daughter's problem is beyond the realm of medical knowledge."

"Please . . . what's wrong with her?" Kathleen reached out her hand and placed it on his arm. His flesh beneath the white shirt was hot . . . radiating a fevered force that traveled through her fingers like an electrical shock.

She dropped her hand and stumbled a step backward, afraid of him . . . and afraid of her incredible need for him.

"I told you what was wrong before. She's a traveler," he said.

"I don't know what that means." Tears of frustration burned her eyes. Why couldn't she find somebody to help her . . . help Gina?

"She's astral projecting."

She stared at him in bewilderment. Astral projecting? The spirit flying without the need of the body? She'd heard of it

71

before, but she had never really believed in such a thing. It sounded so ridiculous, so incredulous.

And yet as she thought of the way Gina had described seeing her own body lying on the bed, then the sensation of flying, it made a kind of horrifying sense. But how could this stranger understand her daughter's experiences?

Lucas seemed to recognize her confusion and his penetrating gaze intensified. He took a step closer to her, his nearness causing her heartbeat to pound painfully against her ribcage. It was as if he commanded the air around them, and he made it almost impossible for her to breathe in enough oxygen.

"It's not important whether you believe me or not. What is important is that you understand that your daughter is in tremendous danger. She's traveling into dimensions she's unprepared to handle."

His features were taut with suppressed emotion, and his eyes burned with an infernal flame. Highlighted by the red glow, he looked completely, utterly mad. "If you don't do something to help her, eventually she will disappear and never find her way back to you."

Kathleen felt as if she stood on the precipice of an uncharted, unexplored netherworld and with one misstep she could plunge into the abyss and never again escape. "I . . . I don't know what to do," she whispered.

"I do." There was a calm assurance in his tone, one that reached inside her, sought out her anxiety and soothed it seductively. "I can help her."

"How?"

"She must be trained. Right now another force is attempting to control her. She has to be taught to channel her energy, master her talent. It must be done quickly."

He stepped closer still, his breath warm on her face as heat from his body pressed in around her. "We must act quickly if we are to save the child. I will need to spend time with her, teach her. I'll need to be there whenever she travels, day and night."

A quick protest rose to her lips. Open her home to this man? Impossible. She knew nothing about him. What if he was just another nut?

Still, even as this thought arose, a mental vision of Gina filled her mind. She saw her daughter's eyes . . . green eyes tormented with the kind of fear a little girl shouldn't have to experience.

She closed her eyes, knowing she would do anything, risk everything to find her daughter some peace, to keep her safe from harm. She opened her eyes and looked at Lucas Connelly . . . afraid to give in to him, afraid not to. "Okay." Her voice was a mere whisper in the silence of the hallway. "When can I expect you?"

"Tomorrow morning." Without saying a word he turned and disappeared into his dressing room.

Kathleen expelled a deep, tremulous sigh and fought against the shiver of apprehension that threatened to race up her spine. For just a moment, before he'd turned to walk away, his eyes had lit with what had looked like a flare of triumph, and that had frightened her more than anything.

She closed her eyes and swayed against the wall. She should be feeling a certain amount of relief, but she didn't. She felt as if *she* stood at the mouth of that dark tunnel and instead of helping Gina find her way out . . . she'd only managed to get them both more hopelessly lost in the darkness.

* * *

Belinda stood in the deepest shadows of the hallway, watching as the dark-haired woman left and Lucas went into his dressing room and closed the door.

She'd been too far away to hear what the two had been saying to each other, but she'd felt the electricity that sparked in the air. She'd tasted the tang of desperation that had radiated from the woman and felt the more subtle energy of sexual attraction that had emanated between them.

She narrowed her eyes, still smelling the expensive perfume of the woman. What had she wanted with Lucas? There had always been a number of groupies who after the performance threw themselves at Lucas, women he turned away with a charming smile.

But this one hadn't fit into that category. She hadn't been some young wild thing out for the thrill of a quick screw with the star of the nightly entertainment. Nor had Lucas responded to her with his usual casual charm.

There had been an intensity radiating between them, an intensity bred of familiarity. Was the woman a past love? Was her intention to come back into his life, displace Belinda?

"Over my dead body," Belinda murmured softly. There was no way she intended to lose Lucas. No way in hell. Besides, she had Thanatos's blessing. He'd promised her that Lucas's soul would belong to her for all eternity. If she couldn't take care of that bitch, then Thanatos would.

"You are out of your mind." Despite Bill's hushed tone, his anger was apparent in the flare of his nostrils, the wrinkles that cut deep into his broad brow.

He paced the length of the living room, stopping with every step to glare at Kathleen. "You can't do this. You don't know anything about this man. He could be some pervert, a nut . . ."

"Bill, please." Kathleen rubbed the center of her forehead, trying to suppress the pain that blossomed there. "Please, just sit down and let me explain."

"There's nothing to explain. You waltz in here in the middle of the night and tell me you've invited some stranger . . . some two-bit magician to move in and help you with your daughter. Jesus, Kathleen . . . think about it."

"I have. I thought about it on the way to the club, and I thought about it all the way home." She rubbed her forehead again. "Bill, I'm out of options. Lucas Connelly is the only person who seems to know what's going on. He's the only one who has offered to help Gina."

"And you know absolutely nothing about him."

"I know what I need to know. When I looked into his eyes I believed in him. I believe he can help us." She looked down at her hands.

There were other things she couldn't explain, like the fact that when she'd stared into Lucas's dark eyes, she'd been struck by a haunting sense of familiarity.

She'd looked at his mouth and had known how his lips would feel, fevered and hungry against her own. She'd had the distinct feeling that it had not been a fantasy, but rather a distant memory echoing from a distant past. She frowned, wondering if she had finally lost her grip on sanity.

"Kathleen, I can't condone you doing something so crazy as opening your home to this man."

She stood, fighting against a sudden burst of anger. "You don't have to condone or approve of anything I do," she said stiffly.

"At least let me find out about the guy. Let me run a

background check on him before you allow him to come here and be around Gina."

"You do what you think is best, but he's coming here first thing in the morning and I don't intend to turn him away."

"Dammit, Kathleen, you're being unreasonable. Give me a week, two at the most to find out what I can on him."

"I don't have a week or two to gamble," she returned angrily. "I don't know if I have another day. For all I know Gina could have another attack tonight and never wake up."

She stood and walked to the front door. "Go home, Bill. I'm tired. I don't have the energy to fight with you anymore tonight."

"Then stop arguing and listen to me. I don't want this man in your house. This is foolhardy at best."

"I don't need this from you, Bill." She opened the front door. "Just leave me alone. Let me deal with the result of my actions."

Bill was angrier than she'd ever seen him. His face was florid. "Fine, but don't call me when things are out of control and you realize you've made a mistake inviting this . . . this . . . magic man into your home." Without waiting for a reply, he stalked out of the house and disappeared into the darkness.

Kathleen slammed the door and locked it, her anger instantly seeping away. She sank down on the sofa and thought about calling Theresa, just to talk, but instantly changed her mind.

She hadn't seen or heard much from her friend since Theresa had started dating John Riley. As usual when Theresa was involved in a new relationship, everything else fell by the wayside.

What upset her more than anything was that Bill had spoken aloud her own fears, fears she refused to acknowledge because she so desperately needed the hope the magician offered.

She knew absolutely nothing about Lucas Connelly. But he was the first person who'd said anything that made any kind of sense. Other than that, she had no idea what kind of man he was.

She wrapped her arms around herself as she remembered that moment when his dark gaze had locked with hers, when she'd felt his presence, his energy deep inside her.

For that moment she'd been lost . . . helplessly lost to the power and command of his eyes. He had owned her as their gazes had remained locked.

She shivered. In allowing Lucas Connelly into their home was she really allowing in help? Or had she invited the very devil himself into their lives?

Bill drove home like a bat out of hell, his anger bowing to a more volatile emotion: fear.

The whole thing scared him. What did Kathleen know about this Lucas Connelly? That he worked in some East Side nightclub and performed tricks of magic? It was hardly a glowing recommendation.

For all he knew, the man was a con, or an abuser who preyed on single women and helpless children.

He pulled into his driveway, shut off the engine, then reached into the glove box. Shaking out two antacid tablets, he popped them in his mouth, then got out of the car. The fight with Kathleen had upset his stomach. Bitter acid rose up the back of his throat.

He got out of the car and sank down on the front stoop. The sweltering heat surrounded him. It was so hot even the insects that normally sang in the night were quiet. He stared up at the moon, the surface partially obscured by wispy night clouds skirting across the sky.

Looking deep within himself, he recognized the source of his fear, and it shamed him. He was afraid that the magician would be able to do what everyone else could not . . . heal Gina. In doing so Lucas Connelly would become Kathleen's hero. And Bill so desperately wanted to be her hero.

One thing was certain. First thing in the morning he was going to place some calls. He intended to do that background check on Mr. Lucas Connelly.

He was determined to learn everything he could about the magician as quickly as possible. And if the magician brought more harm to Kathleen or to Gina, then Bill intended to see the magician dead.

"I have to go away," Lucas said as he folded clothes from the closet and placed them in a large suitcase.

"What are you talking about?" Belinda asked, her heart pounding the rhythm of fear and suppressed rage. She sat on the edge of his bed and stared at him. "What about your job? You can't just walk out."

He didn't look at her but continued packing. "I spoke with Arnie and told him I need some time off starting immediately."

Belinda grabbed one of his arms, forcing him to stop his motions and look at her. "Lucas, wherever you're going, take me with you."

He shook his head. "You need to go home, Belinda. I'll be leaving early in the morning, and there are things I must do tonight."

"What things? Where are you going?" She reached up and

cupped his face with her hands, frantic as she saw the distance in his eyes. "Lucas, please talk to me. Tell me what's going on."

"I wish I could." He took both her wrists and gently pried her hands away from his face.

His dark eyes bore into hers and in their depths she saw a strength, a power she'd never seen before. "Belinda, you're a nice woman and I've enjoyed our time together, but I told you from the very beginning that there was no future with me. You need to move on."

"It's her, isn't it?" Belinda hissed. "That woman who was at the club tonight. Who is she, Lucas? Tell me, I want to know who the hell she is."

"This has nothing to do with you, and it doesn't matter what you want, doesn't even matter what I want." He released his hold on her and continued packing the suitcase.

Fear once again swept through Belinda. "Lucas . . . please . . . don't leave me. Please . . . I need you."

This time he reached out to her. He ran his hand down her cheek and she turned her face into the warmth of his hand like a cat seeking a caress. "Belinda, I have no choice in this. There are powers at work here . . . powers greater than you, greater than me."

"I don't understand."

"Nor do I," he said softly, and again his eyes grew distant, as if his mind had taken him away to a place where she couldn't follow. "Go home, Belinda." He gave her a gentle push toward the door. "Go home and forget about me."

She stared at him, tears burning as despair transformed into rage. "You bastard," she hissed. She twirled on her heels and left his apartment, but didn't go far.

She stood in the shadows of the building across from Lucas's and prepared to wait. He'd said he was leaving early in the morning and she intended to follow him.

Her eyes narrowed as she stared up at Lucas's penthouse. Thanatos had promised her. She had Satan's pledge that Lucas belonged to her. "It's not over until I say it's over," she whispered.

Chapter Seven

Keith stood outside the Westside Methodist Church. The church, by New York standards, was small. However, the aged stone construction and ornate gothic style spoke of longevity. It was a neighborhood church tucked in between a small park and a large brownstone.

Despite the early morning hour, half a dozen kids were already playing in the park, their childish voices filling the air with sounds of merriment.

He'd spent all yesterday talking to the police officer in charge of the most recent spate of church desecrations. The officer had been able to give Keith very little information. They had no idea who was responsible for the vandalism, although he did have a file full of pictures that had been taken at the scene of each crime.

Keith had studied the pictures with interest, noting one unusual commonality. Black balloons and black crepe paper decorated each of the sites.

The churches themselves were in all five boroughs of the city and within the surrounding suburbs in Connecticut, New Jersey, and Long Island. Catholic, Protestant, Methodist . . . no denomination was spared from the revelers' blasphemous vandalism. Only those damned black balloons and crepe paper tied the crime scenes together.

Keith had gotten a call early that morning from the officer in charge, telling him that another church had been hit in the night.

For a long moment Keith lingered on the front step, reluctant to go inside and face the defilement of a holy place. He breathed deeply and let the children's shouts and laughter fill him up. There was no sound in the world more filled with hope than that of a child's laughter.

Would he ever hear Sharon's laughter again? Would he ever see her eyes lit with happiness? He shoved these thoughts away and concentrated on the matter at hand.

He dug out the piece of paper with the name the officer had given him. Reverend John Bascomb. With the name firmly in mind, he shoved the slip of paper into his pocket and opened the church door.

The interior of the church was darker and cool, a relief from the intense heat and relentless sunshine outside. He stood in the back, scanning the rear of the rows of pews and the colorful stained-glass windows.

Growing up, Keith's family had attended a Methodist church much like this one. As a sixth-grader, he'd gone to Sunday School an entire year without missing a Sunday and had earned himself a pretty lapel pin that he'd worn proudly on his suit jacket.

He couldn't remember now why he'd stopped going to church. Despite the fact that it had been years since he'd last officially worshipped, he'd always considered himself a religious man. His Methodist upbringing had served him through his adulthood . . . until Sharon had become sick.

It was then that Keith had realized faith was easy when your life was untroubled; the real test came when those close to you seemed to suffer needlessly. In the last couple of weeks Keith had gained a new respect for Job.

He was pulled from his thoughts by a scraping noise coming from the front of the sanctuary. He walked up the center aisle, noting for the first time the black balloons and crepe paper that littered the floor, the spray-painted symbols and words that marred the walls. Ahead of him on the wall above the altar, a crucifix now hung upside down.

Keith had viewed a desecrated church before. He'd seen an altar smeared with feces, frilly underpants donning a Madonna, black candles mocking purity and goodness. But he'd never witnessed a desecration that included crepe paper and balloons, as if a perverted party had taken place. And for some reason, this particular form of profanity bothered him more than the other cases he'd observed.

He reached the front of the pews and saw a jean-clad young man scraping a slash of red paint off the area just to the left of the sanctuary. Keith cleared his throat, startling the man, who whirled around and stood. "May I help you?" he asked. He dropped the putty knife he'd been using and wiped his hands down the sides of his worn jeans.

"I'm looking for Rev. John Bascomb."

"You found him. What can I do for you?"

Keith introduced himself and waved his hands to encompass the area. "Quite a mess," he noted.

The reverend nodded and in the blueness of his eyes Keith saw the kind of wisdom and peace he'd expect to find in the eyes of a much older man. "I pity the ones who did this. They are lost souls, damned for eternity."

"There's been an epidemic of church break-ins in the last couple of months. You care to make a comment?"

"On the record?"

Keith nodded and John frowned thoughtfully. "On the record, I think the kids in this neighborhood need more constructive avenues for their energy and time."

"So you think kids are responsible for this?"

John shrugged, as if unwilling to make a firm commitment. Keith studied the bloodred spray paint that defiled the walls. There were pictures of the mystical third eye, swastikas and inverted crosses. Blasphemous words were scrawled like joyous graffiti on the side of a subway car.

The destruction was unsettling, more because Keith didn't believe it was the result of bored or wild kids. The balloons were a common denominator, telling him that whoever had defiled this church had also been responsible for at least a dozen others. The whole operation was too big, too far-reaching to be the work of youngsters.

He paused in front of one particular word written in red across the wall. "Thanatos? What does that mean?"

The reverend's face darkened perceptively. "Thanatos is a god of death in Greek mythology."

"Educated vandals?"

Again, John shrugged. He leaned down and picked up his putty blade. "We've got painters coming in later this afternoon. We're lucky that nothing was broken or stolen."

Keith kicked at one of the black balloons, watching as it drifted up in the air, then sank back to the ground. He looked back at the reverend, who had gone back to work. "On the record you intimated that you think kids are responsible for all this. Off the record, what do you think?"

"Off the record?" John sighed and turned to face Keith. This time his eyes weren't filled with the wisdom of godliness. Instead, Keith saw fear.

"I think an incredible evil held a party for the damned in this church. And I think that evil was celebrating its growing power on earth. Dark days are coming. Darkness and death." With a suddenness that startled Keith, John turned back around and returned to scraping at the red paint. "That is strictly off the record."

They both turned as an older woman entered, her forehead furrowed with wrinkles. "Reverend Bascomb, could I speak to you for a moment?"

"Certainly." Excusing himself from Keith, the reverend joined the woman for a brief conversation. He finished talking to her, then moved back to the front of the church. "I'm sorry, I have to leave," he said to Keith as he folded up the dropcloth beneath where he had been working. "I'm needed at the hospital."

"Nothing serious, I hope."

"I'm not sure. One of my young parishioners went into some sort of a coma last night. His family needs me."

Adrenaline soared through Keith. "Would you mind if I tagged along to the hospital?"

John looked at him skeptically. "These people don't need a reporter sniffing around for a sensational story."

"My interest has nothing to do with a story," Keith hurriedly protested. "It's personal . . . my . . . my daughter is in a coma. Please, I promise not to intrude on them."

John studied his face, his gaze seeming to peer deep into Keith's eyes, as if discerning the condition of his soul. After a long moment he nodded slightly, as if satisfied with what he discovered. "Come along then."

Kathleen awoke to the sun beating a brilliant path of heat through the window. Damn the heat, she thought, plucking at the sheet that stuck to her. Would it never break?

The room was not very cheerful even with bright sunshine streaming through the windows. The dark walnut paneling and heavy navy velvet curtains created a somber, almost claustrophobic aura.

The furniture was heavy, sturdy, reflective of Sutton's personality throughout their ten years of marriage. After the shock of Sutten's tragic accident had worn off, she'd contemplated moving out of the brownstone, or at least redecorating. But, before she'd been able to follow through on either thought, Gina's nighttime disturbances had begun.

Rolling over, she checked the clock next to her bed. Only a few minutes after eight. Surely it would be hours before Lucas arrived. He'd finished his show late the night before, and even magicians needed sleep.

With a sigh, she swung her legs over the side of the bed. She had a lot to do before Lucas Connelly showed up. She needed to air out and dust the spare bedroom, prepare it for a guest.

A guest . . . Lucas didn't really fit that description. No, in truth he was as unwanted as the plague, but he also represented her last vestige of hope.

He'd known too many things about Gina. His inexplicable knowledge both frightened her and filled her with hope. She didn't care what he pulled out of his bag of tricks as long as he healed her daughter and returned her to a normal, happy, healthy child.

She immediately checked on Gina, content to see she was sleeping peacefully. How little it took to make her happy these days, she thought as she showered. As long as Gina slept like a normal child, Kathleen was satisfied.

She dressed in a pair of navy slacks and a pale yellow and navy floral blouse. With deft fingers she braided her long, dark hair, then headed for the kitchen to make coffee.

Within minutes the kitchen smelled of the fresh-ground hickory brew. She poured herself a cup and sat down at the table. Her thoughts scattered as she anticipated the arrival of Lucas.

Oh, how she wished Sutton were here for her to lean on. She needed his quiet strength, his calm influence, his steadying authority. There had been times in their marriage when she'd wanted to rebel and fight Sutton's control over her, but now she longed for somebody else to take charge. She was tired of fighting this battle all alone.

She stood and walked over to the window, pleased to see a scattering of clouds gathering in the north. Perhaps it would rain. It was only July, but the grass was already burnt brown as if it were the end of the summer days.

Through the thin pane of glass she heard the sound of dried, withered leaves scratching their way down the street as they rode the morning breeze.

The forlorn noise seemed an appropriate accompaniment to her despair. She felt like a dead leaf, tossed and scattered on the wind with no control of direction or destination. She could do nothing but follow the whim of the wind, and she feared the place where she'd finally land.

Turning away from the window she finished her coffee, then headed upstairs to prepare one of the spare rooms for Lucas. She'd changed the sheets and had just finished dusting when Gina stumbled in, rubbing her eyes with the back of her hands.

"Good morning, my little gumdrop," Kathleen said. A curl of worry uncoiled in her chest as she noted her daughter's unhealthy paleness and the dark circles that shadowed the area beneath her eyes.

Gina sat down on the edge of the bed. "What are you doing in here?"

Kathleen hesitated, unsure what she should tell Gina about Lucas. "We have a guest coming to visit for a little while," she finally said.

"Who?" A flicker of interest animated Gina's face. Kathleen had known Gina would be curious. Other than Theresa, there had never been an overnight guest in the house.

"His name is Lucas. He's a magician, and I'm hoping he really can pull a rabbit out of his hat," Kathleen finished more to herself than to her daughter.

Gina's forehead wrinkled in bewilderment. Kathleen laughed and grabbed her daughter's hand. "Never mind. Come on, let's go get you some breakfast."

They had just finished eating when there was a knock on the door. Kathleen froze, her heart seeming to stop its beating. This is a mistake, the rational side of her brain screamed. *Bill is right. You don't know anything about this man and you're inviting him into your life, into your daughter's life.* And yet despite these sobering, logical admonitions, her heart raced with hope. He'd said he could help Gina and that was what was important.

"Mom, aren't we going to answer the door?" Gina asked as she wiped off her milk mustache with a napkin.

Kathleen nodded and together she and Gina left the

kitchen and went into the foyer. Taking a deep, steadying breath, she opened the front door.

Lucas stood there, a study in contrasts as the sunlight dappled one side of his face and the other remained in shadows. He gripped the handle of a large, battered suitcase in one hand. Clad in a pair of jeans and a white, long-sleeved shirt, he looked positively, wonderfully normal.

However, for a moment, as she gazed into his dark eyes, she felt the same curious sense of time displaced, space compressed that she had felt the night before when in his presence.

The spell was broken as one of his dark eyebrows quirked upward and she realized she'd been staring at him. "Mr. Connelly, please come in." Kathleen moved aside to allow him to step into the large, marble-floored foyer. Gina stood behind Kathleen, peeking out from around her mother to stare up at the stranger.

Lucas set his suitcase on the floor and bent down so he was eye level with the little girl. "Hi, Gina. I'm so glad to meet you." His voice was deep and gentle, and he held out his hand to her.

Gina stepped out from behind Kathleen as if pulled by an invisible strand of silk. Kathleen was surprised when Gina placed her hand in his and smiled shyly. Normally Gina had nothing to do with strangers. It usually took her a very long time to warm up to people she didn't know.

"Hi, Mr. Colony," Gina said.

Lucas laughed, a pleasant rumbling sound that somehow surprised Kathleen. "You can just call me Lucas." He released Gina's hand and touched the tip of her nose. "I hope you and I will become wonderful friends."

He straightened up and snapped his fingers. His hand instantly filled with a nosegay of flowers. Gina gasped in delighted surprise. "I always bring flowers to the people I hope will become my friends."

He presented the tiny bouquet to the little girl, then turned to Kathleen. He swept his hand behind his back and pulled out a handful of red roses. With a courtly bow he offered them to Kathleen.

She took them, their sweet fragrance surrounding her. Droplets of dew still clung to the blossoms. She offered him a cool smile.

She was impressed, but if he thought he could bedazzle her with sleight-of-hand illusions, he was sadly mistaken. She expected a different level of magic from this man, and if he couldn't offer her some solid help, he'd be out in the blink of her eye.

The pupils of his dark eyes seemed to dilate, as if he'd read her thoughts and relished the unspoken challenge. He smiled and Kathleen's heart convulsed at his attractiveness.

Feeling a flush rise to her cheeks, she pulled her gaze away from him. "Why don't I show you to your room," she suggested. She placed the roses on the marble stand, then turned on her heel and took Gina's hand as she led the way up the stairs.

"You have a magnificent home," he observed as they climbed the wide staircase. His hand lingered on the ornate banister. "Do you know the history of it?"

"It was my husband's family home for several generations," she replied. She paused on the landing as Lucas finished ascending the last couple of steps. "Several times in the last couple of months I've thought about selling and moving to a smaller place, but at the last minute I can't seem to make the break."

Once again she found herself discomfited by the intensity of his gaze. It was as if he didn't so much listen to what she said, but rather looked into her soul to discern answers to unspoken questions.

"Mommy said she hoped you could pull a rabbit from your hat," Gina told him. "But you don't even have a hat," she observed with obvious disappointment.

Kathleen felt her face flush warmly as Lucas smiled his irritating, knowing smile. "I have a magic hat right here in my suitcase. Perhaps later we'll see if I can pull a nice, furry bunny out of it."

"And could I keep the bunny for a pet?" Gina asked.

Lucas frowned. "Hmm, that sounds like a mommy question to me. Besides," he looked back at Kathleen. "Maybe we should wait and see if I really can create the kind of magic that's necessary."

"Okay," Gina agreed.

Kathleen knew his words were meant more for her than for Gina, and she nodded. Yes, they would see if he had the ability to help Gina . . . then they would talk about a pet bunny.

She led him into the guest room. "It's rather sparse," she said, looking around the room. "Sutton and I didn't do much overnight entertaining." They had done little entertaining at all.

"It's fine," he assured her and set his suitcase on the bed.

"Well, I guess we'll let you get settled in." Kathleen hesitated. She didn't know what to say, what to expect from him. What did he have in mind to help Gina?

"I'll just unpack. Then we can discuss some sort of schedule."

She nodded and together she and Gina left his room. As

Kathleen walked down the stairs toward the kitchen, she realized Lucas had brought new life into the house. Since Sutton's death it had seemed empty and forlorn; it now vibrated with a new energy and life force.

Gina seemed to feel the new energy, to draw on it, and she danced down the stairs with an animation she hadn't shown in months. "Mommy, don't forget your flowers," Gina reminded her as they passed through the foyer.

Kathleen picked up the roses, their scent sweetening the air, and carried them into the kitchen. She didn't know how he'd managed to hide the roses and not crush a single petal. But they looked as fresh and lovely as if they'd been carefully carried from the florist directly to her.

She found a vase beneath the counter, then filled it with water and added the bright red beauties. "Do we need to put mine in water?" Gina asked.

"No, honey. Yours are silk. They don't need water to stay pretty," Kathleen explained. She finished arranging the roses, then gestured for Gina to sit down at the table.

She knew she needed to tell Gina something about Lucas . . . about why he was in their home and what part he would play in their lives for the next days or weeks.

How did you explain to a child that you'd lost all faith in science and could gain no answers from the medical doctors? How did you explain to a six-year-old that the very last hope she had was a man she didn't know, a possible charlatan who may or may not be a complete nut.

"What's wrong, Mommy?" Gina looked at her worriedly. "You've got a big frown on your face."

"Nothing, honey. I was just thinking." Kathleen smiled reassuringly. "I want to explain to you what Lucas is doing here. He's come to help you."

"Help me?" A frown deepened across her little forehead. "Is he a doctor?"

"No, he's not a doctor." Kathleen saw the relief that passed across her daughter's face. Kathleen's heart threatened to break.

In the past few months Gina had been poked and prodded, probed and tested by doctor after doctor. It was no wonder the little girl was leery of people in the medical profession. "Lucas is a friend who is going to teach you some things that might help you."

"I knew he was coming," Gina said softly. "The voice in my sleep told me. The voice told me to be afraid of him, but I'm not. Will he teach me how to stop flying when I sleep?"

"I'll teach you how to be in control." Lucas stepped into the kitchen and immediately the dimensions of the room seemed to shrink.

He slid into the chair next to Gina at the table, his gaze lingering on her. "Tell me about your night flights."

Without hesitation, Gina explained to him all that she remembered experiencing each time she left her body to fly. Kathleen was amazed by Gina's lack of reticence. The doctors had had to pull each and every word from Gina. She'd offered nothing easily. But with Lucas there was no evasiveness, no vacillation. Her gaze never wavered from his, and she spoke softly but earnestly.

This, indeed, is magic, Kathleen thought as she saw her daughter unconsciously leaning in toward Lucas. Since her father's death and in the last few months of her night disturbances, Gina had grown more and more withdrawn. But there was no sign of shyness with Lucas.

"Do you recognize the voice that speaks to you?" he asked her.

Gina frowned and slowly shook her head thoughtfully. "When I hear it, I know it. But when I wake up I don't remember who it is."

"Is it a man or a woman?"

"It's a man. He calls to me. He wants me to come to him." She studied Lucas for a long moment. "He told me to be afraid of you, but I'm not. I think the voice lies."

"Gina, why don't you run up and make your bed and do your morning chores so I can talk to Lucas for a few minutes," Kathleen said, deciding it was time to find out exactly what Lucas had in mind.

Gina smiled goodbye to Lucas, then left the kitchen.

"She's a beautiful child," he said, his dark eyes focusing on Kathleen.

"Yes, she is. The past couple of months have taken their toll on her." She felt an unexpected hot sting of tears pressing at her eyes. "First the death of her father and now this. I'm . . . I'm so frightened for her."

His expression grew even more serious. "You should be," he replied softly.

"Why is this happening to her?" Kathleen leaned forward. "Who calls to her?"

"There are some questions I can't answer. Not yet."

"I want answers now. I need to know what's happening. I need to understand." Her anger flared as months of frustration and fear rose to the surface. "That's why I allowed you to come here."

"I know and I'll do my best to answer your questions when the time is right. In the meantime you're just going to have to trust me."

"And why should I do that?" she asked.

He leaned over the table, so close to her she could feel the warmth of his breath on her face, see the unusual silvery rings that circled his black pupils. Once again it was as if the air around them had thickened and drawing a breath seemed almost impossible.

"You have to trust me because I'm all you've got. I can help Gina, but it has to be my way . . . in my time."

For a brief moment as she stared into his eyes, she had a curious sense of déjà vu, as if she'd known this man before, in another place, another time.

Something about him was suddenly as familiar to her as her own heartbeat. Something about him struck a chord of familiarity that both threatened and enticed her.

Heat undulated inside her and she had a desire to reach out and stroke his cheek, run a finger across his sensually full lips. She knew exactly how those lips would feel against hers . . . hot and eager and all consuming.

She scooted back in her chair, effectively breaking the peculiar spell. It was crazy. She'd never met this man before in her life. If she had, she'd remember. There was no way she could have forgotten those intense, unusual eyes or the haunting angular beauty of his face.

"So what are your plans? What kind of things are you going to teach Gina?" she asked, realizing so far he'd done nothing to assuage her mistrust of him. "What brought you here to my home that night? How did you know about Gina's problems?"

He reached across the table and enveloped her hand in his. "Kathleen, my purpose will become more clear in time. But you must give it time. You must give me time." His thumb moved back and forth, caressing the back of her hand. "There are powers at work here, awesome powers with evil intent.

Gina is a special child and somehow she called to me in her dreams."

She stared at him in disbelief. Awesome powers? Communication through dreams? Evil intent? Did he really expect her to believe all this?

"Kathleen, you have to trust me, not just with your head, but with your heart. I'm going to do everything I can to save Gina."

"Save her from what?" Kathleen asked, wanting to pull her hand away from the evocative heat of his, and yet at the same time reluctant to do so.

"I don't know." His gaze possessed her, holding her captive. "I only know for sure that something or someone is threatening her, and they come at her when she is most vulnerable, when she's sleeping."

He released her hand and she took a deep breath. She felt dizzy, as if she'd been deprived of oxygen for too long. "So how do we fight this . . . this whatever it is that's threatening her?"

He raked a hand through his hair. "The first thing I need to do is teach Gina some meditation and concentration techniques."

Kathleen frowned. "Is that possible with a six-year-old?"

Lucas smiled and the gesture warmed his features, momentarily removing the dark mystery from his eyes. "Children make the best pupils in these more alternative treatments. Their minds haven't been filled with impossibilities. They are willing to try all suggestions, trusting in their imaginations, which have yet to be constricted and bound by logic."

Kathleen nodded, knowing at least this much was true. She'd once read that children were most apt to experience psychic phenomena because their minds were completely open.

Gina had always been an imaginative child, and Kathleen had always been surprised that Sutton, who was pragmatic to a fault, had encouraged Gina's creative streak. "You talk like this is a person or an entity that's threatening Gina. I've always told her there are no such things as bogeymen or monsters. Was I wrong?"

Lucas looked down at the tabletop. When he lifted his gaze the darkness was back in his eyes ... darkness that seemed to yawn frightening and cold, as if it radiated from his eyes and pulled at his handsome features, changing them to a mask of hard intent.

He reached out and took her hand again. This time his touch was cold, his fingers unyielding as they coiled around hers.

"Was I wrong?" she repeated, her throat suddenly achingly dry.

For a long moment he stared at her, and she had the feeling of something probing inside her mind, invading her very soul.

"Yes," he said softly.

Kathleen felt a shiver of fear sweep through her.

Chapter Eight

His lips plied hers with heat and his tongue sought hers, swirling into her mouth to deepen the intimacy of their kiss. Kathleen had never been kissed so deeply, had never wanted a man as badly as she wanted him.

Her hands raked down the smooth, warm flesh of his back. She'd thought him thin, but she'd been wrong. His naked chest and back were firmly muscled, and she loved the feel of those sinewy muscles beneath her fingertips.

As his hands moved to cup her bare breasts, she gasped with the delicious pleasure that swept through her. His thumbs razed over her taut nipples, intensifying the sweet sensations.

Flames she'd never felt before leapt to life inside her. Every inch of her body burned with want . . . with need.

"Lucas," she moaned against his mouth.

"Kathleen," he whispered, his lips moving from her

mouth, down her jaw line and lingered at the sensitive skin behind her ear. "I want you."

"Yes . . . yes. I want you, too." She thought if he didn't take her, didn't possess her completely she might die. Without his touch her body would wither and be swept away on a wind of despair.

Again his mouth took possession of hers as he moved to position himself between her thighs. He broke the kiss and gazed down at her, his dark eyes burning with his desire. "Do you love me?"

"With all my heart . . . with all my soul," she replied.

"And when the dawn of morning chases away the night and shines on your heart, will you feel the same?"

"Always and forever," she said, and pulled at his shoulders, wanting to feel him inside her, to be one with him.

"Always and forever," he repeated, his eyes hot and intense. He lowered himself and entered her.

She cried out in exquisite pleasure . . . and woke up.

Frantically, she sat up and looked around the moon-drenched room, surprised to find herself alone in the bed and still clad in her white cotton nightshirt.

She was breathless, panting shallowly as if she'd just indulged in intense physical pleasure. Again she looked around the room, unable to believe she was truly alone.

My God, had it only been a dream? It had all seemed so real. She could still smell him. Her skin still burned from his heated caresses. She reached up a hand and touched her lips. They felt slightly bruised and swollen from his kisses.

Her body held a hunger the likes of which she'd never known. She ached with a need she'd never before experienced, and it both thrilled her and frightened her.

She threw the sheet back, knowing that any more sleep would be impossible for a while. She swung her feet from the bed to the floor, but didn't stand, feared she couldn't with the wave of residual sensations still coursing through her.

Swiping a hand through her heavy hair, she felt the perspiration that dampened her neck and moistened the hollow of her throat.

Why on earth would she dream of making love to Lucas? Granted, his presence in the house had unsettled her, but what would cause the kind of erotic dream she'd just had? Her blood still pulsed hot in her veins and her limbs still felt weak from exertion.

Drawing a deep breath, she finally got out of bed and walked on unsteady legs to the window, where she pulled the heavy curtains aside and peered out.

Aureoles of humidity pooled around the illumination from the street lamps. Still hot. Still humid. Her skin was damp and fevered, as if she'd been standing in the outside elements. But she knew it was the lingering effects of the imagined love-making.

She left her bedroom, deciding she needed a cold drink, then perhaps she would be able to settle into an undisturbed sleep. Before going down the stairs, she checked on Gina, who was sleeping peacefully.

In the kitchen, still feeling off-center and shaken by her crazy dream, she poured herself a large glass of orange juice.

Looking at the clock on the oven, she noted it was just after two. The house was silent, and she assumed Lucas, like her daughter, slept undisturbed.

She rolled the cool glass across her forehead, then brought it to her lips and took a sip, hoping the chilled liquid would diminish the lingering heat of her dream. She carried her drink through the living room to the French doors that opened onto a small private garden.

Turning one of the knobs, she frowned, surprised to discover it wasn't locked. Usually, she was quite diligent about securing all the doors. But before going to bed she'd been so unsettled with Lucas in the house she couldn't remember if she'd checked them or not.

Stepping outside, she drew a deep breath of the heavily humid but sweet-smelling air. The moonlight couldn't breach the thick branches of the trees that surrounded the garden, so the small, private area was shrouded in darkness.

The sound of bubbling water from the concrete fountain soothed her as she made her way through the ebony shadows to a stone bench by the fence.

"Couldn't sleep?"

She squeaked in surprise at the deep voice and realized Lucas sat on the bench where she'd been headed. "You scared me," she exclaimed.

"Sorry." He stood. "I saw this garden from the window earlier in the evening. I hope you don't mind my enjoying it."

"No, not at all," she hurriedly replied. "I was going to sit out here for a few minutes myself but the air is uncomfortably thick, isn't it?"

"Yes, it is," he agreed. "In fact, I was just about to go back inside."

She wondered whether the night air would be less oppressive if she wasn't sharing it with him. But it would be churlish of her not to go in with him since she'd just commented on the sweltering heat.

"That juice looks good," he observed as they stepped into the living room.

"There's a pitcher in the refrigerator," she replied, grateful that her nightshirt reached her knees and was hopefully opaque.

Her dream still vivid in her mind, she was far too aware of him as he followed her into the kitchen. He was clad in a pair of navy jogging pants and a white T-shirt that exposed firmly muscled forearms and stretched across the width of his chest.

Her face warmed as her fingers tingled with the memory of his heated skin beneath them. A dream. It had been only a crazy dream, she reminded herself.

She poured him a glass of the juice, then joined him at the small table in the breakfast nook. She could smell him, a clean male scent that was instantly familiar. How was that possible? How could she so readily know his scent?

"My mother always believed a big glass of orange juice would heal anything," he said after he took a sip of the liquid. "Got a cold? Drink orange juice. Got the flu? Drink juice. Broken heart? Anything could be cured by the power of vitamin C."

Kathleen felt herself relaxing. "So you had a mother," she said, the thought oddly comforting.

His sensual lips curved upward. "Yes, and a father. What did you think? That I was spawned from a crystal ball or pulled out of a hat?"

Kathleen laughed, the sound surprising her. She couldn't remember the last time she'd laughed. "You have to admit, all this . . . you being here . . . is not exactly normal."

His smile fell away, and he looked into his glass for a long moment. She couldn't help but notice the thick length of his eyelashes. "I left normal behind about a month ago." He returned his gaze to her, his eyes once again dark and fathomless. "A dream woke you, didn't it?"

She couldn't hide her small gasp. She wanted to tell him no, that the heat had awakened her, that worry had kept sleep away altogether, but instead she found herself nodding.

His gaze held hers intently. "It was a dream about the two of us, wasn't it? A . . . A dream of intimacy."

"Yes." The word hissed from her, and she felt the heat of a blush sweep up her neck and take over her cheeks.

He nodded, as if unsurprised. "I think we shared the same dream."

"How . . . how is that possible?" she asked, her stomach doing a flip-flop.

"I stopped asking myself that question weeks ago." He leaned back in the chair and swiped a hand through his thick dark hair. The gesture, so simple, so normal, so . . . human, eased some of the tension that had gripped Kathleen since she'd encountered him in the garden.

"I don't understand anything that's happening," she said softly.

"I wish I could help you understand it, but I can't. I'm as clueless as you." He leaned forward and wrapped his hands around his glass of juice. "A month ago I was just a mediocre magician lucky enough to be working in a decent club. An ordinary man struggling through life like every other normal person in the universe. Then the dreams began."

Kathleen felt herself leaning forward, drawn into his story. "Dreams?"

He nodded. "I dreamed of a little girl with bright green eyes . . . a little girl in terrible danger."

"Gina," Kathleen said softly.

Again he nodded. "When I came here that night, I came because I thought I was losing my mind. Night after night I dreamed of her, and then somehow I knew her name and I knew to come here. And that night, when you opened the door, I knew I wasn't losing my mind, that it was something far worse than that."

"What?" she asked half breathlessly.

"Fate. Destiny. Whatever you want to call it." He reached out and captured her hands in his. His fingers were momentarily cool from the juice glass, but warmed quickly against her own.

Instantly she remembered the feel of those slender fingers caressing her throat, capturing her breasts and sweeping her to heights of passion she'd never known existed. She mentally shoved against the memory of her dream and tried to focus instead on what he was telling her.

"Kathleen, I can't explain to you what I'm doing here or what forces have driven me here. I can only tell you that you and I have no control in this, that we're merely pawns in a battle that's been predestined for thousands of years."

He saw the confusion in the depths of her eyes, understood it because that same confusion resonated inside him. "I only know for certain that I have to be here, Kathleen . . . for Gina . . . and for you."

Her fingers squeezed his and as he gazed into the sweet blue of her eyes, he remembered the passion they'd shared in their dream, the heated eagerness of her lips against his, and he was granted a single shining vision of truth. He was destined to love Kathleen Marlowe.

And she was destined to betray him.

Chapter Nine

Moments later, alone in his room, Lucas re-examined the crazy knowledge that had felt so true minutes before.

She was destined to betray him.

Now the thought seemed melodramatic and ridiculous as did the notion that it was his destiny to love Kathleen. Granted, he found her extremely attractive, and the dream that had awakened him from his sleep had stirred him in a way he'd never known before.

But he wasn't here to make love to Kathleen. He wasn't here to sate any hunger he might possess for her. He was here to save Gina from a nameless, faceless monster.

He moved to the window of the room, a cold knot growing in the pit of his stomach as he thought of the little girl.

Although he had a feeling that time was of the essence, that the danger surrounding her was imminent, they'd spent the day doing little to prepare her for the fight to come.

He'd played half a dozen games of Old Maid with Gina,

then had entertained her with simple card tricks, eventually showing her how to perform them herself.

Kathleen had watched them interact, and he'd sensed her enormous frustration, but he knew the first step in the battle was gaining Gina's complete trust and there was no way to rush that particular process.

He stepped away from the window and paced the floor in front of the bed, aware that it would take him some time to wind down and return to sleep.

The room where he was staying was rather oppressive. The bed frame was an antique mahogany, a huge monstrosity that matched the dresser in style. There were no pictures on the walls, no little knickknacks of decoration. Heavy navy curtains hung at the windows, thick enough to give the impression of trying to keep something out, or hold something in.

It had taken Lucas only a few minutes in the house to recognize that there was no heart here, that there seemed to be a coldness that emanated from the very foundation itself. The only room that resonated with life and warmth was Gina's, a typical little girl's room done in pinks and whites.

He turned off the bedroom light, kicked off his jogging pants and slid beneath the sheets. The moonlight streaming through the tree branches just outside the window danced in the opened curtains to cast spiderweb–like shadows on the walls.

He had the feeling that he, Kathleen, and Gina were all like helpless flies caught in a sticky web, awaiting a life-or-death struggle against an entity whose sole desire was to destroy them.

What or who was making war on a child? Who called to Gina in the tunnel? And why? He fell asleep with the questions whirling in his head and dreamed no more that night.

106

He awakened just after eight the next morning and as he descended the stairs he heard a deep male voice talking to Kathleen. Judging from their strained tones, the conversation wasn't a pleasant one.

He hesitated in the kitchen doorway, unsure whether to intrude on Kathleen and the man seated at the table. The decision was made for him when the stranger spotted him and immediately stood and approached Lucas with an outstretched hand. "You must be the magician," he said, a touch of belligerence in his overly loud voice. "I'm Bill Abrahms."

Bill Abrahms was not handsome was Lucas's first thought as his fingers were squeezed far too tightly in the man's handshake. His nose was too large, his chin rather weak, and his lips far too thin to be attractive.

"Lucas Connelly," Lucas replied, recognizing in Bill's pale blue eyes an adversarial light of challenge.

"Lucas, please join us." Kathleen gestured to the chair next to her at the table. "We were just about to have some coffee."

Lucas sat in the place she'd indicated as she got up to fill coffee mugs. Bill lowered himself back into his seat opposite Lucas, watching Kathleen with a proprietary air that instantly told Lucas everything he needed to know about the man.

Bill Abrahms was in love with Kathleen.

"Did you sleep well?" Kathleen asked as she set a cup of fresh brew before him.

"Fine," Lucas replied. "Gina is still sleeping?"

Kathleen placed a cup of coffee in front of Bill, then joined them at the table. "Yes, she's still sleeping." She sighed. "There was a time when she was an early bird, but since all this . . . this . . . upset, she's been sleeping later and later."

Bill reached out and covered one of Kathleen's hands with his own, his gaze going to Lucas as if to make certain he saw the familiarity in the touch. "She's going to be fine, Kath," he said.

She nodded and smiled at Lucas. "Yes, I think she will be with Lucas's help."

Bill pulled his hand from hers and frowned at Lucas. "Just what is it you think you can do for Gina that all the medical specialists and psychiatrists can't?"

"I can save her," Lucas replied simply.

"Save her from what?" Bill didn't wait for a reply. "She's a sick little girl," he said as he stood and paced in front of the table. "She's suffering from a serious illness, and she should be seeing more doctors, not some half-baked magician."

"Bill . . ." There was a steely warning in Kathleen's voice.

"I'm sorry, Kathleen, I can't help but be worried," Bill continued despite the chill in Kathleen's eyes.

"If it's any consolation, Bill, I would never do anything to hurt either Gina or Kathleen," Lucas said.

Bill gazed at Lucas coldly. "I don't know you and I have no reason to trust you."

"That's enough." Kathleen slammed her hands down on the table. "You don't have to trust him," she said to Bill. "It's enough that I do."

At that moment Gina called to her mother, and Kathleen stood. "Bill, I think perhaps having coffee this morning wasn't such a good idea. If you would just let yourself out, I'd appreciate it." With these words, Kathleen left the kitchen.

Bill stared at Lucas, not pretending anything remotely resembling civility. "I don't like you being here, and I intend to do everything in my power to get you out."

Lucas nodded. "We all have our destinies to fulfill, Bill.

Just as I must fulfill mine, you must fulfill yours."

"As long as we understand each other," Bill said, then he turned to leave.

A few moments later Bill stepped out into the morning sunshine, an overwhelming sense of despair sweeping through him. The magician had only stayed in the house one night, and Kathleen was already starting to turn away from him. She wouldn't listen to his warnings; she'd even had the audacity to ask *him* to leave the house. Not the stranger she'd only known a few days but him, the one man—the only man—she should be turning to for support.

Bill also couldn't deny that the man was a handsome cuss. Lucas Connelly had the kind of lean, dark, dangerous looks that women seemed to love and certainly Kathleen didn't appear invulnerable to the man.

He pulled his keys from his pocket and headed down the driveway. He'd just unlocked the car door when she appeared beside him.

"Mr. Abrahms?"

"Yes?" He frowned at her curiously. She was a beautiful young woman, with long deep red hair. Clad in a lowcut sun dress, she displayed a prominent amount of breast and long, shapely legs. He'd never seen her before in his life. He definitely would have remembered her.

"My name is Belinda Samuels, and I think we need to talk."

"Talk about what? I don't even know you."

"That's true." She smiled. "But, I think we both want the same thing."

"And what would that be?" Bill asked.

"We both want Lucas Connelly out of that house as soon as possible."

Bill looked at her in surprise. Then he remembered the trusting way Kathleen had looked at Lucas and another wave of despair eddied through him.

He studied the house thoughtfully, then gazed back to the woman. "There's a little diner not far from here. How about I buy you some breakfast and we can talk about our mutual problem."

"Sounds like a plan," she said and walked around to the passenger side of his car.

"So how do you know Lucas?" Bill asked as he buckled his seatbelt.

"I know him because he's mine, and I don't like to share." She smiled at Bill, but there was something in her smile that gave him a nauseating chill . . . a chill that usurped all the heat in his body.

He fought a shiver of apprehension as he pulled out of the driveway.

"You know he's in love with you," Lucas said as Kathleen poured him a second cup of coffee.

She didn't need to ask whom he was talking about. "I know," she replied. She glanced over to Gina, who was sitting on a bar stool in front of the portable television on the kitchen countertop. She appeared to be completely absorbed by the antics of the Road Runner as she ate her bowl of cereal.

Kathleen put the coffeepot back on the burner, then rejoined Lucas at the table. "He's been a good friend since Sutton's death, but he's gotten a little intense over the last couple of months."

"Sutton? That was your husband?"

Kathleen nodded. "He died almost a year ago in a car accident. He and Bill grew up together and were good friends, so when I married Sutton, Bill was part of the package deal."

"He doesn't want me here. He's afraid, and frightened men are dangerous." Lucas held her gaze. "He's going to do his best to discredit me. Will you be strong enough to trust me no matter what others say? Will you be strong enough to trust me no matter what you hear or see?"

Kathleen stared at him for a long moment and although she wanted to answer him in the affirmative, she couldn't. "I will trust you as long as I believe you're helping Gina. Beyond that, I don't know."

He nodded. "I guess that's the best I can hope for at this time."

She shrugged. "It's the best I can offer."

Lucas finished his coffee and looked over at Gina, who had finished her cereal but was still absorbed by cartoons. "I want to work with her in her room this morning. It would be best if we were alone."

Kathleen opened her mouth to protest, but Lucas circumvented her. "Kathleen, I need Gina to trust me, to listen to me and if you're there it diffuses everything."

Kathleen looked over at her daughter. She would be turning her daughter over to a man she hardly knew, a man who had appeared from thin air with the promise of help. "All right," she relented, taking comfort in the fact that Gina was old enough to tell her if anything inappropriate or frightening occurred.

"Gina, honey, are you ready to work a little bit with me?" Lucas asked.

"Okay," she said and slid off the stool.

Kathleen watched as the two of them left the kitchen. She sank down at the table, his words to her whirling around in her head. *Will you be strong enough to trust me no matter what others say? Will you be strong enough to trust me no matter what you hear or see?*

Basically he was asking her to accept him on faith, on the simple strength of his word that he was here to help. Under normal circumstances, she would have never allowed him into their home, but things weren't normal.

When this was over and Gina was well again she'd take her to Disney World. Maybe before the summer was over. She took a sip of her coffee and imagined Gina's joy at going on the rides, meeting Mickey and Goofy and the whole gang of characters.

Her head filled with a vision of Keith Kelly's daughter lying in the hospital bed, and Kathleen swallowed against a sob of anguish. By the end of the summer would she and Gina be enjoying the magic of Disney, or would she be keeping vigil by the side of her daughter's hospital bed?

Lucas had to help them. But it was far too soon for her to know whether his being here was a blessing . . . or the biggest mistake she had ever made in her life.

Chapter Ten

Keith Kelly was on to something. It had been a week since he'd gone with Rev. John Bascomb to the hospital where one of his little parishioners had fallen into an inexplicable coma.

True to his word, Keith had kept his distance from the family, but he'd ached for them as he'd seen the confusion in their eyes . . . the fear and the need for answers that nobody, not even the medical professionals, seemed to possess.

He knew exactly how they were feeling, remembered in haunting detail the night he and Rosalyn had rushed Sharon to the hospital.

It had been a one-way journey for Sharon.

As he'd sat in the waiting room, catching snatches of conversation that confirmed this case was almost identical to Sharon's, visions of the church desecration played in his mind.

Funny, that as a child had slipped into a strange coma, not

far away an unholy group was having some sort of dark celebration.

He'd slipped out of the hospital and headed to the police station to talk to the officer who had responded to the call to the church. As he'd suspected, the officer had little to offer him as to who might be responsible for the break-in.

The next day, armed with a list of addresses of all the churches that had been vandalized over the last six months, Keith began his in-depth investigation.

Over the next several days he spoke with Catholic priests, Baptist preachers and a Jewish rabbi. He looked at police file photos, spoke to officers and took copious notes.

After studying five churches and one temple that had been hit, he'd come away with the gut-chilling certainty that this wasn't the work of bored teenagers. It was something much more organized and frightening.

While religious denomination seemed to play no part in the crimes, other similarities existed. Each church had been decorated with black crepe paper and balloons and at each site the word Thanatos had been spray-painted on a wall.

Was it the work of some new cult? Keith had written an article on cults a couple of years earlier, and he knew how powerful and destructive such groups could be. They were highly organized and their ability to successfully prey on their members' insecurities made them difficult to combat.

But Keith's major discovery hadn't come until he was driving to the fifth church on his list. He'd turned down the wrong street and realized he was only a block away from where Danny Stovall lived. Danny was the second child Keith had discovered who'd experienced the same nightmares his Sharon had, and like Sharon, Danny was now comatose in the hospital.

Although he thought it was a crazy idea that would probably come to nothing, Keith checked the timing of the desecration against the timing of Danny's final fall into endless sleep.

To his surprise, he discovered they had occurred on the same night . . . just as the most recent coma and desecration had coincided.

Energized, Keith began to check the records of all the children he knew who had suffered Sharon's fate. What he discovered astonished him.

On the night that each of the children had slipped into a coma, the church closest to their home had been vandalized. Had he only found this coincidence once, he might have dismissed it as just that . . . coincidence.

But in the cases of all five children who he knew were in the same condition as Sharon, five children who had feared going to sleep and had spoken of flying and tunnels, the church desecrations coincided in both time and proximity to where the child lived.

They were connected. He didn't know what it meant, but he'd discovered an important piece in the puzzle, and it scared the hell out of him.

He now sat in his office at home, re-reading the notes he'd taken about the children and the churches. It was late, Rosalyn was in bed, and the house was silent except for the faint hum of his computer.

Thanatos. He typed the word into his search engine, then waited to see what the name might bring up on the Internet. To his surprise, a listing of more than a dozen sites appeared.

More than half were related to a heavy-metal band of some sort. Several had links to hospice organizations for terminally ill people.

One particular site sent his adrenaline flowing. The home-page Keith pulled up was black with the word THANATOS in bright red letters, oddly similar to the spray paint in the churches.

A doorway bid him entry, but when he clicked it, he got a box asking for his password and member code.

Keith certainly wasn't a computer guru and he wasn't even sure the site held anything of interest, but he was definitely intrigued by the fact that he couldn't explore past the initial screen.

He made a mental note to talk to Judd Kirshman, a friend of his who was a computer programmer and expert hacker. If anyone could find a back door to the site, Judd would be able to.

In the meantime, Keith noticed there was an e-mail icon to contact somebody on the site, so he e-mailed and asked for information.

He doubted anything would come of it, but he couldn't leave a stone unturned, not when he might discover a way to help his daughter.

He wondered how little Gina Marlowe was doing. He hadn't talked to her mother since that night at the diner. Had Gina lapsed into a coma yet?

It was time for another visit with Kathleen. As long as Gina clung to consciousness, Keith felt there was still hope . . . hope that he could save his daughter from whatever madness gripped her.

At that same moment Gina Marlowe was the object of much more sinister thoughts. Thanatos stood at a floor-to-ceiling window and frowned out into the night.

She was proving difficult. The others had been so easy, his

voice guiding them through the tunnel of darkness, like a shepherd with his sheep.

He'd been the Pied Piper, playing the tune that had mesmerized the children. But the last little girl . . . the most important of them all, refused to follow.

Instead of weakening beneath his assault, he felt her strength growing and knew there was somebody beside her, teaching her. Thanatos's foe had found the child and now aided her in resisting him.

Damn him. Damn him to a torturous hell of unspeakable pain. Of course he would fail. Eventually the child would succumb to Thanatos's power. But Thanatos was growing weary of waiting.

He was impatient for the end to be upon them all . . . the time when he would rule the earth as Satan's right-hand man.

He had no choice; he would raise the stakes.

A week.

Lucas had been in her house a full week, and Gina hadn't suffered a single episode. For the first time in as long as Kathleen could remember, Gina had gone to bed on her own, unafraid of what the night might bring.

It was Kathleen who had become afraid of what the dark might bring in the past week, for almost every night since Lucas had moved in she'd had erotic dreams of them together, dreams that had made it difficult to look him in the eyes the next morning.

And what frightened her more than anything was how much she'd come to look forward to those dreams, how lost she felt when the dream ended and she awoke alone in her bed.

She now sat curled up on the sofa, a glass of brandy in

hand. Clad in her nightshirt and a long, light-weight cotton robe, she was comfortable, but dressed respectably enough should she encounter her houseguest.

Lucas had gone upstairs after dinner. When she had tucked Gina in bed, his bedroom door had been closed. He'd apparently decided to have an early night.

She leaned her head back and tried to relax. The house was silent around her, but it was a different kind of silence since Lucas had moved in.

It felt charged with energy . . . as if everything held its breath in anticipation. But in anticipation of what?

She jumped as the phone rang and quickly grabbed the receiver. "Hey girl, how's it going?" Theresa's familiar voice filled the line.

"Theresa, I was beginning to think you fell off the face of the earth," Kathleen exclaimed.

"Ah, you know how it is with me. I fell in love, got my heart broken, and I've been nursing my wounds for the last week."

"Oh, I'm so sorry," Kathleen said, sympathizing with her friend who seemed so desperate for love, yet never able to find it.

"No big deal," Theresa replied flippantly. "On to the next one, that's my motto. So how's Gina doing?"

"Holding her own at the moment," Kathleen said, debating whether she should tell Theresa about Lucas.

"I hear you have a houseguest."

Kathleen sat up in surprise. "How did you find out?"

"Dudley Do Right came to see me the other day."

"Bill came to see you?"

"I know, amazing, isn't it? He's worried about you, Kath. He told me you've got some hocus pocus man living there

118

and he's worried sick. So wanna tell me what's going on?"

"Bill's overreacting," Kathleen said, surprised to find she was reticent to tell Theresa too much about Lucas and how he came to be living in her house. "Lucas is an old friend, and he's trying to help get to the bottom of Gina's problem."

"An old friend? How come I've never heard of him before?"

Kathleen sighed. "Theresa, I really don't want to go into this right now. I'm doing what I think is best and that's really all I can tell you. What did Bill think you could do about the situation anyway?"

"Remember Sam Crane—the cop I dated last year? Bill wanted to see if I'd ask Sam to run a background check on Lucas."

Kathleen sighed heavily and rubbed her forehead, tired beyond belief. "Nothing is going to change my mind right now about Lucas. He's my very last hope." She felt her muscles tense as the object of their conversation came down the stairs. "I don't want to talk about this anymore," she said.

"Okay. I just called to tell you that if you have a guy living in your house, I hope he's a sexy hunk."

Kathleen laughed. "You're incorrigible." She motioned Lucas toward the bar, indicating he should help himself.

"That's why you love me," Theresa replied. "I'll let you go. I just wanted to give you a heads up on what Bill was doing. At least he didn't ask me to get in touch with one of my old biker boyfriends to break some bones."

As the two women said their goodbyes, Lucas sat in the chair across from the sofa. Even from across the room his presence affected Kathleen, set her on edge. She fought the impulse to smooth her hair, irritated that he made her so aware of her femininity.

"I thought you'd decided to have an early night," she said, trying not to notice how his dark navy T-shirt exposed firmly muscled biceps and forearms. His hair was tousled, giving his masculinity a boyish appeal that only strengthened his magnetism.

He sampled his brandy, then smiled. "You know how it is, you're exhausted so you go to bed, but the moment you lie down, your head spins with thoughts and sleep proves completely elusive."

"I've had those kinds of nights . . . lately more than I care to remember," she admitted. She took a sip of her drink, then looked at him once again. "That was my friend Theresa on the phone. Bill went to see her this morning, wanted her to get a cop friend of hers to run a background check on you."

"That's not surprising. If I was in his position, I'd probably do the same thing." He savored another mouthful of brandy before setting his glass on the coffee table between them. "He's going to be fairly disappointed in what he finds. No outstanding warrants, no felony convictions. Hell, I can't even remember the last time I got a traffic ticket."

The smile that had lit his features moments before fell away, and his eyes grew dark with shadows that evoked an edge of fear in her heart.

"But if Bill is looking to dig up dirt from my past, if he digs deep enough he'll find it." He stood and walked over to the sofa and sat down next to her.

Her fingers trembled slightly as she placed her brandy snifter next to his on the coffee table, then leaned back, instantly electrified by his nearness. Although she knew it was ridiculous, she felt him not only at her side but all around her, as if he engulfed her with his closeness.

Her pulse quickened and she tried to tell herself it was because she feared what "dirt" he was talking about, rather than as a result of his physical proximity.

"I'd prefer to tell you about my past than have you hear it second- or third-hand from somebody else."

"Lucas . . . it really isn't necessary."

He held up a hand to cut off her reassurances and leaned forward. He was so close to her she could see the unusual shimmering silver that ringed his dark irises.

His scent surrounded her, the scent of clean male and spicy cologne with a hint of something wild that affected her on a visceral level.

She relaxed a bit as she realized the darkness in his eyes didn't whisper of something horrific, but rather of painful memories.

He drew a deep breath and released it slowly. "I was twelve when my mother committed suicide, and I was raised by my father who was mentally ill. He died a year ago in a hospital for the insane."

Relief accompanied by deep compassion swept through her. "Oh, Lucas . . . I'm so sorry. That must have been horrible for you." She frowned thoughtfully. "But that's certainly not dirt on you. Your parents' problems don't reflect on you and the man you've become."

He reached out and took her hand in his. The moment his warm fingers closed around hers, an electric current vibrated within her. She tried to ignore it, desperately wanted to focus on the man and not the exciting sensations his touch produced.

"I don't know. There are some who might try to make a case about mental illness being hereditary. There are some who would say living with my father made me crazy." His hand tightened around hers. "And in truth, over the last several weeks there have been times I thought I was going mad."

His eyes filled with a deep anguish that Kathleen felt in her heart, that resonated in her very soul. He released her hand and stood abruptly.

"When I first started seeing the visions of Gina, I feared I was going crazy. I thought I was suffering the same kind of insane hallucinations, the same kind of killing madness that had taken my father's mind and eventually took his life."

"But you weren't," she said softly.

He nodded and raked a hand through his hair, his eyes haunted as they held her gaze intently. "There are times I feel a prickling in my scalp, a tickling as if something is trying to get inside my brain."

Kathleen stood and walked over to him. "If you're insane, then I've entered your world of madness, Lucas," she said.

She wasn't sure later whether he reached for her first, or she for him. She only knew that his arms around her felt reassuringly familiar and as his lips sought hers she responded with a hunger that felt as if it had been building for weeks . . . months . . . lifetimes.

Chapter Eleven

His lips plied hers with heat and his tongue sought hers, swirling into her mouth to deepen the intimacy of their kiss. Kathleen had never been kissed so deeply, had never wanted a man as badly as she wanted him.

It was like her dream . . . exactly like her dream. Only this wasn't a dream, and the sensations that swept through her were frighteningly more vivid than what she'd experienced in her sleep at night.

Kissing Lucas felt at once remarkably alien and yet achingly familiar, and the conflicting emotions confused her.

How could she remember what she'd never before experienced?

When his lips had first touched hers, his arms had been at his sides, but now they wrapped around her, pulling her close against him.

Rational thought became impossible as the kiss continued and his hands stroked up and down her back. She was vaguely conscious of a pounding in her ears and realized it was her heart beating a frantic rhythm. One of his hands tangled in her hair as his mouth continued to plunder hers.

Her arms were around him, and beneath her fingertips she could feel the play of sinewy muscles in his back. So long . . . it had been so long since she'd felt a man's lips on hers. It had been so long since she'd felt the fires of sexual desire roaring to life inside her.

Sutton had been dead for almost a year, but for several years prior to his death there had been little physical intimacy in their marriage.

She was a woman starved, and the force of the hunger that raged through her both intimidated her and thrilled her. She wanted not just the taste of his mouth, but also the feel of his warm, naked flesh next to hers, the pleasure of him taking possession of her.

But then he broke the kiss and stepped back from her, his eyes momentarily holding a wildness.

"That probably wasn't a good idea," he said, his voice deeper, huskier than usual.

"Probably not," she agreed, mortified by the fact that he could have taken her right there on the living room floor. She would have let him—she would have encouraged him.

"I should go check on Gina," she said, wanting—needing—to escape.

"She's all right. I would know if she was flying."

She looked at him in surprise. "What do you mean? How would you know?" She was grateful to focus on anything other than the mind-numbing sensations his embrace had shot throughout her.

He sank back down on the sofa, his gaze not leaving hers. "I'd just know."

"She hasn't had an episode since you've been here." Kathleen paced in front of the sofa, too wired to sit and needing to keep distance between them. She stopped pacing to look at him once again. "Maybe it's gone. Maybe whatever it was that was trying to get at Gina has given up, moved on, disappeared."

Lucas shook his head and frowned. "No, it hasn't given up. It's waiting . . . biding time and gaining strength."

Kathleen wished she were back in his arms once again. For a moment as he'd kissed her, the chill that had taken up residency in her body months ago had been banished. But, now the chill was back and she wrapped her arms around herself in an attempt to ward it off.

She finally sank down in the chair opposite the sofa. "You and Gina have spent a lot of time together this past week."

He smiled and she felt the force of its magnetism in the pit of her stomach. "She's a remarkable little girl. She's very bright."

"She gets that from her father."

Lucas picked up the glass he'd set on the coffee table earlier. "Tell me about him."

"About Sutton? What do you want to know?"

Lucas shrugged. "Where'd you meet him? What was he like?"

"I was nineteen when I met him. I was going to college and Sutton was invited to speak as a guest lecturer. I didn't attend his lecture, which was for one of the medical classes. I was majoring in interior design and had no clue who Sutton Marlowe was."

She stood, again too restless to sit while she spoke of the man she had married. "Anyway, we met in the courtyard and struck up a conversation."

"And it was love at first sight?"

Kathleen laughed. "Not even close. I thought he was incredibly arrogant and more than a little bit rude. But he pursued me with a single-mindedness that was amazing."

She moved to the fireplace mantel and straightened a picture of Gina, then adjusted a burgundy pillar candle a fraction of an inch to the right. "I married him for all the wrong reasons," she said and turned back to look at Lucas.

One of his dark eyebrows quirked upward. "And what were those reasons?"

She walked over to a marble-topped table that held a large vase and an arrangement of silk flowers. She pulled out one of the flowers and reinserted it, her mind racing with thoughts of the man she had married.

"Sutton was dynamic, self-possessed, and I was at a point in my life where I was drifting. I wasn't sure what I wanted to do. I didn't really want to be in college, but I certainly didn't want to go back and live with my parents."

She turned back to Lucas and flashed him a quick smile. "You weren't the only one who grew up in a dysfunctional family."

He leaned forward, interest lighting his features. Again Kathleen was struck by his handsomeness. "Tell me," he urged, then grinned with a delightful boyish expression. "I always like to hear others' war stories when it comes to parents and family dynamics."

She settled back on the chair facing him. "Misery loves company, right?"

"Something like that," he agreed.

She thought of the two people who had raised her. "My parents weren't bad people," she began. "They were just kind of sad . . . ineffectual."

She frowned, trying to find words to describe her mother and father. She had never really connected with them, nor felt they had connected with her. "Mother was like a wraith. She always seemed to be in the shadows, never quite a part of life but just drifting around the edges. My father was like her . . . timid and afraid all the time. He couldn't keep a job, so we moved a lot."

"Sounds like there was a lot of instability," he observed.

She nodded. "And I think that's part of why I jumped into marriage to Sutton so quickly. He offered me stability." She frowned once again and looked down at her hands in her lap, idly noting that her nail polish was chipped.

"Of course, I didn't realize it at the time. I married Sutton because I thought I was in love with him, because he overwhelmed me with his forceful personality. But now I think I married him because I'm a lot like my parents."

"I don't understand."

She looked up at him once again. "Sutton made it so I only had to be a wraith, flirting at the edges of life but never having to really participate, never really having to take any chances. He took care of everything. With him I was just like my parents: safe—but in the shadows."

"What exactly did Sutton do?" he asked curiously. "You mentioned that he was lecturing to medical students. Was he a doctor?"

She nodded. "When we first met, he was mostly doing research work. I really don't know too much about it. He was a very private man. I never met any of his colleagues, and we certainly didn't entertain. Then, when I got pregnant with Gina, Sutton quit his research work and opened a small practice in obstetrics. He delivered Gina." She smiled at the memory. "I think that was the happiest I'd seen him in all the years we were married."

"How did he die?"

She stood and walked over to the coffee table where she'd set her glass earlier. She picked it up and moved to the bar where she poured herself an inch of brandy. "Sutton had a place in upstate New York . . . a cabin that had been in his family for years. On the weekends he often went there."

"You never went with him?"

She returned to the chair and sipped the liquor before answering. "Sutton made it clear to me at the beginning of our marriage that he was a man who required private time and the cabin was where he went to be completely alone. Anyway, he was driving home from there one Sunday night and his car went off a bridge and down a steep embankment. The gas tank ruptured and the car burst into flames. They told me he probably died instantly."

"I'm sorry. His death must have been difficult on both you and Gina."

She nodded and took another taste of her brandy. "So now you know my tale. What about you, Lucas Connelly? Ever been married?"

He smiled, that easy grin that made her pulse accelerate despite her intentions to the contrary. "No. I've never even come close to marriage. There have been women in my past, but nobody I could see myself spending the rest of my life with."

"Why magic?"

"Several months after my mother died, an uncle of mine gave me a book on magic. It was a wonderful world to escape into—a place where I could perform great feats that stupefied people, a fantasy world where I was the all-powerful magician who could change my surroundings with the swirl of a magic wand. As crazy as it sounds, magic was the only stability I had in my life."

"Have you always worked as a magician?" she asked, finding the conversation comforting. It was the first real, normal conversation they'd held and it was oddly reassuring.

"No. Up until a year ago I was working full time as a union carpenter and only doing my magic act on the weekends in various Manhattan clubs."

"What made you decide to become a full-time magician?"

"My father died a year ago." It was his turn to get up and splash a little more brandy in the bottom of his glass. "My father was completely and totally insane, but somehow he managed to die an extremely wealthy man." He paused a moment to take a swallow of the brandy, then continued. "Apparently there was a lot of insurance money when my mother died and my father had put it all into stocks."

He laughed, a dry, humorless laugh. "I worked weekends and nights to pay so that my father could get the best possible care, then discovered when he died that he had more money than I could spend in a lifetime."

"So, you quit your job as carpenter and have been spending his money ever since," she replied.

He finished the last of his brandy, placed the glass in the sink, then turned back to her with a grin. "I quit my job and have spent the past year honing my craft, attempting to become the best magician New York City has ever seen. I live comfortably, but certainly not particularly extravagantly."

There was an edge of defensiveness in his tone, and Kathleen realized she had insulted him with her comment. She gulped down the last sip of her brandy, then got up and carried her glass to the sink.

"I'm sorry if I offended you." She turned and nearly jumped out of her skin at his proximity to her.

He stood so close she could once again see the unusual silvery rings around the dark pupils of his eyes; she could feel the heat that radiated from his body and smell the scent of him that drove her half crazy with desire.

"You didn't offend me," he said softly, his brandy-scented breath intoxicating. He reached out and touched a strand of her hair, rubbing it between two fingers as if memorizing the texture.

She stood, still as a statue, knowing she should move away from him, yet unable to do so. The magnetic shine of his gaze and the caress of his fingers through her hair held her in place. But more than anything, it was the memory of her dreams of making love to him that held her hostage.

"Inevitable." His voice was a mere whisper, the expelled air the greatest of touches against her hair.

"What?" she asked breathlessly. "What is inevitable?"

"We will become lovers, Kathleen."

She wanted to deny his words, to tell him there was no way they would ever be lovers—except in her dreams—but the words refused to form on her lips, and she heard herself murmur a soft yes.

At that moment, Gina screamed.

Chapter Twelve

Kathleen took the stairs two at a time, but Lucas was two steps ahead of her. As he entered Gina's bedroom, he flipped on the light and at the same time Gina launched herself from her twin bed into his arms.

In the back of Kathleen's mind she was surprised to see her daughter molded against Lucas, her slender legs around his waist, her skinny arms wrapped tight around his neck. Apparently in the past week Lucas had successfully overcome all trust issues with Gina.

"What's wrong, honey?" His voice was low and soft, and he stroked his hand through her hair. "Did you have a bad dream?"

Gina shook her head vehemently, her face hidden against the crook of Lucas's neck. "A man was outside my window," she said, her voice partially muffled by Lucas's shirt. "He was a bad man."

Lucas frowned and looked at Kathleen. She frowned as

well. Gina's bedroom was on the second floor of the house. Kathleen approached where Lucas and Gina stood.

"Honey, are you sure it wasn't a dream?"

Gina raised her head and turned her tear-streaked face toward her mother. "I wasn't sleeping, and it wasn't a dream," she said. "I saw him and he looked mean and he was trying to get into my window." She shivered, her lower lip trembling uncontrollably.

Lucas motioned for Kathleen to take the child from his arms. "Maybe it would be fun if Gina and I traded bedrooms for the night,". he suggested. "She can sleep in my bed and I'll sleep in hers."

Gina eyed Lucas hesitantly. "And the man can't get into your bedroom window?" she asked, her voice quivering slightly.

"Nobody is going to get into any of our windows," Kathleen said firmly, then added, "but, maybe it *would* be fun for you to sleep in Lucas's room tonight."

Gina sighed, a sigh far too great, far too deep for a child and Kathleen tightened her arms around her. "Do you need Reggie Rabbit to sleep in here with you?"

Lucas looked at her bed, where the bedraggled stuffed animal was tucked beneath the sheets, only his floppy ears and his button eyes showing. "I think maybe Reggie Rabbit would like to sleep in my bed, too," he replied. He picked up the bunny and handed it to Gina.

She cuddled it to her heart and yawned, the trauma of the past few minutes passing swiftly, as did most emotional upsets in childhood. "Mommy, will you tuck me in?" she asked.

"Of course I will." With a nod to Lucas, Kathleen left Gina's bedroom and went down the hall to the room where Lucas had been staying.

It smelled of him, the heady mixture of spicy cologne and clean male and an underlying subtle scent of primal wildness that was intimately appealing.

The room was neat, the bed carefully made, so it took only moments for Kathleen to fold down the bedspread and pull back the sheet to allow Gina to crawl in.

For just a moment, Kathleen fought the desire to get in beside her daughter, between the sheets she knew would retain the smell of him. For just a moment, she wished she were back in his arms, his lips plundering hers with simmering desire, his arms wrapped tightly around her, his heartbeat thundering against her own.

In his arms she would momentarily forget the uncertainty that now marked her world, the terror that was always just a tiny breath away would be banished at least for a little while.

She pulled a chair up to the side of the bed and stroked Gina's forehead, chiding herself for her crazy thoughts. The last thing she needed was any sort of relationship with Lucas Connelly.

The man had blown into her life on a blistering hot wind of mystery, bringing with him more questions than answers, and a blatant sexuality that was as threatening to her peace of mind as everything else that had been happening in her life.

She shouldn't trust him . . . at least not entirely. She didn't really know him at all, knew only the little bits of his past he'd been willing to share.

Logic told her it was important to maintain reservations where he was concerned. But something about Lucas Connelly made it difficult to think logically.

Realizing Gina was sleeping peacefully, Kathleen moved the chair back where it belonged and started to leave the room. She paused in the doorway and examined the room, seeking some personal item, some clue that might tell her more about the man who was staying here. But there was nothing.

She returned to Gina's room to find Lucas seated on the window sill, his upper body outside the window. He saw her through the pane of glass and leaned back into the room, his expression grim.

"Did you know that big old oak tree has limbs perfect for climbing right into this window?" He stood and slammed the window closed, then turned to look at her, his eyes dark and impenetrable. "Gina wasn't dreaming. Somebody did try to get into this window. There are marks where he used some sort of tool in an attempt to pry the window open."

She stared at him for a long moment, trying to comprehend his words. To her horror, unexpected tears suddenly burned hot and thick at her eyes.

She'd handled Sutton's unexpected death stoically, had dealt with all the legal and emotional issues that a tragic death entailed.

She'd coped with Gina's illness, the endless trips to the specialists, the hours of sitting and watching her daughter sleep, and she hadn't fallen apart.

But this, the knowledge that somebody had tried to break into Gina's bedroom, was her undoing. She sank to the bed, a rush of emotion overtaking her. As the tears fell faster and faster, she hid her face in her hands, appalled by her utter lack of control.

Lucas gently pulled one of her hands from her face and forced her up from the bed. "Come on," he said softly, his hand clasping hers firmly. He pulled her out of the bedroom.

"Wha—what are you doing?" she asked, her voice thick with tears still needing to be shed.

"I'm taking you to bed," he replied.

She stiffened and halted in place. He smiled, his eyes momentarily lit with amusement. "Don't worry, Kathleen. My only intention is to tuck you in, not ravish you." The heat of his gaze blazed a little bit hotter. "At least not tonight."

Her cheeks warmed, and she allowed him to lead her to her bedroom. Tears still trickled down her cheeks, and as she watched him turn back the heavy bedspread, she realized she had never felt so exhausted in her life. It was as if an entire year of stress and sleeplessness had crashed down around her in the last few minutes.

"What you need right now is rest," he said as he approached where she stood. Her breath caught in her throat as he raised his hands to the buttons of her robe.

Her tears stopped flowing as his fingers undid the fastenings, starting with the one at her collarbone and moving down to the button between her knees.

He stood so close she could feel his body heat warming her, see the silvery flecks in the dark pupils of his eyes . . . flecks that made his gaze magnetic.

As he pulled the robe from her shoulders, his words came back to her. *We will become lovers, Kathleen.*

She knew he was right. Sooner or later she would be unable to deny the intense chemistry between them. Sooner or later she would be unable to fight the need, the want he evoked in her. Eventually, they would become lovers.

But for now, the desire to escape into sweet slumber was far greater than anything else. Docile as a child, she allowed him to take her hand and lead her to the bed. She crawled in beneath the sheets, the familiarity of the mattress and her pillow like welcoming arms.

He pulled the covers up just beneath her chin, then kissed her softly on the forehead. She wanted to ask him why somebody would try to break into Gina's room, had it been some sort of a coincidence or was it tied to her night traveling and whoever called to Gina in her dreams?

Apparently he saw the questions in her eyes, for he placed a finger over her lips. "Shh, go to sleep. I'll keep an eye on Gina for the night and we'll talk about everything in the morning. Just for tonight, don't worry. Rest."

She thought she might have nodded but wasn't sure, for sleep claimed her immediately.

Lucas turned off the bedroom light but remained in the doorway for a long moment, the light from the hall casting just enough illumination for him to watch her sleeping.

Her dark hair fanned out against the pale pink pillowcase and his fingers itched, knowing those shiny strands would be as silky as they looked.

There was nothing remotely sexy about the knee-length cotton nightshirt she wore, and yet when he'd taken her robe off and seen the white material against her golden skin, he'd thought she looked incredibly desirable.

He started to turn away, but gripped the doorjamb as a wave of dizziness struck him. Everything spun—the walls, the ceiling, the floor. He closed his eyes, waiting for the vertigo to pass.

When it did, he drew a deep, steadying breath and looked back into the bedroom. His breath caught in the back of his throat.

What he saw had nothing to do with reality. The bedroom had disappeared, transformed into what appeared to be a hayloft. The pale walls were now wooden planking, knotted and cracked. The air was rife with the scent of straw and horseflesh, of leather and feed.

The massive king-size bed was gone, replaced by bales of hay piled in irregular-sized stacks.

Kathleen lay on a bed of fresh hay, clad in a simple white cotton shift. Her cheeks were pink and her lips were swollen. Her nipples were erect, pressing against the thin material of her gown, and he knew with a certainty they had just made fiery love.

He also saw himself, standing at the hayloft window, looking out on a sea of prairie grass. He was clad in buckskin trousers and a cotton shirt and his long black hair was tied at the nape of his neck with a strand of deer hide.

He turned to her, his eyes burning with intent. "Come with me," he implored.

She broke eye contact with him and looked down at the dusty floor. "I cannot."

In three long strides he stood before her and reached down to take her hands in his. "You must. You don't belong here with him. You belong with me." He squeezed her hands in a silent plea. "Come with me, and we'll go west. We'll build a life together in the new frontier."

She pulled her fingers from his, her eyes filled with tears as she gazed up at him. "I can't . . . I'm afraid," her voice was a pained whisper.

"If you remain here you will have the creature comforts he can give you, but you'll wither away from lack of love. If you come with me, I can't promise every luxury that you have now, but I can promise that you will never starve, that you'll have clothes on your back and a roof over your head. I can offer you my passion, my heart, my soul."

As quickly as the vision had come upon him, it vanished, leaving behind only a deep well of despair that resonated through his entire body. Once again he looked at Kathleen, peacefully sleeping against the pink-hued sheets.

Had she shared the same vision in her dreams? Somehow he didn't think so, for he felt alone, racked with a grief he didn't understand, torn by the need to make love to her yet needing to keep himself isolated from her.

He left the doorway and headed back to Gina's room, his thoughts spinning wildly in his head. He had come to understand that in helping Gina he fought against some sort of insidious force, a force that strove for the ultimate prize: Gina's soul. He wasn't sure how he knew it, but the knowledge was rich and true inside him.

Now he wondered if the same power he battled for Gina's soul was also responsible for the monumental desire he felt for Kathleen.

Were his emotions really his own? Or was he being subtly manipulated by some evil outside source? The same source that threatened Gina?

He checked on the little girl, who was sleeping peacefully, then returned to her room. He turned off the light and went to the window. Staring out, he watched high clouds steal across the face of the half moon, then directed his gaze to the street below.

Although it was just after ten, the street was as deserted as if it were long after midnight. He ran his hands along the frame of the window, wondering who had tried to get in and why?

He didn't believe the incident wasn't tied to everything else that had been going on. He didn't believe that it was coincidence that a burglar chose this window in this house to try to enter. It was something much more frightening than simply an attempted robbery.

How much of his suspicions should he tell Kathleen? Each moment of each day he spent in her company heightened his desire for her. The visions he occasionally saw, the steamy dreams of making love to her were only sharpening and deepening his longing. But each vision, each dream, also brought with it a gnawing, painful sense of loneliness and despair.

Leaning his forehead against the windowpane, he told himself that he had to be wary, that it was possible his feelings for Kathleen were false, a diversionary tactic employed by whoever wanted Gina.

He knew his power and knowledge were growing by leaps and bounds; he felt as though he were being prepared for a battle where his strength and enlightenment would be necessary.

He wondered whether the first real challenge he would face would be with himself, a battle for the strength and self-control to stay physically and emotionally detached from Kathleen.

Kathleen awoke slowly, leaving behind the sweet oblivion of distant, unremembered dreams and surfacing to the smell of fresh coffee and midmorning sunshine streaming through her window.

She looked at her alarm clock and shot to a sitting position in shock. After ten. She couldn't remember ever sleeping so late. She got out of bed and went to the top of the staircase. From the kitchen drifted the sounds of cartoons and the clink of silverware. She heard Gina's voice, then Lucas's in reply, and she relaxed. Apparently everything was all right. They had gotten through the dark hours of the night without incident.

She returned to her bedroom and grabbed clean clothes, then went into the master bathroom for a quick shower. As she stood beneath the hot spray of water, she was pleased to realize she felt rested after her long sleep and cleansed by the tears she had shed the night before.

She was prepared to take on whatever the day might bring. She intended to call and have a security system installed immediately.

Minutes later clad in a cotton sundress with her hair pulled back into a ponytail, she left the bathroom and went downstairs. She paused in the kitchen doorway, taking in the scene before her.

Lucas stood at the stove, his back to her. Clad in a white T-shirt that stretched across his broad back and a pair of Khaki shorts that displayed tan, well-developed legs, he looked completely at ease flipping pancakes.

Gina sat at the island, her attention glued to the television where the Powerpuff Girls were busy saving the world.

"Good morning," she said as she stepped into the kitchen.

Lucas turned and flashed her a smile. "Ah, the lady of the manor awakens just in time to try a stack of my famous blueberry pancakes."

"They're yummy, Mommy. I already ate three," Gina said.

"Three? They must be yummy!"

"Help yourself to the coffee and have a seat. This batch is almost done," Lucas said.

She did exactly that. With a mug of coffee in hand, she took her place at the table and gazed out the window while she waited for the batter to cook.

It looked as if it was going to be a gorgeous summer day.

Over the past week the intense heat had snapped and temperatures had been more normal for this time of year. Warm, but not excessively hot.

It was the perfect weather for a day at the beach with Gina. She closed her eyes and for a moment, she could feel the warmth of the sun on her face, smell the brine of the ocean waves.

Gina had always loved the beach, had showed a remarkable imagination in building intricate sand creations along the shore. And if circumstances were normal, that's the way they would have spent a lazy summer day.

But things were not normal. She opened her eyes as Lucas set a plate of pancakes before her. "What about you?" she asked as he joined her at the table with a cup of coffee.

"I ate earlier. Did you sleep well?"

"Like a log. I think I woke up in the same position I fell asleep in."

"Good, you needed it."

She took a minute to prepare her pancakes, slathering on butter, then adding a liberal amount of syrup. "I'm going to call this morning and get somebody to install a security system," she said, keeping her voice low enough so Gina wouldn't hear.

"That's probably not a bad idea."

"I've intended to do it ever since Sutton died, but it never seemed as important as it does now."

He nodded and cast a quick glance at Gina, then back at Kathleen. "I think somebody is desperate to reach Gina—any way they can."

"So you don't think the attempted break-in last night was just a coincidence?"

"Do you?"

She sighed and cut into her breakfast. "No, I suppose not, although it would be less frightening if I didn't believe it was related to Gina and her night travels."

"For some reason she's important to somebody." He took a sip of his coffee, then continued. "Have you ever noticed her possessing any strange powers? Psychic abilities? An unusual energy?"

Kathleen shook her head. "No, nothing like that. Until this craziness began, Gina was a perfectly ordinary child. She was brighter than some, quite creative, but well within the average range."

Lucas frowned and she knew he was thinking the same thing she was: What made Gina special? Why was some evil force threatening her daughter not only mentally and spiritually but now perhaps physically as well?

He shoved her plate closer to her. "Eat," he commanded. "Eat first and we'll try to figure things out later."

She nodded and took another forkful of food, self-consciously aware of his gaze lingering on her. "These are very good," she said. "Do you like to cook?"

"Learning to cook was a survival technique for me. When my mother died, my father was in no shape to take care of me. Rather I became his caretaker, cooking meals and keeping the house clean."

"Not exactly a normal kind of childhood," Kathleen replied, then glanced at her daughter, wondering what kind of childhood memories she would retain.

"Kids are wonderfully resilient," he said softly, as if he read her thoughts. He reached out and covered one of her hands with his. "We're going to get through this, and she's going to be just fine."

There was an edge of steel in his voice and with the warmth

of his hand covering hers, with the intensity of his gaze boring into hers, she believed him. She had to believe him in order to hold on to her own sanity.

Gina left the stool at the island and came to stand next to her mother. "Mommy, do you like Lucas's pancakes?"

Kathleen wrapped an arm around her daughter. "Yes, I do."

"So do I." Gina smiled at her mom. "And you like Lucas, don't you?"

Kathleen felt her cheeks warm, and she was surprised to see that Lucas looked as embarrassed as she felt. "Yes, I like Lucas," she finally replied.

Gina nodded, as if she'd known the answer all the time. "I think Lucas should live with us all the time. He could be my new daddy and we could be a family all together."

Kathleen was unsure who was more stunned by Gina's words, herself or Lucas. It was Lucas who recovered first. "Gina, honey, I'm here to be your teacher and a friend to your mother. And now, are you ready to get to work?" He stood and placed a hand on Gina's shoulder.

If he'd intended the change of subject as a diversion, it worked. He looked back at Kathleen. "We'll be upstairs for the next hour or so."

She nodded and when they left the room she got up from the table. She'd eaten all that she could, and she was eager to contact a security company and get the house set up with a good alarm system.

It didn't take her long to make an appointment for later that afternoon with a reputable security company. She had just poured herself a second cup of coffee when the doorbell rang.

It was probably Theresa, eager to get a look at the man

who was sharing her home. She looked out the peek hole and was surprised to see Bill on her porch.

She unlocked the front door and opened it to greet him. "Bill," she said.

"Hi, Kath . . . Can I come in?" He shifted from foot to foot as if uncertain of his welcome.

She hesitated a moment, unable to forget that the last time he'd been here there had been some moments of unpleasantness between him and Lucas before she'd told him to leave. "Bill, I don't want any more hassles," she finally said.

He grimaced. "I'm not here to hassle you, but I do need to talk to you. Kathleen . . . please." He reached out and grabbed her hand in his. His skin was papery dry and icy cold, and his eyes were paler than she'd ever seen them. "It's important. I think you're in terrible danger."

Chapter Thirteen

Kathleen and Bill left the house, went out to the backyard, and sat on the concrete bench. She noticed that Bill looked exhausted, as if he'd not had a minute of rest in the week since she'd last seen him.

Bill had indicated he wanted to speak to her in private and here there was only the sound of an occasional birdsong and the dull roar of a lawnmower in the distance.

"I know you contacted Theresa to get the name of the ex-cop she used to date to get information about Lucas," Kathleen said, deciding to take the bull by the horns. "I know about Lucas's past, about his mother's suicide when he was young and his father's mental illness, so if that's what you came to tell me, you're wasting your time."

He sighed and leaned back against the bench, looking as depleted as a balloon that had been pricked by a pin. "But doesn't that worry you? That he was raised by a mentally ill father?"

"Why should it worry me? Mental illness isn't contagious, Bill," Kathleen replied dryly. She ran her fingers across the rough concrete of the bench. "Gina hasn't had an episode since Lucas has been here."

Bill looked at her for a long moment, his eyes sadder than she'd ever seen them. "You're in love with him, aren't you, Kath?" His voice was low, filled with pain that radiated intensely from his eyes.

Kathleen broke eye contact with him and instead focused on the tree that reached thick branches up toward Gina's bedroom window. "Don't be ridiculous," she scoffed. "I've only known him a week."

"But it's in your voice and in your eyes when you say his name."

She looked back at him. "There's something there," she confessed uneasily. "I don't know what it is . . . an energy, a pull of some kind. I wish I could explain it but I can't. I just know it's there."

Bill nodded and sighed once again. He looked up at the blue sky overhead, then directed his gaze back at her. "You know I've always loved you, Kathleen. But there's never really been any hope of anything developing between you and me, right?"

Again Kathleen felt his pain, and her heart ached for him. He was a good man, a kind man. He'd been a good friend throughout the years first to her and Sutton, then to her after Sutton's death.

She took his big, rough hand in hers. "Bill, I've been selfish, especially since Sutton died. I've loved having your friendship, your dependability and caring in my life, but I've been incredibly unfair to you." She squeezed his hand. "It's time for you to find a nice woman, Bill—a woman who will love you like you deserve to be loved." She hesitated a moment, then added, "And I'm not that woman."

He nodded, a weary resignation on his face. "Somehow I always knew that I didn't have a chance in hell with you . . . but I had hoped." He smiled, a sweet, gentle smile that let her know he'd come prepared to hear exactly what she'd just said to him.

He released her hand. "I can't help but worry about you, Kathleen . . . you and Gina. Please take care, and don't trust anyone unless you're sure they're worthy of your trust."

She frowned, an uneasiness sweeping through her. There was an intensity in his eyes that let her know he had more to tell her, and she wasn't at all sure she wanted to hear what it might be.

She drew a deep breath, steeling herself for whatever might come. "Bill, you mentioned that I was in danger. What exactly did you mean?"

He stood and shoved his hands into his pockets, staring toward the house. "Ask Lucas about Belinda."

"Belinda?" Kathleen's heart beat an unnatural rhythm at the unfamiliar name. "Who's Belinda?"

He pulled his hands from his pockets and looked at her once again. "According to her, she was Lucas's lover until the day he packed his things and moved in here with you."

Kathleen was once again struck by how little she knew about the man she was living with, the man who invaded her dreams and incited a lust she'd never experienced before. She didn't like the tiny arrow of jealousy that pierced through her heart.

"Whatever Lucas was doing before he came here, whomever he was with isn't important to me," she finally replied and stood as well.

Bill took a step toward her and put his hands on her shoulders. "It has to be important to you, Kathleen." His hands squeezed her shoulders painfully tight, and she winced from the pressure.

Instantly he dropped his hands to his sides. His face was a palette displaying confusing, contrasting emotions. Worry battled with unhappiness and overriding both of those expressions was a chilling indication of deep, abiding fear.

"I met Belinda last week when I left here," he said. "She was waiting for me out by my car. She introduced herself and said she wanted to talk to me."

He sat on the bench once again, and Kathleen sank down next to him. "We had breakfast together. At first I felt sorry for her. She told me she was in love with Lucas and didn't understand what he was doing here with you and Gina." He smiled without humor. "I felt a bond with her, you know unrequited love and all that stuff."

He looked down at the ground. "I have to confess, I met with her several times this week to try to get information that would make you throw Lucas out of here. But yesterday when I met with her I realized I needed to tell you about her."

"Why?"

He lifted his head and looked at her, his pale blue eyes haunted. "I think she's crazy, Kathleen. Bad crazy."

The chill of the fear that had been on his face seeped up her spine, and she fought against a shiver. "What do you mean? How is she crazy?"

"She's very intense, and she believes Lucas belongs to her, that he was promised to her by Satan."

"By Satan? That's ridiculous," she scoffed uneasily. What kind of people had Lucas had in his life before coming here?

"Maybe, but she believes it and I think she could be dangerous."

"What do you mean? Dangerous how?"

"I don't know. She's just . . . odd . . . and very focused on Lucas."

Again a chill tried to work up Kathleen's back. Was it this Belinda who had tried to break into Gina's room last night? Just how dangerous could a delusional woman be?

"I'm having a complete security system installed later this afternoon," she said.

"Good, I've been telling you for months you needed to do that." He stood once again and reached for one of her hands. "I've got to go now. I'm taking a little vacation over the next couple of weeks and I fly to Florida later this evening."

Kathleen knew he wasn't just telling her that he was going on vacation; he was also telling her he was moving on with his life.

Relief tempered with regret fluttered through her. Although she knew Bill was doing the right thing, that he needed time away from her, she would miss him.

She stood and he pulled her into a hug. "I'll be retrieving my messages from my phone so if you need me all you have to do is call," he said as he released her. "And be careful, Kathleen. I worry about you and Gina. This Belinda woman could be really dangerous. Just don't take any unnecessary chances, okay?"

Kathleen nodded, not willing to share with him that she had the same bad feeling. She walked him to the door, where they said their goodbyes. Then she watched him get into his car and disappear down the street.

A large part of her past was driving away. It was a little scary, contemplating a life without Bill. He'd not only been a friend, but he'd also been a financial advisor, a companion, and a broad shoulder.

Now, only the future loomed before her—an unsettling future with an unsettling man and some evil entity trying to destroy her daughter.

"Trust me, Mrs. Sutton, nobody is gonna get into a window or a door without you knowing about it with this system in place."

George Tindale, one of four men from Allied Security smiled confidently and patted the master control on the kitchen wall. "This baby is top of the line. If a squirrel farts outside the window, this system is going to sing to our monitoring team."

"And when it does sing to your monitoring system, what happens?"

"Two things happen immediately," George replied. "A dispatcher contacts the police, and we attempt to contact you by phone. If the alarm goes off and you're aware that it's a false alarm, then we request that you call us immediately." He handed her a folder stuffed with paperwork. "This should answer any questions you might have."

She walked with him to the front door, surprised at the amount of relief she felt knowing the house was now electronically guarded. She'd just closed the front door behind George and his crew when Lucas came down the stairs.

"Where's Gina?" she asked as they moved into the living room.

"I left her in her room playing with her Barbies."

Kathleen sat on the sofa and sighed tiredly. She'd battled with herself all day, trying to decide whether she should ask Lucas about Belinda.

150

She had no right to question him about his personal relationships, he owed her no explanations, no answers about the women he'd dated in the past or might date in the future. But if what Bill had said was true, that this Belinda might be dangerous, then how could she not ask Lucas about her?

He sat down next to her. "You've got something on your mind?"

It unsettled her, how he seemed to be able to sense her moods and thoughts. She pulled off her ponytail holder, allowing her hair to spill over her shoulders, hoping to alleviate the headache that had begun to throb at the base of her skull.

"Bill stopped by earlier this morning when you were working with Gina," she began.

He nodded. "I saw you from Gina's window. Was everything all right with him?"

She hesitated a moment and rubbed the back of her neck. "He's leaving this evening for a vacation in Florida." She cast Lucas a faint smile. "I'm hoping he'll meet some wonderful, lonely widow and fall desperately, madly in love with her."

"So you cut him free." His dark eyes held a touch of sympathy.

"It was the right thing to do. I never felt remotely romantic toward Bill, but by allowing him to continue to be such a big part of my life, I was feeding some hope that he had about us."

"But sometimes it's hard to do the right thing," he observed softly.

She smiled. "I have to admit, there are a lot of things about Bill I'll miss. He was steady as a rock, and I always knew he had my best interest at heart." Her smile fell away and she once again rubbed the ache at the base of her skull. "He mentioned something else that I think I need to tell you."

She felt the tension that suddenly filled him, a heightening of the pulsating energy that always seemed to surround him. "What?"

"He told me about Belinda."

He frowned and appeared to relax. "Belinda? What about her?" His puzzlement looked genuine.

"Apparently she met Bill last week when he left here. They had several meetings. She told him she was your lover." She felt her cheeks burn with a touch of embarrassment. "I'm not telling you this because I think you owe me any explanation about your personal relationships, but rather because some of the things Bill said about her I found disturbing."

Lucas leaned back against the sofa cushion, looking as sleek as a panther, but his gaze was troubled. "What was Belinda doing out here?"

Kathleen shrugged. "I gathered from Bill that she's here trying to get close to you."

He sat up. "Turn around," he said.

She frowned. "What?"

"Turn around. I'll massage your neck for you. Apparently it's bothering you."

Kathleen realized she had been rubbing her neck again and she dropped her hand to her lap. "That's really not necessary."

"Turn around, Kathleen, I can ease some of the pain." His voice rang with a soft command.

She moved so her back was to him and pulled her hair to one side of her shoulder. His fingers were warm and strong as they began to rub the base of her skull in circular motions. She dropped her head forward, allowing him full access.

For a few minutes neither of them spoke. His fingers found the sore place and firmly massaged away some of the pain.

But as the tension in her head ebbed somewhat, a different kind of ache began to build in her body.

She could feel his warm breath against her neck, the heat that radiated from his almost intimate nearness. She wished his hands would move from her head to her shoulders, from her shoulders down her back.

She wished he'd wrap his arms around her and put his hands on her breasts. Her nipples hardened at the thought of how his fingers would feel caressing her body.

Breathing from her mouth, her heart banged against her rib cage in a rhythm that had nothing to do with relaxation. Every nerve ending in her body felt electrified, and she knew if she didn't do something to break the spell of his nearness, his touch, things could quickly flare out of control.

"Thanks, that's much better," she said as she scooted out of his reach. She was appalled to hear that her voice had a breathless, trembling quality, and she cleared her throat as she turned to face him once again.

His dark eyes gleamed with a knowing light that both thrilled and irritated her. "Now, would you tell me about Belinda? Is it possible she might have been the person who tried to break into the house last night?"

The gleam in his eyes faded, and his expression was thoughtful as he once again leaned back. "I can't imagine Belinda climbing a tree for any reason. She isn't exactly the wholesome outdoorsy kind of woman. What exactly did Bill tell you about her that has you worried?"

"That she was your lover and she believes you were promised to her by Satan." She half expected him to laugh and when he didn't a new fear swept through her.

Instead, he rose from the sofa, a deep frown slashing across his forehead. He paced in front of her for a moment, then stopped. "Belinda was a waitress at the club where I was working. But the term lovers implies an emotional connection between us that wasn't there."

He raked a hand through his raven hair and began to pace once again. "We had an intense physical relationship for a couple of weeks, but she knew the score—that I wasn't in it for anything long term."

"Well, apparently she thinks she made some sort of pact with the devil that you didn't know about," Kathleen replied.

He sat back down on the sofa next to her. "It's more important than ever that we keep an eye on Gina."

Kathleen's heart jumped with dread. "Do you think Belinda might have something to do with what's going on?"

"I don't know," he confessed. "But if Bill is telling the truth about what she told him, we can't dismiss a possible connection."

"Are we fighting against the devil?" Her voice trembled again, this time from fear rather than from desire.

He reached out and took her hand in his. His skin was warm and as his fingers entwined with hers she welcomed the simple touch.

"I don't know," he said. "I will tell you this: There is no doubt in my mind that we're fighting something inherently evil. Whether it comes from the devil or something else doesn't matter. The fact that whatever it is attacks Gina spiritually and now perhaps physically only means we have to be vigilant until we figure out what is going on, until we can assure Gina's safety—until we can win this battle or whatever you want to call it." He released her hand, and she fought against a sense of loss.

"Gina has been looking forward to going to a birthday party up the street tomorrow. I hate to tell her she can't go."

She sighed. "She's been so isolated from her friends since this all began. Since she hasn't had an episode for a while, I thought it would be okay for her to attend."

Lucas frowned thoughtfully. "Is it possible you could go to the party with her?"

"Gina would be mortified," she answered.

His features lightened and he laughed softly. "Yes, I suppose she would be. You said the party is just down the street?"

She nodded. "Three houses away at the Banfields'."

"And you know them?"

"Yes, Lisa and Gina have been best friends since they were four, and Melissa Banfield and I were room mothers together last year for first grade and the year before in kindergarten. Melissa would never let anything happen to Gina."

"We'll take Gina to the party, then pick her up afterward. You'll need to let Mrs. Banfield know that she isn't to release Gina to anyone other than the two of us."

Relief swept through her. She'd been afraid that he might try to talk her into not letting Gina go. While Gina's well-being was her first priority, there were times in the night when she was overwhelmed with sadness because Gina was losing days, weeks, months of a normal happy childhood.

At that moment the object of her thoughts came flying down the stairs, a brightly clothed Barbie doll in each hand. "Barbie says she's hungry. Is it time for supper yet?"

Kathleen got up from the sofa. "Does Barbie have anything in mind for supper?" She'd noticed that in the past week, without any of the dreadful episodes, Gina had some of her color back and looked healthier than she had in weeks.

"Hot dogs and macaroni and cheese."

"Hmm, my favorite," Lucas said, also getting up from the sofa. With a mock growl, he grabbed Gina in his arms and swept her up in the air, then set her on his shoulders.

Gina giggled with delight, the delightfully normal, girlish sound wrapping its way around Kathleen's heart. If she did ever allow herself to fall in love with Lucas Connelly, part of the reason would be because he'd given Gina back her laughter.

Chapter Fourteen

"I think it's time I start working with you as well as with Gina," Lucas said as he and Kathleen walked back from the Banfield house, where they had just left Gina for the birthday party.

"Working with me? What do you mean?" she looked at him curiously, trying to ignore how vital, how handsome he looked with the bright sunshine sparkling off his black hair and emphasizing the strength of his features.

He was clad in a T-shirt and jean shorts and looked wonderfully virile and sexy.

"I want to teach you how to astral project," he said.

She stopped in her tracks. "Why?"

"Because there's no stronger instinct than that of a mother to save her child. Because if Gina goes into that tunnel and can't get out, perhaps the two of us together will have the strength to fight what tries to hold her." His eyes glinted with a touch of amusement. "There's nothing to be frightened about, Kathleen."

She stiffened her back. "I'm not afraid. I'd do anything for Gina . . . anything."

He nodded. "And that's why I think it's important." They resumed walking again.

"Is astral projecting something that can be taught?" she asked.

"The techniques can be taught, and if one is open enough, accepting enough, anyone can astral project."

They reached the house and Kathleen unlocked the front door, then stepped inside and quickly punched in the security code to assure the alarm would not sound. She re-armed the system, then turned back to Lucas.

"When do you want to start working with me?"

"I'd say now is the perfect time. With Gina gone, we can concentrate completely on you."

Kathleen rubbed her hands down the sides of her cotton dress, her throat slightly dry as she realized this was the first time the two of them had been alone in the house.

"All right," she agreed. "Uh . . . where do you want to do this?"

His dark eyes showed no emotion. "We can either do it in your bedroom or in mine, but it's best accomplished if you're lying down and comfortable."

He's talking about teaching you, not ravishing you, she told herself as she tried to calm the racing of her pulse. "My bedroom," she said. There was no way she wanted to be lying in his bed, where the scent of him would cling to the sheets.

She walked up the stairs, far too conscious of him just behind her. As they entered her bedroom she was grateful she had made the bed. It seemed less intimate for him to be in here with the comforter neatly pulled up and the pillows artfully arranged. Exposing bunched up sheets and a rumpled duvet cover would have seemed too personal.

She opened the curtains that had been drawn across the windows, as if the bright sunshine streaking through the glass would prevent any untoward behavior between her and Lucas. Intimacy and lovemaking happened at night, when darkness reigned.

Turning to face him she once again ran her hands down the sides of her dress. "What now?"

"The first thing you need to do is take a couple of deep breaths and relax." He smiled with a gentleness that did nothing to alleviate her tension. "I promise you, Kathleen, I'm not going to let anything happen that you don't want to happen."

His words didn't exactly make her feel better, for she wasn't sure at all what she wanted to have happen. He gestured her toward the bed, and she stretched out on her back as he instructed.

She was intensely aware of herself—of the fact that the cotton dress she wore was thin and loose, but suddenly felt tight and restrictive. Her breathing was far too rapid and every inch of her body felt electrified.

Lucas pulled a chair up next to the bed and leaned toward her, but didn't touch her in any way. "Close your eyes and let your shoulders relax into the mattress. Take some deep breaths, Kathleen. The first step in astral projection is learning how to reach complete and total relaxation."

She nodded and did as he bid. With her eyes closed, she drew in deep gulps of air and released them slowly. After several moments of deep breathing, she felt herself begin to relax.

"Good, that's good." Lucas's voice was seductively soft and low. "Now, imagine a calm and peaceful setting in your mind. Maybe you're lying on a quiet beach with the heat of the sun warming you or snuggled beneath a blanket in front of a roaring fire. Whatever scene is tranquil to you, get it firmly in your mind."

She focused on the thought of a crackling fire, the faint pleasant scent of hickory smoke in the air. She was naked beneath a soft comforter and Lucas was beside her, warming her as effectively as the flames before them. His mouth was almost savage with need against hers as his hands stroked up and down the length of her.

Her eyelids snapped open and she gasped. Instantly she knew that Lucas had been privy to her vision. There was no mistaking the emotion in his eyes . . . passion, hot and hungry flared in the depths.

"Lucas . . ." His name slid from her lips softly and she was unsure in her mind whether she meant it as a protest or a plea.

He apparently took it as a plea. Standing up from his chair, he leaned over her and covered her mouth with his. She knew at that moment he'd been absolutely right—their joining was inevitable. She was lost and had no desire to be found until she'd tasted and felt and savored him to the fullest.

She wound her arms around his neck and pulled him to the bed next to her. He came willingly, wrapping his arms beneath her to hold her tightly against him as he deepened the kiss with his tongue.

Kathleen lost track of time as his mouth took possession of hers. After what seemed a blissful eternity, he slowly retreated, gently nibbling at her lower lip. Then he raised his head to gaze deep into her eyes. "I told you I wouldn't have you do anything you didn't want to do," he said. "But I can tell you right now, I want you. I've wanted you since the moment you opened your door to me in the middle of the night."

In reply she pulled his head back down and took his lips with her own. Her heart beat frantically as he released his hold on her and instead stroked both hands down the sides of her face.

Hot. His fingers were fevered with heat as he moved them across her collarbone, then splayed them so they were precariously close to her breasts. And dear God, but she wanted them on her breasts.

She moaned with displeasure as he once again broke the kiss and sat up. In one sleek movement he pulled his T-shirt over his head, then rolled to the side of her. His broad chest gleamed with sunlight dancing in the window, and she forced herself to lay still despite her desire to touch the smooth, bronzed skin.

He propped himself up on his elbow and studied her, his eyes filled with an appetite that caused a tightness in her chest. "You are so beautiful," he whispered, his breath warm and caressing against her neck.

He ran a finger across her brow, down the curve of her cheek and across her lower lip. She captured his hand in hers and not breaking eye contact with him, drew his finger into her mouth.

She sucked with a soft pressure and watched the flare of desire in his eyes intensify. It was the most wanton thing she could ever remember doing in her life, but she wasn't ashamed or embarrassed.

This was right. This was destined. She knew it in her heart, in her soul.

He pulled his finger from her mouth and moved his hands to the buttons that ran down the front of her ankle-length dress.

She felt as if she'd stopped breathing, as if breathing wasn't necessary at all as long as Lucas was touching her. He unfastened the buttons slowly, as if he had all the time in the world and the slight pressure of his hands moving down her body only served to increase the thrumming in her veins.

When he'd finished, he swept the material to her sides, baring her to his hot gaze. In that moment she was grateful she'd decided to wear her pale pink lacy bra and matching lace bikini panties. Funny, she usually saved the expensive set for when she dressed up.

Had she suspected in the back of her mind that this was going to happen? When she dressed this morning, aware that Gina would be gone from the house for several hours, had she known she and Lucas would spend those hours making love? She'd hoped.

Once again his lips sought hers as his hands moved to cup her bra-covered breasts. He tasted of something wild and primitive and she reveled in his kiss. Through the thin lace of her bra she could feel the heat of his hands, but it wasn't enough. She wanted him against her bare skin, and she wanted him beneath the covers on her bed, where the scent of him would linger long after he'd left her room.

This time it was she who broke the kiss and gently pushed him away from her so she could sit up. He appeared to know what she intended. As she shrugged off her dress and reached behind her to unfasten her bra, he took off his shorts and boxers, leaving him splendidly, beautifully naked beside her.

Before she could remove her panties, he pulled her back into his arms. His warm skin against hers caused her pulse to quicken so fast she thought she might die. And when his hands moved up to cup her breasts she moaned with pleasure.

Her legs tangled with his as her hands splayed across his back. Her skin loved his as he crashed his mouth to hers in a near savage kiss.

His thumbs moved across her nipples and they responded, becoming turgid and full. "Lucas," she moaned against his mouth. She wanted to ask him how it was possible that although they had never made love before, his arms, his skin, his mouth felt so familiar.

"Kathleen," he replied, her name like a reverent prayer on his lips. One hand left her breast and moved with aching slowness down her ribcage to her lower abdomen. He traced the skin just above her panty line and she arched against him with need.

She was on the verge of losing all control and somewhere in the back of her mind she was amazed that he seemed to have so much patience. He moved his hand from her abdomen to her inner thigh, lightly caressing the sensitive skin but still not touching her where she needed him most.

She moaned again as he used his thumbs on either side of her hips and pulled her underwear off and tossed them to the floor by the side of the bed. Still he tantalized her, kissing her mouth then down her neck, licking her nipples and stroking her thighs and her hips.

Her blood had never been so hot inside her as currents of pleasure coursed through her. He knew what he was doing to her. His eyes glowed with pleasure as she writhed against him.

Somewhere in the back of her mind she realized two could play at this game. She ran her hands down his firmly muscled chest, across his flat stomach and stopped just short of holding him intimately. She heard the hiss of his breath as she teased his inner thigh, careful not to brush against him anywhere else.

They stroked and kissed and touched, feeding the building frenzy inside one another. The only sounds in the room were the sighs and moans of pleasure. It wasn't until Kathleen reached down and grasped him in her hand that the last modicum of control snapped.

Lucas had intended to maintain control, to make love to Kathleen slow and easy, savoring every sensation, each of her responses. He knew in his heart, in his soul, that their coupling had been destined, but he had no idea what tomorrow would bring. He only knew he had this single moment in time with her and he meant to make it last as long as possible.

But when her fingers wrapped around him, all rational thought fled from his head. He pushed her hand aside and positioned himself between her welcoming thighs. Trying to be gentle, yet filled with raging need, he pushed into her, sighing as he felt the moist, velvet heat of her surrounding him.

She gripped his shoulders, arching herself up so he could fill her completely. He pulled back, then thrust forward and felt her fingernails biting into his skin. He remained still for a moment, afraid that if he moved again he might lose it all together.

And he wasn't ready for this to be over so quickly. It had been lifetimes since he'd made love to her, and he knew it might be a hundred lifetimes before he got the opportunity again.

Still, despite his desire to the contrary, he couldn't help his instinctive, primal need to move his hips against hers, to take total possession of her and allow her to possess him.

He thrust deep and hard and she met him thrust for thrust, tiny cries falling from her lips as they moved faster and faster, racing to an all-consuming crescendo.

She reached her climax first, shuddering uncontrollably against him with the violent force of her pleasure and that sent him over the edge. He stiffened against her, swelling inside her as her name ripped from his throat.

They remained unmoving for long minutes, their bodies still tangled together, their skin cooling from the fever that had gripped them as their breathing resumed a more normal rhythm.

Somewhere in the back of his mind, Lucas knew nothing good could come from this new development in their relationship. The last thing he needed was to be distracted from his task of helping Gina. He couldn't allow himself to become emotionally attached to Kathleen because he had no idea what painful choices he might face in the future.

He finally rolled to the side of her and propped up on his elbow so he could see her lovely face. She smiled at him, her eyes the blue of endless summer days. Her lips were lush, red and slightly swollen from his kisses. The desire to have her again claimed him in its heady grasp.

What he needed was distance. He felt as if they were playing out a tragedy of the past, a tragedy of love that would never be resolved, but rather would continue to haunt them both throughout eternity. The power of his emotions scared him. Were they real or part of his new consciousness? He refused to be a pawn in someone else's game. Until he knew more he had to maintain strict control of his actions. He had to stay away from Kathleen's influence.

Abruptly he sat up, disturbed by his thoughts, more disturbed by the fact that making love to her had done nothing to sate his hunger for her. "We'd better get dressed. It won't be long before we need to walk back to get Gina."

The sweet smile on her face, the bright sparkle in her beautiful eyes faded. He knew she was disappointed. She'd wanted flowery verse, to bask in the sweet afterglow of their lovemaking, but he knew to give her that would be akin to offering her false promises about some sort of future together. He knew better.

If he didn't manage to save Gina, Kathleen would hate him. If he did manage to save her, he would forever be a reminder of this time of horror.

If their present life played out like all their past lives, she would eventually reject him, so what was the point of becoming emotionally involved?

As he pulled his T-shirt over his head, he was conscious of her sitting up and raking a hand through her thick, luxurious hair. He felt her confusion, her hurt radiating from her as she rose from the bed. He fought the impulse to turn and wrap his arms around her, give her the words, the afterglow, the promises all women wanted.

"I think I'll take a fast shower," she said softly and disappeared into the master bathroom.

Lucas breathed a deep, troubled sigh. This had been a mistake. The scent of her still clung to his skin, filling his senses and stirring the desire he'd thought sated.

Making love to her had been the wrong thing to do . . . so why was he thinking of doing it again? He pulled the T-shirt he'd just put on off again and walked into the bathroom.

Steam shrouded the large wall mirror and rose above the shower enclosure. Through the slightly mottled glass he could see the shape of her body—the curve of her lush breasts, the slender waist and hips, the long length of her legs.

His knees weakened as he remembered the feel of her warmth surrounding him. It hadn't been just a physical warmth, it had been a warmth that had fluttered through him, seeping into his heart, into his soul.

Just one more time, he told himself. Just one more time. He opened the shower door. She turned in surprise. Then those gorgeous eyes of hers flared wide as she recognized his intent. She stepped aside to let him join her beneath the hot spray of water, and once again Lucas was lost.

Chapter Fifteen

Making love to Lucas had been all that Kathleen had dreamed, all that she had imagined. What she hadn't imagined or experienced in her dreams was his withdrawal from her after they had made love not once, but twice.

By the time they'd gotten out of the shower and dressed again, they'd had to go back to the Banfields' to retrieve Gina.

The walk home from the birthday party was filled with Gina's happy chatter, but Kathleen couldn't help but notice that Lucas seemed distant and far away.

There had been magic in his arms. First in bed, then in the shower, but like a sleight-of-hand trick, the magic had disappeared the moment they'd finished.

"Jeremy Matthews brought a bag of gummy worms and he put them all in his mouth then pretended like he threw up," Gina said. "It was kinda gross and kinda neat at the same time." She smiled thoughtfully. "Jeremy is sorta cute. I think when I get big I might marry him."

Her words evoked the haunting questions that had plagued Kathleen for the past couple of months. Would Gina survive whatever this madness was? Would she grow old and eventually marry and have a wonderful life?

Suddenly consumed by a need to hug her daughter, Kathleen reached down and swung Gina up in her arms. "No matter how cute Jeremy is, I absolutely forbid you to marry him for at least a year."

Gina giggled and wrapped her arms around Kathleen's neck. "Don't worry, Mommy. I'm not going to leave you for a long, long time."

As they stepped up to the front door, Kathleen handed Lucas the key. He unlocked the door, punched in the code, then smiled at them both. But the smile didn't reach his eyes.

"Gina, maybe we can do a little work together before supper," he said. He looked to Kathleen. "Unless your mommy needs help cooking."

"No, that's all right. You two go ahead. I'm just going to broil a couple of steaks and make a salad." She was almost grateful when he left with Gina and she went into the kitchen alone.

Where the tension that had existed between them before had been an exciting, anticipatory tension, what resounded between them now was decidedly uncomfortable.

As she began the meal preparations, a flutter of anger began to build inside her. What was he afraid of, that she'd turn into some clinging, needy woman just because they had made love? Was he afraid that somehow she would expect or demand something from him that he was unwilling to give?

She vented some of her anger by tearing into a head of lettuce, shredding it into bite-sized pieces. She'd been alone for almost a year, really much longer than that if she considered the state of her relationship with Sutton before his death.

All she wanted from Lucas Connelly was for him to keep Gina safe. She pulled a green pepper from the refrigerator and chopped it with more force than necessary.

By the time she had cut up carrots and celery, tomatoes and cucumber, most of her anger had dissipated. She seasoned the steaks, then sank down at the table with a glass of iced tea, deciding that what she needed to do was assure Lucas that their lovemaking had changed nothing between them.

He was here to do a job, to teach Gina whatever tools she might need to fight whatever force attempted to possess her. Making love to him had been an incredible experience, one that had touched not only her body, but her heart and soul as well. But he confused her, and if she looked deep within herself she recognized that he also frightened her just a little bit.

There were moments when his eyes glowed more silver than black, when she sensed something other-worldly about him. Uneasiness swept through her as she wondered if his magic was good or bad, if he was really here to help them or if she was a fool to trust him.

She got up from the table and slid the steaks beneath the awaiting hot broiler. She couldn't second guess her decision to have Lucas here now, nor could she second guess the man himself. She had to focus on the fact that since Lucas had been here Gina had suffered no episodes, and although life hadn't returned to anything remotely resembling normal, things were better than they had been before he arrived.

Dinner was a quiet affair. Gina was obviously exhausted from the birthday party. She picked at her food without interest, her eyelids drooping heavily. Lucas appeared preoccupied, focusing solely on the act of eating.

Kathleen ate little herself, hungry only for a bit of warmth in Lucas's eyes, a hint of a smile on his lips.

"Why don't I clean up the mess and you can get Gina ready for bed. She looks like she's about ready to fall over," he said once they had finished the meal.

"I'm tired," Gina said and took Kathleen's hand.

"All right, sweetheart, I'll take you upstairs." She looked at Lucas. "I'll be back down in a little while." He nodded, already at work clearing the dishes from the table.

As Kathleen fixed warm water for a bath, Gina stripped off her clothes, yawning. Although it was fairly early, just after seven, it was obvious she was more than ready to go to sleep.

"So you had fun at the party?" Kathleen asked when Gina sat in a tub of strawberry-scented bubbles.

"It was lots of fun. We played games and I didn't even care that I didn't win any of them. When I have my birthday can we have a party here and I can invite all my friends?"

"Of course," Kathleen agreed. "We'll decorate the backyard with balloons and crepe paper, and we'll have a wonderful celebration." Gina smiled, sinking deeper in the water.

"Come on, munchkin, let's get you into bed before you fall asleep right here in the tub."

Nearly half an hour later, Kathleen went back downstairs and found Lucas seated in the living room, a glass of brandy in his hand.

She walked to the bar and poured herself a glass, then settled in the chair opposite where he sat on the sofa. "Lucas, you don't have to worry about me getting all crazy on you just because of what happened earlier."

He offered her an enigmatic smile. "I'm not worried about you getting crazy." The smile faded and he swirled the brandy

171

in the bottom of his snifter. "And although making love with you was wonderful, it shouldn't have happened."

He set his drink down on the coffee table and looked at her once again, his eyes as dark and mysterious as she'd ever seen them. "For the past couple of days a feeling of urgency has possessed me . . . as if we're about to enter a hellish storm. I have a feeling the danger to Gina, to all of us, is mounting. You are a beautiful, breathtaking distraction. But I can't allow myself to be distracted. What we shared today can't happen again. We both need to be clear-headed and unemotional for what is coming."

His words chilled her to the bone. She'd thought things were getting better. She jumped as the sound of the doorbell pealed.

She got up to answer it, aware of Lucas following her. "It's Keith," she said after looking out the peek hole.

"Keith?"

"Keith Kelly," she replied, realizing she hadn't told Lucas about the reporter and his daughter. She opened the door to greet the man. "Keith, please come in."

He offered her a tired smile and stepped into the foyer. "I was so grateful when I pulled up and saw lights on. Gina is doing okay?"

"She's holding her own. And Sharon?"

His brown eyes softened. "The same. I've been doing a little digging and have some information I thought you might find interesting." He cast a curious look at Lucas.

Kathleen quickly introduced the two men. "Please, let's go into the kitchen and I'll put some coffee on."

While they waited for the coffee to brew, Kathleen explained to Lucas how she had met Keith and about his daughter.

"It's bigger than just Sharon and Gina and a couple of other kids," Keith explained when they were all seated at the table with coffee mugs before them. "I have now found twelve children in comas. I talked to their families and have discovered all shared the same experiences before lapsing into the comas, flying, the tunnel, a voice calling to them."

"Twelve," Kathleen repeated in horror. Twelve children in deathlike comas, twelve families torn apart by some unknown force.

"Exactly what are the children's physical condition?" Lucas asked.

"Their bodies seem to be doing okay. They're all breathing on their own, but they're being fed intravenously and physical therapists massage their muscles to prevent atrophy." Keith frowned. "It's like they're in a deep state of hibernation."

"You said you had some interesting information." Lucas leaned forward, his gaze dark and intense.

Keith shot a quick glance to Kathleen.

"It's all right, Keith. Lucas is here to help. He believes that Gina is astral projecting, and he's trying to teach her to control it so she won't be lost in the tunnel," she explained.

"I'll tell you like I've told Kathleen. I'm not sure what brought me here, I'm not sure what's going on. All I know is that I had to come here and try to help Gina." Lucas frowned thoughtfully. "I know it sounds crazy, but there are some things I can't explain and me being here is one of them."

Keith stared at Lucas for a long moment, but Lucas felt no censure, no challenge from the man. Rather he recognized the weary resignation of a man who'd experienced too much and was open to anything anyone could do to offer hope.

Keith broke the gaze as he picked up his briefcase from the floor and opened it on the table. He pulled out a sheaf of paperwork, then closed the case and set it on the floor.

"A couple of weeks ago I was assigned to write a piece about some church desecrations," he explained. "While researching the story, I discovered something interesting . . . and rather frightening." He looked first at Lucas, then at Kathleen. "The break-ins have taken place in all five boroughs of New York City and in all denominations of churches."

He paused a moment and took a sip of his coffee, as if to ward off a chill, then continued. "All the desecrations involved crepe paper and balloons."

"Crepe paper and balloons?" Kathleen frowned.

Keith nodded. "Black crepe paper and balloons to be exact. There was the usual spray paint and minimal vandalism, but in every church I've investigated, it looked as if a party had been thrown—a party for the damned." He wrapped his hands around his mug. "But that's not the really interesting part."

A well of trepidation pooled in the bottom of Lucas's stomach. He had no idea what was coming, but felt every nerve ending in his body tightening with a portent of dread.

"On the night each church was desecrated, a child slipped into a coma." Kathleen gasped and Lucas thought he might throw up. Keith frowned and pulled a sheet of paper from the stack before him. He slid it across the table in front of Lucas.

"That's a list of the children I've been able to find who have lapsed into these inexplicable comas. Beside their names you'll see the date they went into the hospital and the church near their home desecrated on the same date."

Lucas leaned toward Kathleen so they could read the report

at the same time. Lucas's senses suddenly seemed more acute. He could smell not only Kathleen's perfume, but the fainter subtle fragrance of the soap she'd used earlier in the day in the shower.

A chorus of rhythmic pounding filled his ears—his heartbeat, her heartbeat, and Keith's from across the table. As his gaze swept over the list of names, he felt tiny beads of perspiration pop out on his brow.

Twelve names, twelve churches, and twelve celebrations of the damned. And he knew now it wasn't just Gina's fate he held in his hands, but the fate of all the children who had been lost before her.

"It all has to be connected," Keith said. "It's just too great of a coincidence not to be."

"Oh, it's connected," Lucas replied softly, the dread inside of him reaching almost unbearable proportions.

"I've taken pictures of the damage at the last three churches to be hit," Keith said, once again shuffling through the papers in front of him. "I scanned the pictures and made color copies." He handed a sheet with a composite of pictures to Kathleen, then one to Lucas.

The first photo showed the balloons and crepe paper Keith had described. The second was of crosses turned upside down. The third was of a wall sprayed with red paint.

"Thanatos . . . what does that mean?" Kathleen asked.

The name thundered painfully in Lucas's head as a riveting slice of lightning splintered through him. The perspiration that had begun as small dots above his brow now trickled from his forehead, raced down the small of his back, and dampened his underarms. At the same time, he was gripped by a hand of ice, chilling him to the bone despite his sweating body.

"Thanatos is from Greek mythology," he said, his voice sounding strange and faraway to his own ears. "He was the god of death, son of night and twin brother to Hypnos, the god of sleep."

The words tumbled from him, coming from some unknown source, some strange knowledge not his own. "Thanatos is the personification of death. His mission is to eventually bring each living soul to the underworld."

Both Keith and Kathleen looked at him in shocked surprise. "Don't ask me how I know all this. I just do."

Lucas raked a hand through his hair. Now he knew the enemy's name—Thanatos. It once again boomed in Lucas's brain, bringing with it the aching wail of a desolate wind, the stench of plague and death, the beating of thousands of locust wings and a gut-wrenching terror that knew no bounds.

Lucas now knew his role, understood fully the path laid out before him. The strange powers he'd gained, the strength he felt growing inside him, all were to prepare him for the battle to come. And the battle would be waged between him and the one known as Thanatos.

If Lucas won, the children would be saved. But if he were not triumphant, all would be lost.

Chapter Sixteen

For endless moments the three sat not speaking. As Kathleen studied Lucas, fear gripped her.

His eyes glowed that haunting silver, and in the depths of them she saw a glimmer of challenge. They were a warrior's eyes before battle, void of pity, filled with a blood-thirsty need and for a second she didn't know whether she was afraid *for* him . . . or *of* him. The look lasted only a fleeting instant, then disappeared.

Lucas stabbed a finger at the name Thanatos visible in the picture. "This is our enemy." He glanced at Keith, then at Kathleen. "This is who calls to Gina."

"But is this a man, or an entity, or what?" Kathleen asked in confusion. "And why does he call to Gina?"

"I don't know." Lucas leaned back in his chair and raked a hand through his hair in frustration. "He could be a man, but if he's mortal, he's been given enormous powers by the devil himself. Perhaps he once was a man, but now he's something much more."

"And the children . . . why the children?" Keith asked.

Lucas frowned. "I don't know. I don't have all the answers yet."

"So how do we find this Thanatos?" Kathleen asked.

"We don't. He'll find us." Again Lucas's eyes glowed with the other-worldly shine. "If we can keep Gina from going to him in her sleep, he'll have to come to get her another way."

"You think that was what the attempted break-in was about?" she asked.

"I think it's very possible," Lucas replied.

"Break-in?" Keith raised a questioning eyebrow, and quickly Kathleen explained what had happened.

"So what do we do now?" Kathleen asked.

"What we've been doing. I'll keep training Gina. I still need to work with you on astral projecting so together we have the power to keep Gina from following the voice." Lucas turned to Keith. "And you keep digging. Maybe something with these church desecrations and the celebrations will give us some important information."

"Actually, I do have one more thing to tell you about," Keith said. "I found an interesting web site." Again he pushed a piece of paper before them.

The page was black except for a bright red name in the center. The name of Thanatos. As Kathleen stared at the name, fear once again swept through her.

"I've got a buddy of mine working to try to hack into the site, but so far he's had no luck. He says he's never seen so much security on a web site before. But he's good. Eventually he'll break through. I contacted the site asking for information and this is the e-mail I got back."

The message read: Danger. Go Away. This is a private site.

"It's possible it's nothing more than a bunch of kids," he added.

"Maybe," Lucas conceded, "but I'd like to know what your friend finds out if he manages to breach the security."

Keith nodded. "I'll keep you posted." His brown eyes darkened with pain and he gazed solemnly at Lucas. "You seem to know more than anyone about what's going on here."

"I wish I had all the answers," Lucas replied.

Again Keith nodded. "I just have one question to ask you. I know you're here to help Gina, that you think somehow you can stop her from falling into the coma that has claimed the other children. Is there still hope? For the others, I mean. Is there still hope for Sharon?"

Kathleen looked at Lucas, her heart aching for Keith and his wife. "There's always hope," Lucas said, his voice soft and low. "I wish I could tell you more than that."

Keith offered him a smile. "That's enough for now." He placed his briefcase back on the table and began to gather up his paperwork. "It's time for me to get out of here. My wife will be home from the hospital soon, and we like to eat a late dinner together."

"Does she know what you've discovered?" Kathleen asked curiously as she and Lucas walked Keith to the front door.

"No. I haven't told Rosalyn about any of this. I didn't even tell her about coming here to talk to you that first time we met. She has enough on her mind keeping vigil over Sharon."

"You'll let us know if you learn anything else?" Lucas asked.

"Of course." Keith shifted his briefcase from his right hand to his left, then held out his free hand to Lucas, who grasped it in a firm handshake. "Thank you," he said. "I don't know who or what brought you to us, but I think you're our only hope to save these children—to save ourselves."

Lucas frowned and released Keith's hand, then excused himself and returned to the living room. Kathleen said her goodbye to Keith, then carefully locked the door and set the alarm system once again.

When she entered the living room she found Lucas standing before the French doors that led out to the garden. His back was to her and something about his posture made him look oddly vulnerable.

She walked up and stood beside him, wondering what it was that held his attention in the darkness beyond the window. He seemed not to notice her presence next to him, but then he spoke. "It was an awesome burden before, believing that I might be responsible for Gina's salvation or damnation. But now it's more than just Gina. It's twelve little souls in limbo."

He turned to study her, as though searching for an explanation, his long-lashed eyes tortured with pain. "I keep asking myself, why me? Why has this huge responsibility been placed on my shoulders?" He stalked away from her and the room filled with his anger. "Why me? I don't need this in my life." He whirled around and glared at her. "I don't know why it's got to be me."

He raked a hand through his hair and the anger seeped out of him. Again he looked vulnerable, racked by an internal war.

She walked to where he stood, his body rigid, his facial expression haunted.

She placed a hand on his cheek, felt him relax a little at

her touch. "I don't know, Lucas. I don't know why it's you. I don't know why it's Keith and all those other children. I don't know why it's my daughter and me. But it is Gina and me and it is Keith and the others and it's you, Lucas. None of us chose to be involved in this, but we are."

She dropped her hand from his face. "I'm scared, Lucas. I've been scared since the first night Gina was lost to me in her sleep. But with you here, I'm less frightened."

He stepped away from her, as if unable to stand her nearness. Terror ripped through her. Was he thinking of turning his back on them all? He couldn't. He was their only hope—her only hope for seeing that Gina didn't end up like Keith's daughter, a shell in a hospital bed.

"I've got to get out of here," he said and started toward the front door.

Kathleen grabbed his arm in sheer panic. "Please Lucas, where are you going?"

"I need some air." He shrugged off her hand. "I need some time to think." His gaze was distant and she knew he'd retreated to a place where she couldn't reach him. He punched off the alarm and opened the front door.

"Lucas . . . will you be back?" she asked, trying to keep the desperation from her voice. "Are you coming back?"

He didn't seem to hear her. He walked out the door without looking back and was swallowed by the darkness.

For a long moment after he disappeared, she remained at the door, overwhelmed by despair. What if he didn't return? What if he never came back?

Would Gina be safe without him in the house? She slammed the door, quickly punched in the code, then raced upstairs to Gina's room.

She stifled a sob of relief as she saw Gina sleeping peacefully. Silently sliding into the rocking chair near the bed, she wondered what she would do if Lucas didn't return.

She felt in her heart that if Lucas wasn't here, then Gina's risk of being lost increased a hundredfold. What she didn't understand, what frightened her almost as much, was the feeling that if Lucas wasn't here, she would be lost as well.

As Lucas walked, heading toward the pounding surf of the ocean, he felt the night air gathering suffocatingly close around him.

Overhead the stars winked brightly in a black velvet sky, but the beauty of the night was lost on him. He strode briskly, driven by a silent rage that had come upon him suddenly.

It had been bad enough when he'd thought he was responsible for Gina's health and welfare. But knowing now that there were more children filled him with both anger and despair. Seeing Keith Kelly's face, his eyes filled with grief had made the other children's plight all the more real for Lucas.

How was he supposed to fight an entity he didn't know? How was he supposed to save the children who had been violated in sleep and left in a deathlike coma?

He was just a cheap, second-rate magician who'd finally begun to live his life after his father's death. Why had he been the one to get the visions of Gina's frightened eyes? Why had he felt the trauma of her terror deep inside his bones?

He should just catch a cab and return to his penthouse in the city, leave all this madness behind. It would be so easy to just turn his back on all of it. Well, perhaps not easy, but possible.

It didn't take him long to leave behind the fancy Hampton homes. The pounding of the surf grew louder and the scent of brine grew stronger. He climbed a small sand dune and when he reached the top, the ocean appeared before him.

Lit by starlight, by moonlight, the silver-tipped waves rolled in, and in the ever present rhythm of water meeting shore, some of his anxiety, his anger, his despair quieted.

He kicked off his shoes and raced toward the ocean. For several minutes he walked along the beach, allowing the waves to break over his feet.

The night was warm and even though he could feel how cold the water was on his ankles, he dove in, needing the physical exertion of swimming in the bracing water to numb his mind. The frigid temperature stole his breath momentarily, numbing his body as well as his brain.

For a little while it worked. As he stroked through the chilling waves, his mind remained blissfully empty. He didn't think of Kathleen or Gina, didn't consider Keith Kelly or the other children. He just swam.

It wasn't until his muscles tired and he was gasping with exhaustion that he headed back to the shore.

As he left the water he saw her. She stood on the dune where he had left his shoes, her long hair blowing in the breeze that blew inland.

He approached her, her features becoming more clear as he drew closer. "What are you doing here, Belinda?"

"Lucas." She hissed his name and raised her arms as if to coil herself around his neck. He grabbed her arms before they could make contact with him and pushed them back down to her sides. "I needed to see you. I needed to talk to you."

"Did you come to tell me about your meetings with Bill Abrahms?"

She broke eye contact with him, as if ashamed. "I was desperate." She looked at him again and in her wild eyes he saw her desperation, smelled it like an animal odor wafting from her. "I miss you."

What had been for Lucas a fairly uncomplicated life a month ago now seemed fraught with complexities. He raced a hand through his wet hair and stared up at the sky overhead.

"Lucas, please. Talk to me. Tell me you miss me, too. Tell me she means nothing to you."

He stared at her. "I can't do that, Belinda," he said softly. "She and I, we're bound together through fate." At that moment he realized he would return to the house. He would fight for Gina's soul because she was Kathleen's daughter, because he couldn't walk away from Kathleen while so much danger swirled around her.

"No, you and I are bound together." Once again Belinda raised her arms toward him, but he sidestepped her embrace.

"Belinda, listen to me. I never made you any promises. Our time together was special, but now it's over. You have to move on. Go back to the city and get on with your life."

Each word seemed to affect her like a slap across the face, and even in the darkness he saw the flush fill her cheeks, the rage spark in her eyes.

"I hate her," she exclaimed. Her eyes narrowed and her teeth gleamed feral in the moonlight. "Her and that kid of hers, I hope they die."

White hot rage swept through him. He grabbed her by the front of her blouse and pulled her to within inches of his body. "If you do anything to harm them, if you hurt them in any way, I'll find you, Belinda. I'll hunt you down like an animal."

"You don't understand." Tears filled her eyes where moments before there had been nothing but hate and anger. "You were supposed to be mine. He promised me."

Lucas's head pounded as he held tight to Belinda's blouse. "Who promised you? Who?" he demanded.

"Thanatos." The word hissed out of her as she wrestled away from his grasp. "He promised you to me," she said, as she backed away like a frightened crab skittering from a predator.

"He can't promise you what is not his to give," Lucas replied angrily. "Who is he, Belinda? Where can I find him?"

She shook her head and turned and ran. "He'll get them, Lucas. Thanatos will have them both—the child and the woman." She disappeared over the sand dune and by the time he reached the top she was nowhere in sight.

Rage swelled inside him. He threw back his head. "Thanatos!" He yelled to the heavens, the name ripping from his throat. "You bastard, Thanatos, where are you?"

The air filled with the stench of rotting vegetation and dead fish. A scorching wind began to blow, howling like a banshee in the darkness. The sand lifted from the beach and blew against him, biting at his legs, his arms, his chest. Overhead the stars disappeared, as if doused by one gigantic candle snuffer.

Above the sound of the screaming wind, he thought he heard a low, deep rumble of laughter, and it unleashed in him a feeling of imminent danger.

He had to get back, back to Kathleen, back to Gina. But the swirling sand disoriented him, stinging his eyes with grit and making it almost impossible for him to breathe.

He stumbled and raised his arm to shield his face. An urgent need to get back to the house filled him; he knew he should have never left them alone.

He recognized now that the doubts he'd entertained, the anger at being somehow chosen to fight for the children were weak emotions—tools of destruction.

If he had been selected for this battle, then so be it. He recognized now he was a part of something much bigger than himself, or Gina, or Kathleen.

He had been chosen to engage in a battle against evil, and he would do his part. He would be a warrior like none before or after him. He would do whatever it took to save the children, to save Gina . . . to save Kathleen.

Kathleen. For a single instant, his mind filled with the memory of making love to her, the wonder of her arms, the joy in their kisses. A buzz began at the base of his skull, a sensation followed by the familiar probe of something alien and yet not so alien anymore.

Power. It surged inside him, filled every pore of his body. He was no longer just Lucas Connelly the man. He was Lucas Connelly the magician. He held the power of magic and something more in his bones . . . in his soul.

He drew a deep breath and waved his hands as if he held a magic wand.

The wind died instantly with a final moan. The sand settled back to the ground and once again the stars twinkled overhead.

He'd stopped the assault, but he wasn't sure how. He only knew that as the chosen one he'd been gifted with the power and strength necessary to match Thanatos.

He didn't stop to wonder what had happened. He simply ran, needing to return to Kathleen and Gina as soon as possible.

Surely nothing had happened in his absence, he thought as he raced back the way he had come. He hadn't been gone that long—forty-five minutes, an hour at the most.

It wasn't until he unlocked the front door and got inside that he glanced at the clock in the entry. Shock riveted through him. After two. He'd been gone for more than four hours.

He raced up the stairs, his heart pounding frantically in his chest. He halted abruptly in the doorway to Gina's room. Moonlight splashed in through the window, illuminating the scene before him.

The child slept peacefully. Reggie Rabbit was tucked into her arms and a childish snore emitted from her with each breath.

He sagged against the door frame with relief, then looked at Kathleen, who slept in the chair next to the bed. He thought he could see the trace of tears that had fallen down her cheeks, and his heart ached with the knowledge that he had been the reason for her tears.

He walked over to her and touched her shoulder lightly. She came awake instantly and he quickly placed a finger over his lips and pointed to Gina.

Grabbing her hand, he took her out in the hallway. "I'm back," he said softly.

"Thank God." She fell into his arms.

He held her tight against him for a very long time.

Chapter Seventeen

"Breathe, Kathleen, slow and easy. Let yourself go."

It had been six days since Lucas left the house in the middle of the night and over that time he'd been trying, without success, to teach her how to astral project.

She was now stretched out on the living room floor. He sat cross-legged at her side. Gina was upstairs with Lisa Banfield, who had come over to play at Kathleen's invitation.

The living room was dark. Lucas had pulled the curtains across all the windows before they'd begun. The only sound she could discern was the occasional mumble of girlish voices drifting down the stairs from Gina's room.

"Feel your leg muscles relaxing, your arm muscles," Lucas's soft voice continued. "Concentrate on releasing all the tension from your muscle groups."

She felt herself relaxing, her arms and legs growing heavier and heavier as her breathing grew deeper and slower. She was on the verge of falling asleep and she didn't try to fight it, but rather gave in to the darkness that surrounded her.

"That's good," Lucas said. "Very good. Now, in your mind's eye imagine you're looking down at yourself as you sleep."

She tried to do what he said, to imagine herself lying on the thick beige carpeting, to picture herself as if she were floating above her body. The darkness of sleep crept closer and closer and she fell into it, no longer able to hear his voice.

A sense of lightness soared through her body. Then she was floating, suspended in the air near the ceiling, and she could see with perfect clarity her body on the floor beneath her. She could see the tiny red buttons that ran down the length of her sleeveless dress, her hair splayed out from her head.

She could see Lucas, clad only in a pair of cotton athletic shorts, his gorgeous, muscled chest bare and his gaze focused intently on her sleeping form.

Lucas! Suddenly fearful, she cried out his name in her mind. He raised his head as if he'd heard her plea. She slammed back into her body and awoke with a gasp.

Struggling to a sitting position, she reached for one of his hands. "I did it," she exclaimed and squeezed his fingers. "I left my body. It was just for a moment, but I did it." Euphoria swept through her.

"That's good, Kathleen. But why did you stop?"

"It scared me," she confessed.

He nodded. "That's why most people don't astral project. Fear of flying." He grinned at her, a smile that caused heat to stir inside of her.

There had been no intimacy between them since the day of the birthday party. Other than the night when he'd returned to the house and had held her in his arms, they had touched very little.

She hungered for him, and there had been moments when she'd seen his hunger for her. But he'd made no move to sate their desire for each other, and rationally she knew that was best.

"You ready to try it again?" he asked.

"Okay." She released his hand and once again lay back.

"And this time if you manage to do it, try to sustain it longer."

"All right." She dutifully closed her eyes and focused on relaxing, but before she could completely lose herself, she heard the sound of little footsteps clopping down the stairs.

She sat up as Gina and Lisa appeared. "Mommy, can Lisa eat dinner with us?" Gina asked.

"It's okay with me if it's okay with Lisa's mom," Kathleen replied. She looked at her wristwatch, surprised to realize it was almost supper time.

"Can we order pizza?" Gina asked.

Kathleen smiled, loving the sparkle that lit Gina's eyes. "Call Lisa's mom, if she says Lisa can stay, then I'll call and order in pizza."

The two girls cheered and hugged each other, then raced to the telephone. Within minutes they had Melissa Banfield's approval, and Kathleen had ordered from their favorite pizzeria.

As they waited for the food to arrive, Kathleen set the table and Lucas sat at the counter, watching her work. She was intensely aware of his gaze and wondered what he was thinking. But one thing she had learned after living with him for fifteen days was that Lucas didn't talk about his thoughts or feelings until he was good and ready.

When she had finished laying out the silverware and napkins she sat on the stool next to him at the breakfast counter. "Lucas, that night you left here, where did you go?" It had been a question that had nagged her for the past six days.

"I thought about calling for a cab and going back to my penthouse in the city. I wanted to forget all about you and Gina and this whole mess."

"Why didn't you?"

"I'm not sure. I wound up down at the beach." He looked past her, his gaze distant and thoughtful. "I swam for what I thought was a few minutes, but it must have been for a long time and when I got out of the water Belinda was waiting for me."

"Belinda? How did she know you were there?"

He focused back on her. "I don't know, I hadn't thought about it until now. Maybe she'd been watching this house and followed me. Who knows?"

"What did she want?"

"Me." His gaze held hers steadily. "She told me that I was promised to her not by Satan, but by Thanatos."

Kathleen sucked in a breath at the name.

"Anyway, I told her he couldn't promise her what wasn't his to give. Then I told her if she harmed you or Gina I would hunt her down and make her pay."

"What did she say?"

"She ran away. I was going to go after her but I decided not to. I don't think we'll see her again."

She knew there was something he wasn't telling her, something that had happened that night that darkened his eyes and clenched his jaw. But before she could dig further, the doorbell rang and she hurried to answer it.

It was the delivery guy and minutes later the four of them

sat at the table eating pizza and laughing as Lucas entertained them with stories about magic.

Anyone peeking into the kitchen window would see a normal family, enjoying a normal meal. Kathleen embraced the image, wondering how long normal would last for them all.

Keith sat in his home office, wearied to the bone, battling to retain a modicum of hope for his daughter.

He'd done everything he could as far as his investigation was concerned, and he didn't know where to go from here. Judd had been unable to break into the mysterious web site. There had been no more church desecrations in the past week and no report from any of his contacts at the local hospitals of any other child falling into an inexplicable coma.

He was at a dead end and he was frightened for Sharon . . . for Rosalyn. If he couldn't figure out what connected all the children, if he couldn't find out any more information about the mysterious Thanatos, then how could he help?

Rubbing his eyes tiredly, he leaned back in his chair and thought over the past week. It frightened him that he and Rosalyn were beginning to find some normalcy in the situation, that they were starting to adjust to their daughter being in a coma.

He and Rosalyn had even made love three nights before for the first time since Sharon had lapsed into her coma. It didn't seem right that the sun continued to rise and set every day, that Rosalyn was back to cleaning the house and cooking meals, that life went on while his little girl slept her endless sleep.

He reached into his bottom desk drawer and pulled out a folder. The tab at the edge simply read: Sharon. Inside were important papers, lovingly drawn pictures and mementos of his daughter's life.

His hand trembled slightly as he placed the folder before him on the desk and opened it. On top lay the first drawing Sharon had ever given him. The cat's face was blue, the crayon scribbles not contained by any of the printed lines. She'd been two when she'd colored it, and he'd thought the bright colors and determined slashes a stroke of genius.

Her social security card, her graduation diploma from nursery school, more pictures, and her birth certificate. Keith picked up the latter, remembering the night she had been born.

It had taken two years of trying for Rosalyn to get pregnant, and never had a child been as wanted as Sharon. They had anticipated her birth like gleeful children. They had shopped for the perfect furniture together, deciding on white for the baby bed and chest of drawers.

While Rosalyn went to her doctor's appointments, Keith worked on the nursery, painting it a pale pink and stenciling white ballerinas around the border.

Unfortunately, on the night Sharon had decided to make her entrance into the world, Keith had been on an assignment out of town and had been unable to be reached. He'd missed the dramatic moment of birth, but he'd tried not to miss anything else in Sharon's life since then.

Tears burned in his eyes as he once again looked at the birth certificate, detailing the particulars. She'd been born at 8:06 P.M. She'd weighed six pounds, seven ounces and had been nineteen inches long. The attending physician had been . . . Keith frowned, suddenly realizing he'd never known who had delivered Sharon.

He stared at the signature of the doctor. Another odd coincidence? He'd stopped believing in coincidences where this particular case was concerned. But how was it possible that this could be connected at all to what was going on now?

With his heart banging an unsteady rhythm, he shoved the file folder aside and reached for his phone.

"That was Keith," Kathleen said as she hung up the phone. "He says he's on his way over. He has something important he wants us to know. He sounded excited but wouldn't give me any details."

"Maybe his friend managed to gain access to that Thanatos web site."

Before Kathleen could reply, a wave of girlish giggles resounded from upstairs.

Gina had begged to let Lisa spend the night and with Melissa Banfield's approval, the sleepover was taking place. The girls had been bathed and pajamaed and put in Kathleen's king-size bed. They were supposed to be sleeping, but last time Kathleen had checked on them they were reading books with a flashlight beneath the sheets.

Kathleen and Lucas had been sitting in the living room, drinking coffee and watching television.

Some sitcom played across the screen, but she wasn't sure if Lucas was paying attention to it or not. She was pretending to, but her mind kept going over and over the events of the past few months, trying to figure out why an entity named Thanatos had singled them out.

She jumped as the doorbell rang.

"That was fast. Keith must have called from a cell phone," Lucas said, rising to his feet.

"No, he said he was at home." Kathleen padded to the door and peered out. It was Theresa, and Kathleen knew her friend had finally gotten around to coming to see the "hunk" who was living with her.

"It's my friend Theresa," she said as she opened the front door. "Theresa," she exclaimed as she was engulfed by a hug.

"Hey, girl. I thought it was about time I came over for a little visit."

Kathleen tried not to be shocked by Theresa's appearance. While always thin and always trendy, and even now clad in a cute pair of shorts and a halter top, she was painfully thin, her legs and arms like sticks and her skin an unhealthy color.

Kathleen introduced her to Lucas. "Have we met before?" Theresa asked, her professionally plucked eyebrows raised quizzically.

Lucas studied her face for a long moment. "No, I don't think so."

Theresa flashed a quick smile. "I don't know why, but you look so familiar to me." She shrugged. "Oh well, my mistake."

As they walked into the living room, Lucas in the lead, Theresa gave Kathleen a thumbs-up sign.

"If you two will excuse me, I have some things to take care of in my room," Lucas said.

Kathleen knew it was a polite lie, that he was giving her time to visit with her friend alone. "It was nice meeting you, Lucas," Theresa called after him.

He waved a hand in response, then climbed the stairs and disappeared from their sight.

"No wonder Dudley Do Right was worried," Theresa said as she sank down on the sofa and patted the space beside her. "God, Kathleen, the man is gorgeous."

"He's been wonderful with Gina," Kathleen replied, but she felt the warm blush that swept into her cheeks. She picked up the remote control and muted the television.

Theresa eyed her knowingly. "He must be pretty wonderful with you, too. There's a spark in your eyes I've never seen there before."

"I'm sleeping better now that Lucas is in the house."

"I'll bet," Theresa replied with a wry grin.

Kathleen took Theresa's hands in hers and looked at her worriedly. "But tell me what's going on with you. You've lost so much weight, Theresa."

"Ah, you know what they say—you can't be too rich or too thin."

"I don't know about the rich part, but you are definitely getting too thin. Have you been ill?"

She pulled one hand free from Kathleen's and waved it dismissively in the air. "I had a bout with the flu, then developed an ulcer, but I'm on the mend. I should be good as new in no time."

It was obvious to Kathleen that was all she intended to say on the subject. "So tell me what's been happening with you? It seems like it's been forever since we've really talked."

"Oh, you know, same old stuff. I've met a few nice guys, but nothing serious has developed. I'm beginning to think there is no such thing as Mr. Right for me."

"Maybe you're looking too hard," Kathleen said. She certainly hadn't been looking for any sort of love interest the night she'd taken a cab to the club to meet with Lucas. She frowned, wondering when Lucas had transformed himself in her mind from Gina's savior to her love interest?

"Maybe," Theresa replied, then grinned slyly at her. "So what's really going on between you and Mr. Magic?"

"Nothing," she answered far too quickly. "He seems to

have a stabilizing effect on Gina. She hasn't had an episode since he's been here."

"Well, that's good news. Where is the little munchkin anyway?"

"She and her best friend are supposed to be asleep, but I would guess they're probably still whispering and giggling."

"I'm glad she's doing better, Kath, and I'm glad to see you looking well."

Kathleen nodded, wishing she could say the same about Theresa. "You want something to drink? Something to eat?"

"Nah, I'm fine. You'd just been on my mind a lot lately, so I figured it was past time to stop by."

"I'm glad you did."

For the next half an hour, the two caught up on gossip, Theresa telling Kathleen about various teachers at the school where they both worked, about planned changes for the next year.

For Kathleen, the conversation was most welcome, reminding her that there was life outside the four walls of her house, dramas being played out in the everyday world that had nothing to do with her or Gina or Lucas. It was refreshing to hear about office politics and scandals.

While they chatted, Kathleen checked her watch several times, wondering why Keith hadn't shown up. She had no idea how long she and Theresa had been speaking when she noticed the news had come on the television. She reached over to push the power button on the remote when Keith Kelly's photo flashed on the screen. She held up a hand to silence Theresa and turned up the volume on the television.

". . . the victim has been identified as Keith Kelly, a reporter for *The Varsity* newspaper. Anyone with any information about this crime should call the tips hotline. And now, to weather." The blond reporter offered a perky smile.

Frantically, Kathleen jumped up and yelled for Lucas, then quickly changed channels, trying to get more information on what had happened to Keith.

Lucas bounded down the stairs and halted at her side. "What's wrong?" he asked tersely, looking from Kathleen to Theresa, who shrugged in bewilderment.

"Something happened to Keith," Kathleen exclaimed, her gaze focused on the changing channels. Then Keith's face filled the screen, and she lowered the remote.

"Keith Kelly, a reporter for *The Varsity*, was found badly beaten behind Mojo's Bar. He's said to be in critical condition and police are investigating the crime. In an unrelated incident, there was a drive-by shooting in . . ."

Kathleen muted the attractive male broadcaster and turned to Lucas. "My God, Lucas, we've got to go see him."

"Is this guy a friend of yours?" Theresa asked.

Kathleen nodded, tears welling in her eyes. "I spoke with him earlier this evening. He was on his way here. I can't imagine what he was doing at Mojo's."

Mojo's was a seedy bar on the water's edge, a place frequented by freaks and bikers. Not the place a man like Keith Kelly would go for a drink.

"I'll go get the girls out of bed," Lucas said. "While I'm doing that, you call and find out what hospital he's been taken to."

"Wait," Theresa exclaimed. "There's no reason for you to wake the girls. I'm at loose ends tonight. I'll watch them while you two go."

Lucas looked at Kathleen, who looked at Theresa. "Are you sure?" she asked. "I can't promise you how long we'll be gone."

Theresa took the remote from her hands and fell back on the sofa. "You have cable, you probably have chips and salsa, hey, I'm good for as long as it takes. Now go, get out of here."

It took Kathleen ten minutes to discover that Keith had been taken to St. Vincent's, a semi-private hospital not far from Kathleen's house where she knew Sharon was also a patient.

Within minutes they were in Kathleen's car, Lucas behind the wheel, rushing to St. Vincent's and Keith. "I can't believe this. I just can't believe it," Kathleen said. "Do you think maybe he was working on some sort of story involving something at Mojo's?"

Lucas's hands tightened on the steering wheel. "If I had to wish for a scenario, that would be it, because the alternative is far more frightening."

Kathleen looked at him sharply. "What do you mean?"

Lucas paused a long moment before replying and when he did finally speak, his voice was deep and troubled. "Keith told you on the phone he was on his way over to tell us something very important. I'm just wondering if it's possible somebody else knew he was on his way over."

As the implication of his words sank in, Kathleen felt the sting of tears in her eyes. Poor Keith. She said a quick, silent prayer. "I hope he's all right," she said aloud.

"Yeah, so do I," Lucas replied, his voice grim. "Not only for the obvious reason, but because if what he had to tell us was important enough to get him nearly killed, then I pray he's in good enough condition to tell us what it was."

"I guess we'll know in a few minutes," Kathleen said softly as he pulled into the parking lot in front of the small hospital.

Chapter Eighteen

The lobby of the hospital held the hushed silence of a library. They walked across the shiny tile floor toward the emergency waiting room, unsure where else to go, hoping they'd be able to find a doctor or a nurse who might tell them Keith's condition.

What they found in the tiny waiting area was Rosalyn Kelly. Although Kathleen had never met the woman before, she recognized her immediately both from the photo Keith had shown her of Sharon, and from the dry-eyed shock that radiated from her.

"Mrs. Kelly?"

"Yes?" Rosalyn looked up at her, her features utterly life-less, as if there were no more emotions left to display.

Kathleen sat in the salmon-colored plastic chair next to her. "My name is Kathleen Marlowe." She gestured to Lucas, who took the chair on the opposite side of Rosalyn. "And this is Lucas Connelly. We've been working on a story with your husband. How is he?"

"I don't know. It's been an hour or so since the last doctor came out to speak with me." She gazed unblinking at the door where a doctor might emerge at any moment. "I know it's bad . . . very bad." Her voice was so soft Kathleen had to lean forward to hear.

"Mrs. Kelly," Lucas said softly. "Your husband called us about two hours ago and told us he was on his way to our house, that he had something important to tell us. Do you know what that might have been?"

She shook her head faintly. "Keith's funny about his work. He never talks to me about it. He always says he wants me to read his articles in print like his other readers." She tilted her head sideways. "You said he was working on a story with you?"

Kathleen nodded. "And he told us about Sharon."

"She's in this hospital, you know. She's sleeping, but I'm sure she's going to wake up anytime now. She'll wake up and Keith will be fine and we'll have a picnic to celebrate. Keith and Sharon love picnics." Her voice cracked and she closed her eyes, but not before Kathleen saw the horror of a mother who had lost her child and was now facing the possibility of losing her husband.

Kathleen reached out and took Rosalyn's hand in hers. "Do you have any family we can call for you?"

Rosalyn clung to her hand as if it were a lifeline and tears began to run down her cheeks. "No, Keith and Sharon . . . they're my only family." Her body shook with suppressed sobs and she hid her face behind a hand.

Kathleen said nothing, did nothing. She wanted to pull

Rosalyn into a hug, but wasn't sure how the other woman would react. Rosalyn's shoulders shuddered and she drew a deep breath and dropped her hand from her face.

She gazed with childlike bewilderment into Kathleen's eyes. "Why would somebody want to hurt Keith? I don't understand this. The police said his wallet wasn't touched, so it apparently wasn't a robbery."

"Mrs. Kelly, we think maybe Keith was attacked because somebody didn't want him to get to us with whatever it was he had learned. Can you tell us if he was home this evening?" Lucas's voice was gentle, but determined.

She nodded. "He was home. We'd eaten dinner, and he went to his office. It's really just the spare bedroom, but he uses it as a home office. Anyway, he went into the office and was in there for just a little while when he came out and said he had to go somewhere and he'd be back before long."

"Did you go into his office after he left? Did you see what he might have been working on or looking at?" Lucas asked.

"No."

"Did he receive any phone calls or messages right before he told you he had to leave?"

"No, nothing like that," she replied. She tensed and stood as a doctor wearing scrubs came through the door. Kathleen and Lucas stood as well.

The doctor's eyes were too somber for it to be good news. Kathleen steeled herself for the worst, her heart aching for the woman who stood next to her.

"Your husband came through surgery," the doctor said without preamble. "But he's not out of the woods yet. He's suffered a tremendous trauma and we've done what we can to stabilize him for now."

"Can I see him?"

The doctor hesitated. "You realize he's unconscious and has suffered quite a bit of damage to his face."

Pain flickered across Rosalyn's features. "I know, but I'd still like to be with him."

The doctor nodded and indicated she should follow him. She took several steps after him, then turned back to Kathleen and Lucas. "I don't know what I can do to help you."

She opened her purse and withdrew a key ring. She quickly removed one of the keys and held it out to Kathleen. "Go on, take it. It's my house key. Maybe you can find a reason for all this in Keith's office." She told them the address of the house.

"I really don't think that's a good idea," Kathleen demurred.

Rosalyn smiled sadly. "If you two are cons and intend to rip me off, good luck. I don't care about anything in that house. All I care about is here in this hospital."

"We aren't cons," Lucas said. "And we want to find out why this happened to Keith as much as you do." He took the key from her. "What do you want us to do with the key when we're finished?"

"Just leave it on the kitchen table. My neighbor has a spare."

"We'll be in touch," Kathleen said as she reached out and grabbed Rosalyn's hand in hers. "And we'll pray for Keith and for Sharon." She released the woman's hand and watched as she followed the doctor through the doorway and disappeared from their sight.

"I still don't feel right about this," Kathleen said twenty minutes later when they pulled up in front of a neat beige ranch with dark blue shutters and trim.

"Me neither, but maybe we can figure out what it was

Keith wanted to tell us by looking in his office." Lucas parked the car, then turned to look at her. "I know this feels weird, but maybe we can come up with a clue to help the police catch whoever hurt Keith."

"Maybe," she said without conviction. What she feared most was that they'd go inside and find absolutely nothing and would never know why Keith had wanted to come over, what information he had for them and why somebody had beaten him half to death.

They got out of the car and followed the sidewalk to the front porch where potted geraniums showed the signs of a tough summer and a bit of neglect. A faint light shown from behind the curtains in the picture window.

Lucas unlocked the front door and they stepped into an attractive living room that smelled of lemon polish and vanilla.

"She said Keith's office is in one of the bedrooms," Lucas said and pointed down the hallway.

The first bedroom they came to was Sharon's. Kathleen's breath caught in her throat as she gazed around the little girl's domain. It was so like Gina's room, done in shades of pink and with a frilly spread.

Kathleen thought she could hear the hushed sobs of a mother's anguish, thought she could taste the salt of a father's tears. She smelled the grief that had taken up residency in the room. She turned to Lucas, who stood next to her. His face was blanched of color and he clung to the door frame as if dizzy. "Lucas?" She said his name softly and when he didn't reply, she said his name again louder.

Lucas was lost, battling against an assault on his senses. The room had begun as a typical little girl's room, but before his eyes had transformed into a vision of hell. Gone was the pretty bed. In its place was an open grave that emitted the sickening odor of death and decay.

Sharon lay in the grave, although it wasn't the image of Sharon he'd seen in Keith's photograph. This was a Sharon with her flesh melting from her bones, maggots crawling from her eyes. Huge black flies circled her head, buzzing incessantly. As he watched, she opened her mouth and grinned, then threw back her head and laughed, the laughter not that of a child, but the deep, depraved laughter of Thanatos.

A lie, he told himself. The vision was a lie, an illusion from the master of tricks. He shut his eyes to escape the horrific scene and heard Kathleen calling his name.

Kathleen, with her sweet scent of spring and her eyes the color of warm summer skies . . . Kathleen with her sensual nature and loving heart.

He opened his eyes and the vision was gone. Once again a little girl's bedroom stood before him. Kathleen peered up at him worriedly. "Are you all right?" she asked.

"Yeah, I'm fine. Let's find Keith's office."

The room across the hall proved to be the study Rosalyn had described. It held floor-to-ceiling bookshelves, a desk, a chair and a floor lamp.

Lucas sat down at the desk and turned on the computer. "Maybe his friend finally broke into that Internet site," he said. "Or maybe he got an e-mail from somebody there."

Kathleen moved to stand just behind him and waited anxiously for the computer to boot up.

"Maybe you should look at those file folders while I'm checking the computer." Lucas indicated a stack of manila folders on the left corner of the desk.

Kathleen grabbed the folder on top of the small stack and

opened it. Instantly she realized she was holding tangible evidence of a childhood.

Brightly colored pictures, Father's Day cards and achievement certificates were neatly organized. Kathleen studied each and every page, feeling as if she were paying a service to Keith by admiring his daughter's work.

Three-fourths of the way through the papers, sentimental keepsakes gave way to legal documents. A social security card, dental records, report cards and a birth certificate.

"I don't see anything unusual in his e-mail," Lucas said. "I'll check his Internet connection history and see if any alarms go off."

Kathleen didn't reply. She picked up the birth certificate. As she came to the name of the delivering doctor, she felt the blood drain from her face and her hands began to tremble.

"Lucas." Her voice sounded far away to her own ears. "I think I found what Keith discovered."

He looked up at her sharply. "What?"

Hand still trembling, she held out the birth certificate. "Look who delivered Sharon."

Lucas took the certificate from her, scanned down and released a small gasp. "Dr. Sutton Marlowe." He reared back in the chair, staring at the name with a frown.

When he looked at Kathleen once again, his features radiated confusion. "But why wouldn't Keith have known this before last night?"

Kathleen took the certificate from him and placed it back in the folder. "I'll bet if you surveyed a hundred fathers and asked them who delivered their children, less than ten percent would know the answer."

"Let's get out of here." Lucas shut down the computer and stood, his expression still troubled.

They set the house key on the kitchen table as Rosalyn had requested, then left the house and got back into the car.

They drove for several minutes in silence. "I don't understand what this might mean," Kathleen finally said.

"All we know right now is that Sutton delivered Sharon and he delivered Gina," Lucas said thoughtfully. "We know that Sharon is in a coma after having been called by something or someone through a dark tunnel. We know that same something or someone is trying to entice Gina through that same tunnel."

Kathleen fell silent, trying to digest this newest bit of information. She stared out the window, where the night seemed darker, deeper than usual. Clouds chased across the sky, obscuring the face of the moon. In the distance she thought she saw a flash of lightning.

"It looks like a storm is brewing," she said as Lucas pulled into her driveway.

"A storm has been brewing for some time," he replied, and she knew he wasn't talking about atmospheric conditions.

As they got out of the car and walked to the house, another, closer streak of lightning appeared, followed by a low rumble of thunder.

They found Theresa asleep on the sofa. She woke up, told them both of the girls were sleeping soundly, then stumbled out the front door with a wave goodbye.

Immediately Kathleen went upstairs to check on the girls, who were, indeed, sleeping soundly. She went back downstairs and shut off the television. It was after midnight, but she wasn't a bit tired and apparently neither was Lucas, who stood at the French doors and stared out into the darkness as if watching the storm approach.

He turned to look at her. "What happened to all Sutton's records when he died?"

"Sutton had an office not far from here. After his death, I boxed up everything and put it in his office in the basement."

"Here in the basement?" Lucas asked, interest sparking in his eyes. She nodded. "Can I take a look down there?"

"Sure. You want to see it tonight or in the morning?"

"Tonight, right now if you aren't too worn out."

She smiled wryly. "I can't think of anything that would allow me to sleep right now. Come on, I'll show you downstairs."

Kathleen rarely went to the basement. It was damp, musty and dark. None of the generations of Suttons who had lived here had made any attempt at renovating this space.

Floor-to-ceiling metal shelves lined one wall, used for storing extra canned goods and holiday decorations. Sutton had been the first to try to make the basement more habitable. He'd claimed a small section, Sheetrocked it in and proclaimed it an office. It was to this area she led Lucas.

She flipped on the light suspended from the ceiling of the small room and gestured to the boxes neatly stacked against the desk. "Those are all the records from Sutton's office." Thunder rumbled ominously in the distance. "And I haven't touched his computer, so I don't know what kind of records he might have kept on it."

Lucas nodded and sat in the chair behind the desk. "We'll start with the computer files and see what we find."

"What are you looking for?" she asked as he punched the power button on the computer and it whirred to life.

He leaned back in the chair and studied her, his eyes as dark and mysterious as the first time she'd met him. "I want to know if Sutton delivered all the children who are now in comas."

"But what would that mean? Sutton is dead."

He held her gaze for a long moment. "Are you positive about that?"

Her reply became a squeal of shock as a thunderous boom resounded, shaking the very foundation of the house. Everything went black.

Chapter Nineteen

"The storm must have knocked out the power," Kathleen said. Lucas could tell she'd moved closer to him. "Sutton used to keep his spare pipe lighters in this top drawer."

He heard her fumbling in the desk, then a click and her beautiful face was illuminated by the faint glow of a small flame.

"Stay here, I'll get a couple of candles," she said. She disappeared from the office, plunging it back into total darkness.

As Lucas waited, he thought of the unexpected storm that had apparently taken out the electricity. Was it a real storm that had blown up as late summer storms often did? Or was it something more sinister . . . a power play to stop any investigation they might have made into Sutton's records?

He rubbed his forehead tiredly. The attack on Keith had shaken him. He'd liked the man the moment he'd met him, had sensed he was an old, kind soul. A man who had already experienced so much tragedy didn't deserve to be beaten half to death and left in a back alley to die. Nobody deserved that.

Kathleen reappeared in the doorway, a lit candle in a crystal holder in each hand. "I guess we'll have to go through these records another time," she said as he took one of the candles from her.

"Yeah, there's no point in attempting to do anything more tonight," he agreed. Together they made their way back to the living room.

"I should go check on the girls, make sure the thunder didn't awaken them and frighten them," she said.

"I'll go with you." He was intensely aware of her as he followed her up the stairs. It was nothing new. He'd been intensely aware of her since the last time they'd made love. But now it seemed more pronounced.

Every minute of every day desire for her thrummed in his veins. Watching her eat breakfast had become an exercise in self-control. Seeing her dust the furniture or play with Gina, or simply seated in a chair relaxing, sent his hormones raging.

He inhaled a cloud of her sweet fragrance, and watched the soft sway of her jean-clad bottom and the slight swing of her dark hair visible in his candle's glow. He knew the silky softness of that hair, remembered well her firm buttocks and welcoming warmth.

He felt as if he'd been fighting against a simmering desire for her forever, afraid to give in, afraid giving in would only muddy the waters.

Now, he wondered if fighting his desire was far more draining than succumbing to it.

She stopped in the doorway of her bedroom and peered in. He stood at her side and followed her gaze to the bed, where the two girls still slept soundly.

She turned to look at him and must have seen his thoughts,

his passion. Her pupils began to glow, as if the candle flame was not in her hand, but rather in the depths of her blue eyes.

"If the girls are in your bed, then where do you intend to sleep?" His voice sounded deeper than usual, filled with the longing that suddenly pierced him.

"I thought I'd sleep in Gina's bed," she said, although whether she was aware of it or not, her voice held a bit of a question.

He took her arm in his hand and led her away from the bedroom door and down the hall several steps. "Gina's bed is awfully small," he observed.

She leaned against the wall, the candlelight bewitching her features into something more than beautiful. "It's big enough for me," she said, her voice breathlessly sexy.

He reached out a finger and trailed it along the side of her jaw, giving into the primal need he'd been struggling against for too long. "It's not big enough for the two of us."

Lightning flashed in the hallway followed by a distant rumble of thunder.

"It sounds like the storm is moving away," she said softly.

"The storm outside might be moving away, but there's a storm building inside me. Spend the night in my bed, Kathleen. Let me make love to you. Sleep in my arms."

She swallowed visibly, her lower lip trembling slightly. "I thought you said that us being together wasn't such a good idea."

"I was a fool." His fingers moved to the top button of her blouse and he saw her pulse throbbing in the hollow of her throat. He leaned forward and pressed his lips against the soft skin and felt her swift intake of breath. He stepped back from her and held out his hand.

She hesitated for only a second, then reached out her hand, her fingers intertwining with his. Together they walked down the hall to his bedroom.

He took her candle and placed it on one nightstand, then set his candle on the other, the glow of the twin flames illuminating the bed.

She stood hesitantly in the middle of the room, watching as he turned down the spread. Lightning once again flashed through the window, the following rumble of thunder nearly indiscernible.

She looked at the doorway, as if unsure how exactly she'd gotten into his room, and he knew he was about to lose her to common sense.

But he didn't want common sense tonight. He wanted nothing more than Kathleen in his arms. Tomorrow would be soon enough for troubling questions and perhaps painful realizations.

For the past six days he'd felt the darkness drawing closer, knew instinctively that the days ahead would be the most difficult he and Kathleen would ever face. He also knew that holding Kathleen in his arms would momentarily keep that darkness at bay.

He walked to her and drew her into his embrace. She came willingly, eagerly, her lips already parted to accept his kiss. He plundered her mouth, drinking deeply of her sweetness.

She molded herself against him, pressing her breasts against his chest, her hips against his as her arms wound around his neck.

Her mouth was hot, hungry, and their tongues battled in a dance of sensual pleasure. It was impossible for him to worry about what the future might bring while his senses were filled with her.

He felt her heart, banging a perfect rhythm against his own and again he knew with undetermined knowledge that they were destined to this moment, destined to give to each other body and soul.

Their kiss seemed to last an eternity. When they finally broke apart, each gasped with the intensity of the kiss.

He'd thought to undress her slowly, exposing her flesh inch by inch to his passionate gaze, but she had other ideas. She ripped open the buttons to her blouse and discarded the outer garment as if she couldn't wait for them to be bare skin to bare skin.

He closed the bedroom door with a soft thud, then followed her lead, tearing his T-shirt over his head, then undoing his jeans and pulling them off as well. By the time he was naked, so was she, and they tumbled onto the bed, flesh against flesh.

Her lips sought his again, and he kissed her long and deep as his hands cupped her buttocks and pulled her tight against his raging need.

He knew their coupling would be intense, frenzied and far too fast, knew the moment he entered her he'd be lost and would reach his climax far too quickly. He also knew he wanted her weak and sated before he finally took possession of her.

With this thought in mind, he rolled her over on her back and rained kisses down the hollow of her throat, across the expanse of her smooth chest, then fastened his lips around one turgid nipple.

He tongued the rosy peak, loving the sound of her gasps and tiny sighs, the way her hands clutched at his back as if she attempted to drag him into her.

He loved the way the candlelight cast dancing golden shadows across her sweet skin. He knew if it were just a little brighter, he'd see that her sky-colored eyes had darkened to the lush blue of desire.

Leaving one breast, he fastened his mouth on the other as his hands stroked down the flat of her abdomen. She moaned, a sweet sound that echoed in his heart.

He loved this woman, had loved her before he'd ever met her, when the memory of her had been just a whisper in the deepest recesses of his head.

He also knew with a chilling, heartrending certainty that this would be the last time he would enjoy the soul-connecting pleasure of making love to her.

As Lucas moved down her body, his mouth making love to her, Kathleen lost all sense of herself. She tangled her hands in his hair and cried out with splendor as waves of pleasure crashed through her.

She shuddered with the intensity of her climax, and then he entered her. With one slick stroke he filled her. She was no longer Kathleen, and he was no longer Lucas. They were one body, one soul, and tears of joy seeped from her eyes as she felt his heartbeat in sync with her own.

Slowly he moved against her. Then ever so quickly he increased his thrusts and the overwhelming sensations began building again, sweeping her higher and higher.

She felt him not just in her body, but in her head, in her heart. She knew without question that what he'd told her was true, that they were old lovers who had found and loved each other lifetime after lifetime.

For the first time in her life she felt whole, as if the pieces that had always been missing were now connected. She opened her eyes to look at him. Their gazes locked, and in the depths of his eyes she saw that he was feeling the same incredible bond that she felt.

"Kathleen," he whispered and the sweet love that was in his voice flooded over her, through her.

"Lucas," she replied. The cords in his neck grew taut as he stroked faster and faster. A light of something primitive shone from his eyes, and she felt a wildness awaken inside her. She met him thrust for thrust, closing her eyes as the pleasure became almost too intense to bear. She cried out his name as she fell over the edge, was vaguely aware of his shuddering against her.

For endless moments they remained unmoving, still joined and clinging breathlessly to one another. Kathleen was surprised to find tears pressing hotly against her eyelids and wasn't sure what caused them.

Was it because for the first time she had to admit to herself the depth of her love for Lucas? Was it because it frightened her just a little? Or were the tears the result of the lifetimes they had shared before this one, lifetimes that she knew instinctively had resulted in heartbreak?

They rolled apart, lying on their backs and staring at the ceiling, where shadows from the flickering candlelight danced playfully.

Kathleen was afraid to speak, afraid the tears that threatened to fall would succeed if she tried to talk to him. Her heart was too filled for words.

He pulled her into his arms and stroked the length of her hair, the tenderness of his touch nearly her undoing. "You're crying," he exclaimed. "Why? Did I hurt you?"

"No, nothing like that." She wiped her cheeks with an embarrassed laugh, then released a tremulous sigh. "I don't understand it myself." He propped himself up on one elbow and gazed down at her in bewilderment.

She frowned thoughtfully. "I don't know, maybe I'm crying for our past lives, where I think we always ended up separated from one another." She placed her palm against his cheek, loving the slightly scratchy feel of new whiskers. "Why is that, Lucas? Why have our souls tumbled through time?"

"If you believe in reincarnation, the theory is that we replay the same dramas lifetime after lifetime until we resolve the issues."

She dropped her hand from his cheek. "And what are the issues we've never resolved?" she asked. "Do you know?"

He rolled over on his back and stared at the ceiling for a long moment. "I don't know for sure, but I can tell you what I feel."

She rolled onto her side, resting against him, gazing down at him. "Then tell me what you feel, because all I know is when I have a dream about you I wake up feeling abandoned and so alone."

He sat up and bunched the pillow behind him, then leaned back again in a sitting position and pulled her to him. He raked a hand through his hair, his gaze not leaving hers. "My sense is that in every other lifetime you've chosen with your head, not your heart."

"What does that mean?" she asked, wanting to understand what forces had ruined things for them in the past.

His frown deepened. "I can't be sure, but when I get the visions of you and me and I know they are of a past life, it's always you denying me, denying our love."

She laid her head on his chest, heard the thundering of his heartbeat in her ear, felt the warmth of his body against hers, and smelled the scent of him that had become so familiar to her.

"I can't imagine anything in this lifetime making me deny you anything, especially my love," she said fervently.

His hand once again stroked her hair. "I love you, Kathleen, as I have loved you in each lifetime of my existence."

She raised her head once again. "Then promise me a future with you. Promise me this time we'll get it right and we'll be together forever."

Once again his gaze went to the ceiling, but not before she'd seen the darkness in his eyes. He sighed deeply. "I wish I could promise you that, Kathleen." He looked at her once again. "But all I can promise is this moment, this night." He pulled her against him and held her tight.

She closed her eyes, wishing the promise of this night was enough. But it wasn't. She wanted a lifetime with Lucas. She wanted him to be beside her as Gina grew into adulthood. She wanted to forget the madness surrounding them, to just be a couple in love.

She fell asleep in his arms and dreamed of getting it right in this lifetime.

Chapter Twenty

Kathleen awoke before dawn and for a long moment was disoriented. Although darkness surrounded her, she knew the bed beneath her wasn't her own, and the memory of a nightmare soured the taste in her mouth.

Then she remembered. She was in Lucas's bed and whatever the nightmare had been, it was nothing more than a night's phantom chased away by consciousness.

She heard the sound of Lucas's deep, regular breathing and knew he was still asleep. Not wanting to awaken him, she crept from the bed as quietly as possible, picked up her clothes from the floor and left the room.

She fumbled her way down the dark hallway to the hall bathroom, then clicked on the light, pleased that the electricity was working once again. She took a quick shower, then dressed in the same outfit she'd worn the night before. Once the girls woke up, she'd go into her room and get clean clothes.

With her hair still damp, she crept down to the kitchen and made a pot of coffee. While she waited for it to drip through, she went to the window and peered out, looking for signs of dawn. But the storm must have redeveloped overnight. Any early morning light was obscured by the dark, ominous clouds that filled the sky.

She poured herself a cup of coffee and sat down at the kitchen table, her thoughts chasing back to the night before and the splendor of sleeping in Lucas's arms.

He'd held her for most of the night, his body warm and molded to hers, and she'd felt as if she truly belonged in the shelter of his arms.

But as much as she believed she loved Lucas, she had to admit that love came with reservations.

She was too smart not to recognize that part of his appeal lay in the knowledge that he alone seemed to be able to keep Gina from the terrifying unnatural sleep. She knew they were not out of danger yet and was afraid what might happen to her love for Lucas if, ultimately, he could not save her daughter.

Still, it was hard to concentrate on any reservations when his words of love still rang in her ears. She recognized that there was a lot she didn't know about Lucas, but she believed she knew his heart, his soul and she loved what she knew.

She wasn't sure how long she sat at the table, sipping coffee, lost in daydreams when she heard the sound of running water from upstairs. Lucas must be up, she thought. She stood to refresh her coffee and jumped as the telephone rang.

A glance at the clock told her it was just after seven. She couldn't imagine who would be calling this early in the morning. She grabbed the phone before it could ring a second time.

"Kath?"

"Theresa!" She carried the cordless phone back to the table and sat. "What are you doing up at the crack of dawn?"

Theresa chuckled. "You probably don't realize how early I fell asleep on your sofa last night. Once I saw the munchkins were down for the count, I was out like a light. Kath, I need to tell you something."

The sudden, serious tone of Theresa's voice set her on edge. "Tell me what? Did something happen last night with Gina?"

"No, no. Nothing like that. I need to tell you something about Lucas."

"What about him?" Kathleen ran a finger over the rim of her mug, trying to control the nerves that jumped like dancing beans in her belly.

"Remember when I was dating Jeremy Tyler? The hunky blond I brought over to meet you one night?"

Kathleen rubbed two fingers across her forehead, trying to remember one hunky blond in the sea of men Theresa had been involved with over the years. "I don't know if I specifically remember him."

"Oh well, it doesn't matter. Anyway, I dated him a couple of times but broke it off when I realized he was into some weird shit."

"Weird how?"

"He invited me to this party and after we'd been there for a while I realized they were all a bunch of devil worshippers or something like that."

Kathleen rubbed her forehead harder. "Theresa, what does this have to do with Lucas?"

"I knew last night, the moment I met him, that I'd seen him someplace before. I racked my brain all night long. Then it hit me. He was there . . . that night at that party."

Kathleen's heart fell. "Are—are you sure, Theresa?"

There was a long pause and Kathleen gripped the receiver painfully against her ear as she waited breathlessly for Theresa's response.

"I—I'm not a hundred percent sure, but I'm pretty sure. I just thought I should tell you, Kath. I wanted to warn you to be careful where he's concerned."

Kathleen became aware that the sound of running water had stopped. That meant Lucas was out of the shower and would be coming downstairs at any moment. "Thanks, Theresa," she said hurriedly. "I need to get off now. I'll talk to you later." Without waiting for Theresa's reply, she hung up the phone.

She set the phone next to her on the table then wrapped her hands around her coffee mug, her head spinning with confusion. Surely Theresa was mistaken. She'd said she wasn't a hundred percent certain.

Again she was struck by how little she really knew about him. He'd been dating Belinda, and she apparently was some sort of Satan worshipper. Where did Lucas's power really come from? A chill threatened to work its way up her spine, but she stood, mentally shaking it off.

No. She had to believe that Lucas was a good man who would never consider selling his soul to the devil. She had to believe that he was here to help her, to help Gina. To think otherwise was to invite madness.

"Good morning."

She jumped and whirled around to see him standing in the doorway. "Good morning," she replied.

He walked over to her and wrapped his arms around her, gazing down into her eyes with such sweetness, such tenderness. How could a man with Heaven in his eyes belong to the devil? "Are you okay?" he asked.

"Of course. Why?"

"You just look tense." He kissed her on the forehead, then released her and walked over to get himself a cup of coffee. "Did I hear the phone?"

She sat back down at the table and nodded. "Yes, it was Theresa. She wanted to know if she'd left her earrings here last night." The lie slid smoothly from her lips.

She couldn't very well tell him what Theresa had said, nor could she ask him if he was in league with dark forces. If he wasn't, he would say no. And if he was, he'd still say no. She picked up the phone from the table. "I was going to call the hospital and check on Keith's condition."

Lucas joined her at the table. "I hope he made it through the night okay."

She got up once again to grab a phone book, then returned to the table and looked up the number to the hospital. It took her several minutes before she was finally put through to a room where Rosalyn answered the phone. She listened as Rosalyn updated her on Keith's condition. After telling the woman they would try to stop by later in the day, she hung up.

"He's still critical, but stable," she told Lucas. "He's slipped into a coma, but they're hoping he'll wake up once his brain quits swelling."

Lucas winced and shook his head. "I hope they find whoever is responsible."

Kathleen nodded. Are you responsible, Lucas? a tiny voice whispered in the back of her head. Did Keith have some sort of information about you?

Lucas sipped his coffee and looked at her. "Are you sure you're okay? You look stressed."

"I guess I am," she admitted uneasily. "Maybe it's the weather . . . so cloudy and gray. I just feel on edge."

He reached across the table and covered one of her hands with his. The physical touch seemed to ease the doubts that assailed her. "I'm afraid things are going to get rougher for you."

"Why? What do you mean?" she asked sharply.

"I mean today we need to check out Sutton's records and see if he delivered all the children in comas."

"And if he did, then what?"

His hand grasped hers tighter. "Then we have to consider the possibility that Sutton is wielding some sort of power over the children."

A humorless laugh escaped her. "But that's impossible. Sutton is dead."

"Are you absolutely positive?"

She pulled her hand from his. "Of course I am. I have a death certificate to prove it."

"People have been known to fake their own deaths before," he observed. "Did you see his body? Did you identify him after the accident?"

She frowned and stared out the window at the gray pall, remembering the day the police had come to inform her of Sutton's accident. "There was a fire when the car went over the embankment. Apparently the gas tank ruptured. There wasn't anything to identify except his personal effects. His wedding ring and what was left of the watch he always wore." She looked back at Lucas. "It had to be him who died that day . . . nothing else makes any sense."

She stood, unable to sit while myriad emotions rolled inside her. "It's a crazy idea. Why would Sutton want to do that to me? To Gina?"

Lucas leaned back in his chair and swiped a hand through his thick dark hair. "I don't know. Maybe the whole idea is crazy."

Their conversation was interrupted as Gina and Lisa came downstairs, hungry for breakfast and giggling the way only best friends can.

It was late afternoon when Lucas and Kathleen finally got an opportunity to check out Sutton's records. Gina was happily entertained with the newest Disney video and waved a hand in distraction as Kathleen told her where she and Lucas would be.

As they walked down the stairs to the basement, a shiver of apprehension raced through Kathleen. She wasn't sure what frightened her more, that they would find nothing or that they would find a link tying Sutton to the nightmare of the children.

Lucas sat down behind the desk and turned on the computer. Kathleen got a folding chair from the storage area and opened it next to him.

As they waited for the computer to boot up, she gazed at his features, as always struck by his breathtaking handsomeness.

If he were some sort of devil worshipper and intended them harm, surely something would have already happened. He'd spent long hours of each day alone with Gina, had been in the house for weeks and had access not only to their physical beings, but their spiritual beings as well.

Theresa had to be wrong about seeing Lucas at that party. Kathleen gripped the edge of the desk tightly. She had to be wrong.

As if he sensed her intense scrutiny, Lucas turned to her and offered a gentle smile. "I know this is hard for you, Kathleen, delving into Sutton's records. I'm sorry we have to do it."

She nodded, shoving aside any lingering doubts about him. He returned his focus to the computer screen. "Uh oh," he said softly.

"What?"

"He's got security on here. Do you know what his password was?"

Kathleen looked at the screen, where a prompter requested a password. "I have no idea." Frustration knotted her stomach. "What do we do now?"

He shrugged. "Maybe we can guess his password."

"And what happens if we can't?"

"Then we see if Rosalyn Kelly knows how we can contact that computer friend of Keith's." He poised his fingers over the keyboard. "We'll start with the obvious. What's Sutton's birth date?"

She told him and he quickly typed it in, but instantly a box appeared stating it was an incorrect password and access was denied. They tried his social security number, Gina's birth date and name, Kathleen's birth date and name, but all to no avail.

With each unsuccessful try, Kathleen's anxiety rose. Suddenly it seemed desperately important that they find what might be hidden in Sutton's computer. She wanted—needed—to know what connection Sutton might have had with the lost children.

Lucas leaned back in the chair and templed his fingers before him, obviously at a loss as to how to proceed. "Can you think of anything else? Hobbies he might have had, favorite places to visit, anything that might have worked as a password?"

Kathleen frowned. "You might try Whispering Pines," she suggested.

"What's that? It sounds like a Girl Scout camp."

She smiled. "Actually, it's the name of the cabin upstate." Her smile fell. "And cabin isn't the right word, either. It's more like a compound with several good-sized buildings."

"You've been up there?"

She shook her head. She'd told him about the cabin before, but apparently he didn't remember their brief conversation about the place. "No, but I've seen pictures."

"It's worth a try." He typed in the name, but it didn't work.

Kathleen sat back in her folding chair, intensely disappointed. "I'm fresh out of ideas." She eyed the boxes stacked against the desk. "If we can't get into the computer, I guess we'll have to go through all those boxes." The task seemed overwhelming. It would take days for them to go through all the paperwork those boxes contained.

She stood. "We'll take them upstairs. I don't want to sit down here any longer than necessary." The basement had always spooked her.

Lucas nodded absently and typed something else into the computer. He gasped softly and looked at her, his eyes dark, his expression unreadable. "I'm in."

"What?" Kathleen quickly sat down again and gazed at the screen, surprised to see that he was indeed into the main screen. "What did you do? What did you type in?"

He didn't answer for a long moment, and in that moment a chill swept through her. "Thanatos," he finally said. "I typed in Thanatos."

Kathleen reeled with the information. Nausea rolled in her stomach and crawled up the back of her throat. She stood, unsteady on her feet. It felt as if the walls of the office were closing in, suffocating her, making it impossible to draw a deep breath.

Lucas stood and took her arm. "Are you all right?"

"No . . . I'm not all right." She shrugged off Lucas's hand and took a step away from the computer. "If Sutton's password is Thanatos, then he *was* involved in all this. And if he's involved, it's possible he might have faked his own death. It's possible he's alive somewhere right now."

"Yes," Lucas agreed softly. "That's a possibility."

Once again she felt the walls pressing in, as if in an attempt to squeeze the life out of her. "I need to get out of here." She stumbled toward the doorway.

"Do you want me to come with you?" Lucas asked.

She shook her head. "No. I need some time alone, some time to think. You go ahead down here. I'm just going to lie down for a little while."

She didn't wait for any reply, but ran from the basement up to the living room. Grateful that Gina had fallen asleep on the sofa, Kathleen hurried up the stairs to her bedroom— the bedroom where she had spent eight years of her life sleeping with Sutton.

How could she have been married to him, shared meals and a bed, a daughter, a life and not known that something evil resided inside him?

She stared at the bed where she had slept night after night beside Sutton. She'd kissed him, made love with him, gotten pregnant by him, and had never suspected the secrets he'd harbored.

She moved to the window, threw back the curtain, and

stared out where the skies were growing darker with each passing minute. The darkness seemed to be everywhere, surrounding her, engulfing her, swallowing her whole.

Anger surged as she thought of Sutton alive and well. How could he have put her and Gina through his death? Damn him . . . how could he have left it to her to tell their daughter that her daddy was gone if he wasn't really gone?

Still, what frightened her most was that she'd known Sutton for almost nine years. She'd believed she knew him inside and out, but apparently he'd fooled her completely.

She dropped the curtain and moved away from the window as she felt the cold darkness creeping into her, suffusing her. She hadn't been this afraid since right before Lucas had moved in. She was adrift in a sea of the unknown, unsure who, if anyone, she could trust.

If the man she'd been married to for over eight years hadn't been the man she believed him to be, then how on earth could she trust anyone?

If Sutton could fool her so easily, then who was to say that Lucas couldn't as well?

Chapter Twenty-one

The minute Kathleen left the basement, the damp chill of the place began to seep into Lucas's bones. There was evil here. It permeated the dank stone walls and the concrete floor. As he began to check the files on Sutton's computer, he was aware of the stench of sickness rising around him and a feeling of dread filled him.

He clicked on one icon, then the next with a sense of urgency. He didn't know exactly what he was looking for and had to scan the contents of each document to make sure he didn't miss anything that might be important.

He wasn't sure how long he'd been working when he felt it: the tingling, probing sensation in the base of his skull. He knew it was a precursor to something happening. Always before when he felt those sensations in his head, he was granted a momentary supernatural power of some kind. It had been what he'd felt just before he'd sent his assistant spiraling to the ceiling of the club, and it had been what he'd felt just before he'd seen the visions of Gina in his mind and knew who she was, where she lived and that he had to get to her.

But this felt different. The fingers that probed at him were icy cold, not warm. And the tingling sensation was not just uncomfortable, but was growing more and more painful.

He shook his head in an attempt to dislodge whatever it was that he sensed was trying to invade his mind and tried to focus on the task at hand. But concentration became increasingly difficult as the pain in his head grew excruciating.

The stench of the basement grew more pronounced, like the air that emanated from an open grave where the departed had begun the process of decay.

Adrenaline pumped through him as he opened a file and found a listing of all the children who were now in comas. Next to their names were their birthdates. The last name on the list was Gina's.

He pushed the button to send the document to the printer, then leaned back in his chair, the pain in his head nearly blinding him.

He closed his eyes and instantly the torture stopped. Instead his head filled with visions of Kathleen. Beautiful Kathleen. Snapshots of her flickered through his brain, a kaleidoscope of images. In each she was dressed differently, and he felt as if he were watching a fashion show through a time machine lens.

Kathleen wearing a Victorian dress, then clad in a simple homespun skirt and blouse. Picture after picture of the woman he loved flashed before him and with each new one he was filled with a deep, abiding sense of loss, a piercing ache of abandonment.

The buzzing in the base of his head increased and he felt

the first stir of anger. Kathleen, his love, his soul mate. In all the lifetimes he'd existed, she'd been a part of him.

Kathleen the enchantress, Kathleen the seductress. She'd reeled him in and stolen his heart, then rejected him and left him empty, bereft.

The bitch.

The buzzing increased as did his anger, building into a rage. Perspiration dotted his forehead as the fury swept over him, through him.

Lifetime after lifetime she'd forsaken him, and he knew this lifetime would be no different. She would leave him again. She would replay the same scenario, breaking his heart as she had so many times before.

Damn the bitch to hell.

White hot wrath filled him. She had to pay—pay for the pain she caused him over and over again. She had to pay for the vast yawning emptiness that filled his soul.

He could kill her. With his bare hands. So intense was his rage at the moment, he knew he could kiss her sweet lips and wrap his hands around her slender throat and squeeze until all breath left her.

But that would be too easy, too quick for her. She needed to hurt like she'd hurt him. And the place where she was most vulnerable was in her love for her child.

Through Gina he would avenge her sins. Through Gina he would sate his thirst for revenge. Through the child he would make the mother pay . . . and pay . . . and pay.

He opened his eyes and gasped as intense pain ripped through him. Grabbing his head with both hands, he tried to stand, but fell to the floor as blackness descended.

Consciousness came slowly. He first became aware of the

cold concrete beneath his cheek and the hum of the computer hard drive. What had happened?

He sat up, surprised to discover he was covered with a sheen of sweat and his heart was pumping overtime. He felt as if he'd just gone twelve rounds in a prize-fighting ring.

The last thing he remembered was printing off the document he'd found in Sutton's files. He pulled himself up off the floor and leaned weakly against the desk. He looked at his wristwatch, shocked to realize he must have been out of it for some time.

Something had occurred, but he didn't know what. All he knew was that he needed to get out of this basement that felt like a grave. An urgent need to check on Kathleen, to check on Gina surged through him.

While he'd been lying on the floor, unconscious and out of commission, what had happened to them? He grabbed the paper he'd printed and left the office at a sprint, taking the stairs two at a time.

Relief flooded through him as he found them sitting at the kitchen table playing Go Fish. The very normalcy of the activity stilled his racing fear.

"Hi," he said.

"Hi, Lucas. Wanna play?" Gina asked.

"No thanks, I think I'll just sit and watch for a little while." He folded the piece of paper he clutched in his hand and stuffed it in his pocket. Now wasn't the time to discuss what he'd found.

It wasn't until later that evening, after they had eaten dinner and Gina was in bed that he and Kathleen sat down at the kitchen table to talk.

He pulled the sheet of paper from his jeans pocket and handed it to her, carefully studying her features. She had seemed distant all evening and for the first time he'd found himself unable to read her thoughts, her expressions.

"It was in a file labeled Stocks," he said. He watched as she scanned the list and knew the moment she found Gina's name. Her fingers tightened on the paper and her cheeks lost some of their color.

When she looked at him her face was once again devoid of emotion. "Okay, so now we know that Sutton was right in the thick of whatever is happening to the children." She stared down at the list of names once again, then shoved the paper back to him. "And I realize it's very possible he's still alive. But what I don't understand is why this is happening? What's wrong with the children?"

Lucas leaned back in his chair and raked a hand through his hair. It was the same thing he'd asked himself a dozen times over the last few hours. "You mentioned before that Sutton was doing research before he became an obstetrician. Do you know exactly what kind of research he was involved in?"

She shook her head. "I told you that he was a private man when it came to his work." She stared at him for a long moment. "Do you think this is some sort of experiment that went horribly wrong?"

He sighed. "I wish I could tell you yes, because that would make sense—that this was all some sort of a scientific research project gone awry." He reached out to cover one of her hands with his, slightly disturbed by the fact that rather than accepting his touch, she moved her hand away.

"But science has nothing to do with church desecrations and Thanatos, does it?" Her eyes looked hollow, so void of emotion that it shot a strand of concern through him. "So in order to get our answers, it would seem to me we need to find my *dead* husband." Her sarcastic emphasis on the word dead was unmistakable, and for the first time he heard an edge of anger in her tone.

"Is it possible he could be at that cabin . . . at Whispering Pines?"

"It's the only place I can think of." She frowned. "I always figured I would sell it, but I just never got around to it. I don't even know how to get there. Bill would know. He's gone up there several times with Sutton." She got up from the table. "I'll call Bill. He said he'd be checking his messages while he's gone. I'll ask him to get in touch with me as soon as he can."

Lucas watched her surreptitiously as she made the call. Something was different about her. There was a distance today that hadn't been there yesterday.

Last night they had made love and slept in each other's arms. Last night he had felt her with him in body and spirit. What had changed? And what the hell had happened to him in the basement?

She left the message for Bill, then hung up the phone and looked at her watch. "I'm going to head up to bed. I'm exhausted. If Bill calls back I can take it in my room."

As she started to leave the kitchen, he jumped out of his chair and stopped her and pulled her into his arms. She held herself stiff, unyielding against him and her gaze refused to meet his.

"Kathleen, what's happened? What's going on inside that head of yours?" he asked softly.

"Nothing . . . I don't know what you're talking about." Still she wouldn't look at him.

He took her chin in his fingers and tilted her head so she had to meet his gaze. "Don't go away from me, Kathleen."

Her blue eyes held his and her lower lip trembled slightly. "I'm afraid, Lucas. I'm just so afraid."

"You have to stay strong—for Gina, for me . . . for us."

He dropped his fingers from her chin and again her gaze left his and he felt the chill of abandonment and another edge of anger well up inside him.

She stepped away from his embrace. "Lucas, I've had to face the realization that my dead husband isn't dead and worse, he is involved with children who have fallen into horrendous comas. And on the list of children in comas is the name of my daughter. I'm overwhelmed at the moment and exhausted."

She offered him a faint smile. "I'm sure I'll be fine tomorrow." He knew the smile was meant to reassure him, but it didn't.

As she left the room he walked over and sank back down at the table. He eyed the sheet that he'd printed off Sutton's computer and once again wondered what had happened to him in the basement. In those minutes he couldn't remember, what had been going on?

He suddenly recalled the pain . . . the excruciating pain that had attacked the back of his head. Had he simply passed out from sheer agony? He had a feeling it was something more sinister than that . . . but what?

Why did he have the sick feeling in his stomach that it had begun—that this was the beginning of the end for him . . . for Kathleen. Why was he suddenly so afraid that there was no hope that they might get it right in this lifetime?

"Kathleen."

The voice called to her in her sleep, a sweetly familiar voice filled with love. *Lucas.* As if in a dream, she opened her eyes and saw him suspended above her. He smiled and held out a hand to her.

"Come, Kathleen. Come fly with me," he said softly.

"I can't fly," she protested.

"Yes, you can. Just take my hand. Trust me and let yourself go."

It's just a dream, she told herself. There's nothing to be afraid of, she thought as she reached for his hand. The moment their fingers touched, she felt a sensation of lightness, as if she were floating in the deep end of a swimming pool.

The ceiling of her room loomed closer and she saw herself sleeping on the bed, the sheet twisted around her middle section, baring her shoulders and her legs.

"Hold tight," Lucas said. "Tonight we're going to take a trip."

She squeezed his hand as they soared upward, out through the window and into the night sky. She looked down and saw the rooftop of her house, then the roofs of neighboring homes. She should have been afraid, but she wasn't.

"Where are we going?" she asked as a gentle breeze stroked her face.

He smiled, his eyes glowing silver. "As close to Heaven as we can get." Almost immediately they were engulfed in a fog so thick she couldn't see him any longer.

"Lucas!" she cried in a panic.

"Don't worry, my love. It's just the clouds. We'll be above them in a minute." Almost before the words left his mouth they exploded out of the gray mist and into a black velvet world lit by big, bright twinkling stars.

The beauty and grandeur surrounding them caused an ache inside her, and she gasped in wonder at the marvelous sight. "Oh, Lucas, it's beautiful."

He nodded and she realized for the first time that there was a vaporous quality to him. She looked down at herself and realized she had the same insubstantial quality as well.

"Your body is still in bed," he said, letting her know he'd read her thoughts. "We're spirits, Kathleen. We've left behind our physical beings to travel together."

Of course, she thought. It made perfect sense. In a dream anything was possible. He gestured around them with his free hand. "This is the second thing closest to Heaven."

"What's the first thing closest to Heaven?" she asked.

His eyes seemed to glow brighter. "This."

Without warning, he wrapped his arms around her and seemed to melt into her. She felt him in every pore, a warmth and sensation as intimate as lovemaking.

She cried out in ecstasy as wave after wave of intense pleasure swept through her. Along with the pleasure came love. It was as if all the love of their lifetimes united at this moment to crash through her, filling her with a completeness she'd never before felt.

The stars spun around them as she clung to him, and she felt as if the entire universe smiled on them. The shining of the stars was inside her heart as irrevocably as Lucas was. His heartbeat was her own, his breaths were her life support. They were one. She was filled with love and warmth and Lucas.

She awoke with a start, her heart hammering against her ribs. Sunshine attempted to crawl into the room around the edges of her curtains and she turned over and looked at the clock, surprised to discover it was after eight and even more surprised by how well-rested she felt.

Minutes later as she stood beneath the spray of a hot shower, she thought of the man who had consumed her dreams. There was no getting around it, her brief conversation with Theresa had shaken the complete trust she'd had in Lucas.

But she had to believe that Theresa was mistaken. Theresa was a bubble-head at best and rarely knew whether she was coming or going. She had to have been mistaken in believing she saw Lucas at a party for a bunch of devil worshippers.

There was no denying that Gina hadn't had an episode since Lucas had been in her house. And wasn't there a saying about children and animals having a sixth sense when it came to good and evil? Wouldn't Gina be the first to know if Lucas couldn't be trusted, if he had evil intentions?

She shut off the shower, dried and dressed and clung to the love she'd felt in her dreams, the absolute trust she'd felt as she'd held Lucas's hand and soared with him through space.

As she went downstairs, she heard Gina and Lucas in the kitchen. As usual, Gina was giggling, as she often did in Lucas's presence. How was it possible for her not to trust a man who could make a child laugh so exuberantly?

"Good morning," she said as she entered the kitchen.

" 'Morning," Lucas replied, his eyes filled with warmth and good humor.

"Mommy, Lucas taught me a new card trick," Gina exclaimed. She held the deck of cards out toward Kathleen. "Pick a card," she instructed, her bright green eyes sparkling. "And don't show it to me."

Kathleen picked a card and looked at it, then nodded. "Okay."

"Now put it on the bottom of the deck," Gina said. When Kathleen had done that, Gina shuffled the cards carefully. "Now, I'll show you which card you picked."

It was an old trick, one that most children learned, but

Kathleen acted appropriately shocked and surprised when Gina chose the card she had picked.

"She's been fed and watered," Lucas said, ruffling Gina's hair affectionately.

"Good, then how about you head up and get dressed and make your bed," Kathleen said.

"And after your bed is made, we'll work together a little while if that's all right with your mom," Lucas added.

"Sounds like a plan," Kathleen agreed as she poured herself a cup of coffee.

"You holler down for me when you're dressed and have your room cleaned," Lucas told the little girl, who nodded, then scampered out of the kitchen. Kathleen sat at the table and wrapped her hands around her coffee mug.

"Are you hungry?" Lucas asked her. "I could whip you up a couple of eggs and some toast."

"No, thanks." She gestured to the mug before her. "This is all I need at the moment." She took a sip, her gaze not leaving his.

"I had the craziest dream last night," she began, but the moment she said the words she knew by the expression on his face that it hadn't been a dream. He sat opposite her, a soft smile curving his beautiful lips. "It wasn't a dream, was it?"

"No."

She leaned back in her chair and frowned thoughtfully. "But you've been working with me trying to get me to astral project, and I haven't been very successful at it. But last night . . ."

His smile widened. "Last night we flew together as if we'd been doing it for years."

"Why was it so easy last night?"

He leaned forward, and she smelled his clean maleness and remembered that breathtaking moment among the stars when he'd been inside her, loving her from the inside out. "Because last night, in the unconsciousness of your sleep, you had no defenses. You trusted me implicitly."

He reached out and took one of her hands in his. The smile that had lit his face moments before was gone. "Kathleen, the storm is getting closer. I feel it closing in on us. You told me the other night that you love me. You have to hang on to that love and trust me no matter what happens."

"Lucas . . ." She uttered a small, uncomfortable laugh and tried to pull her hand from his, but he held on. "You're frightening me."

"No, my love." He squeezed her hand painfully tight. "I'm simply warning you that the worst is yet to come."

Chapter Twenty-two

Kathleen plunged a spade into the rain-softened dirt and attempted to dig out a weed the size of New Jersey. The heat was back, the air thick and sultry, making it hard to breathe. But she'd needed to get out of the house.

Lucas's words had chilled her to the bone, but before they'd had an opportunity to say anything more, Gina had called to him and he'd gone up to work with her.

Almost immediately Kathleen had decided to go out and do some weeding in what was left of the flower garden. She'd grabbed her cordless phone in case Bill called.

The only thing she had done before heading outside was to call the hospital to check on Keith's condition. He was still in the critical care unit and Rosalyn had told her there was little change. He was stable, but still in a coma.

As she pulled weeds, she wondered if maybe Keith was with Sharon. If somehow when he'd first slipped into his coma, he'd found his daughter and now was reluctant to leave her. She prayed he'd wake up. She prayed Sharon and all the rest of the children would awaken.

Gazing up at Gina's bedroom window, she stopped digging for a moment. She hadn't been privy to the training Lucas did with Gina, had respected his explanation that he needed Gina's complete trust.

Usually when she tucked Gina in for the night, she tried to question her daughter about what they had done in their time alone, and always Gina said that they talked, then practiced meditating. It all sounded very benign.

But something was working because she hadn't gone into the tunnel for weeks. She was sleeping well, eating well and had the sparkle back in her eyes.

Kathleen redirected her attention back to the flower bed, trying to ignore the ungodly heat that seemed to be getting worse with each passing minute.

She'd been working for about twenty minutes when the phone rang. She pulled off her muddy gloves, then answered.

It was Bill. "I got your message. Is everything all right?" Worry was rife in his voice.

She considered telling him everything they had discovered about Sutton and his involvement with the children. She thought of telling him that they suspected Sutton was still alive. Then she remembered that Bill had been a good friend and confidante of her husband.

With painful clarity she realized she shouldn't trust Bill as well. "I'm thinking about selling Whispering Pines," she said, "and thought maybe I'd take a ride up there and look around to see what needs to be done before putting it on the market."

"You should be able to get a pretty penny for it," Bill said.

"I was wondering if you could give me directions on how to get there."

"Sure."

"I'm out in the garden. Hang on a minute while I go into the kitchen and grab a pencil and paper. Are you enjoying your vacation?" she asked as she headed into the house.

"Actually, I am," he admitted. "Believe it or not, I've met somebody."

"Really? Bill, that's wonderful. Tell me everything." She entered the kitchen and got a notepad and a pen from one of the drawers. "When's the wedding?"

Bill laughed lightly. "It's far too early to start planning a wedding. Her name is Marilyn and she's a widow. She's teaching me to play bridge, and she's a very nice lady."

"I'm glad, Bill. I truly am. I hope something wonderful comes out of it."

"We'll see," he replied. "Now, you ready for those directions?"

It took him fifteen minutes to give her the directions and for her to read them back to him to make sure she'd gotten them right.

"It's back in the sticks," he explained. "You really have to watch for the turnoffs and pay attention. When are you thinking of going up?"

"I'm not sure . . . in the next couple of weeks or so." She didn't want him to know any exact plans. If he knew that Sutton was alive and at the cabin, if he was somehow involved with everything that had been happening, she didn't want him to know what her plans were.

"Are you going to use a realtor?"

"I haven't thought that far ahead," she replied.

"You know if there's anything I can do, Kath . . ."

"I know, but I'll handle it. All you need to focus on is your bridge game."

He laughed again, and she was glad to hear him sounding happy. She couldn't imagine that he had anything to do with the horror that had befallen them, but she hadn't been able to imagine that her dead husband was actually alive.

They spoke for a few more minutes, then hung up. Kathleen stared at the directions she'd written and felt a pounding in her head, a racing of her heart. A million thoughts careened through her mind.

Had Sutton transformed the cabin into some sort of laboratory? Was he a scientist gone mad, performing crazy experiments on innocent children? Or was he a devil worshipper, following an evil entity known as Thanatos?

Was the cabin the lair of a beast? A den of evil? What would happen if they went there? In a final confrontation, would they be triumphant? A shiver raced through her as she recalled Lucas's words from the night before. *The worst is yet to come.*

How could things get worse? She shoved the question out of her head, knowing that to ask such things was to tempt fate.

Deciding it was too hot to return to the garden, she went into the laundry room and sorted through a basket of dirty clothes. As she came across one of Lucas's T-shirts, she brought it to her nose and breathed deeply of the scent, remembering their flight the night before.

Her heart was filled with love for him, a love like she'd never known before. But her love was tempered with tiny doubts. She didn't want to have doubts. She wanted one person she could count on without reservations. But it would seem the only person she had to rely on one hundred percent was herself.

Interesting, she mused, as she threw a load of dirty clothes into the washer and started the machine. Throughout her entire marriage, she'd depended on Sutton. He'd made all the decisions, taken away every choice, kept her blissfully unburdened by life.

After Sutton, Bill had stepped into the role of taking care of her, easing her through the maze of paperwork generated by a death, making decisions in her best interest, and once again keeping her generally unburdened by life.

It had only been since Gina's illness that she'd gained a new strength and began to make decisions for herself and for Gina. She'd stopped hiding from life and instead was embroiled in it, with all the pain and happiness it brought.

She left the laundry room and went back to the kitchen and opened the freezer, trying to decide what to cook for dinner that night. As she stared at the meager contents, she realized while she'd been dealing with the fear and uncertainty of her life, she'd neglected the mundane things such as grocery shopping.

Now would be the perfect time to make a run to the store. She ran lightly up the stairs to Gina's room, where Lucas and Gina were sitting Indian style across from each other, practicing deep-breathing exercises.

The sunlight streaming in the window glinted off his dark hair and even in repose, the strength in his body was evident. Again Kathleen had a flash of their time together in her dreams, when his body had entered hers and filled her up so sweetly.

They both flashed her smiles as she stood in the doorway. "If you don't mind, I thought while you were working with Gina I'd make a fast trip to the grocery store."

He nodded. "Okay, no problem."

"Is there anything in particular you'd like me to get to eat?" she asked.

"Not for me," he replied.

"Chocolate chip cookies and ice cream," Gina chimed in.

"Oh yeah, that's what I meant to say," Lucas teased and winked at Gina, who giggled.

"I'll see what I can do," Kathleen replied. "I should be back within an hour."

It wasn't until she was in her car driving to the closest grocery store that her thoughts once again filled with Lucas. He was not only seducing her with his body and lovemaking, he was also seducing her through his relationship with her daughter.

The more time the three of them spent together, the more Kathleen saw the promise of what life would be like if they were a normal family. Would they ever get the opportunity to be normal again? She desperately wished she knew the answer.

The minute she entered the store, she had an overwhelming instinct to return home. She flew down the aisles, grabbing the items she knew they were out of, including the cookies and ice cream Gina had requested.

Impatiently she waited in line, the need to be home filling her with a crushing anxiety. Surely everything was all right, she tried to reassure herself, as the cashier most likely to be fired rang her up with excruciating slowness.

She loaded her groceries into the trunk of her car, trying to still the raging dread that seemed to have no real basis and had sprung from nowhere.

She drove home like a bat out of hell, grateful that other traffic seemed to stay out of her way and no police cars whirred their red lights.

As she pulled into her garage, she told herself she was being silly, that nothing could possibly be wrong. Grabbing the grocery sacks from the trunk, she chided herself for her foolishness.

She walked into the kitchen and placed her bags on the countertop. The house was quiet, but if Lucas was still working with Gina, that wasn't unusual.

Leaving the groceries, she crept up the stairs, listening for the murmur of their voices. Nothing. Even the air seemed unusually static.

As she entered Gina's room, she cried out in horror. Her daughter was lying on the floor on her back, and Kathleen recognized in an instant that she was gone . . . lost to the darkness that beckoned her.

She ran to Gina's side, but knew it was too late. Her baby had been taken, and all Kathleen could do was wait and pray that somehow Gina would find her way back to the light as she had in the past.

Lucas. Where was he? Why wasn't he here with her? Kathleen flew from Gina's room to Lucas's room. She stopped in the doorway, a gasp flying from her lips. Lucas, too, was stretched out on his bed on his back.

"Lucas!" She raced to his side. "Lucas—you have to get up. Gina needs you." She touched his arm and instantly recoiled. Cold. He was ice cold.

Then she realized he was gone . . . gone to whatever world Gina was in. Was he there to save Gina? Or had he called her into the darkness?

She backed away, her terror knowing no bounds. This hadn't happened before. Why had it happened now? Because for the first time you left him here completely alone with her, a voice whispered in the back of her head.

Backing out of the room, she fought the tears that half blinded her. In the hallway between Lucas's room and Gina's, she slid to the floor and covered her face with her hands, weeping in despair.

Had Theresa been right about Lucas? Was he some sort of a devil worshipper? A follower of Thanatos? Had he merely been waiting for the perfect opportunity to call Gina into the tunnel and lead her to the place where the other children had disappeared?

There had to be a way to find the truth about him. Swiping her tears, desperate to act, to combat her helplessness, she returned to his bedroom.

Once again she moved to the side of his bed and stared at him. Could such a beautiful face hide the soul of a devil? Hadn't Ted Bundy been described as very handsome and charming, and yet he'd been possessed by internal demons.

"Lucas," she whispered and once again reached out to touch him. He was still cold as death and there was no discernible indication of him breathing.

She drew her hand away from him, her eyes straying to the dresser top. There had to be something here to give her some clue as to what kind of man he was . . . some personal object that would let her know whether she could trust him or if she'd been a fool to open her door to him.

She began her search in the chest of drawers, her hands trembling. She had no idea what she was looking for . . . something—anything—that would ease the terror that ripped through her.

In the top drawer she found socks and underwear. The next one down contained shorts and jeans neatly folded. The rest of the bureau was empty.

She moved to the closet, where his shirts and a couple

pairs of dress slacks hung. His suitcase was on the floor, and after shooting a glance at him to make sure he was still out, she bent down and rummaged through the bag.

Nothing. Absolutely nothing. Again tears pressed hot and furious at her eyes. What forces had driven him to their house on that first night? Had he truly been compelled to come to save Gina? Or had he come to gain Kathleen's and Gina's trust, then destroy them.

She stood and noticed a shoebox on the shelf above the hanging clothes. Her hands still trembled as she reached up, removed the shoebox, pulled off the lid. Paperwork. The box contained a medical card, insurance papers, and bills. All were addressed to Lucas Connelly on the Upper East Side in Manhattan.

With a sigh of frustration, she started to slide the box back where she'd found it, but then paused, noticing there was something else on the shelf, something the shoebox had hidden.

Standing on her tiptoes, she reached up and grabbed two things . . . a fat pillar candle and a small white envelope. Black. The candle was black. What kind of person kept a black candle hidden in a closet?

A devil worshipper.

The words crashed through her head, and she stumbled backward as the candle fell from her fingers to the floor. She had invited him here . . . into her house, into their lives.

With dread filling her, seeping from her pores, she opened the envelope. Hair. Strands of dark hair. They could be hers, or they could be Gina's.

Why would he have their hair in an envelope? Had he lit the black candle and chanted over the hair, sacrificing them to Thanatos?

She glared at his inert form, filled with a rage she'd never known before. She wanted to slap him and kick him. She wanted to tear out his hair and scratch his handsome face. Never before had she experienced the kind of searing rage she felt at the moment.

Had he somehow manufactured the echo of love from past lives she'd experienced to gain her trust? Was he a master magician of dark powers?

Of course he was. How else to explain Theresa believing she'd met him at some weird party? How else to explain the black candle and the envelope of hair?

The fury inside her waned as fear washed through her. Was Gina lost forever? Like Sharon, would she now be transported to a hospital to be fed intravenously and live out her life like a shell?

Pressing her fist against her mouth, she attempted to halt the sob that ripped from her. She left Lucas's room and returned to Gina's. She sank down on the floor next to her daughter and took the child's cold hand in hers.

There was nothing she could do but wait . . . wait to see what, if anything, happened next.

The afternoon passed in agonizing increments of time. The phone rang several times, but Kathleen didn't leave Gina's side, refused to leave until Gina woke up.

The shadows of purple dusk began to seep through the window, and Kathleen felt an overwhelming despair that if her daughter didn't awaken before the night came, she would never wake up.

Over and over she called to her daughter, whispered in her ear, begging her to find her way out of the tunnel and return to her mommy who loved her.

She wasn't sure what made her turn her head and look at

the doorway, but when she did she saw Lucas standing there, looking ill and almost haggard with exhaustion.

Kathleen rose from her position on the floor, the anger that had dissipated over the long hours returning to sweep through her with a vengeance. "Get her back," she demanded.

"I can't. . . . I tried, but I can't."

"Damn you, get her back." She slammed into his chest with her fists as tears trekked down her cheeks.

He grabbed her arms and held her so she couldn't hit him again. "I told you, Kathleen. I've been trying to get her back, but I haven't been able to." He dropped his hands from her.

"I want you to pack your bags and get out."

He stepped back as if she'd slapped him. "What?"

"You heard me. Get your things and get out."

"You don't mean that," he said softly.

"Oh, but I do." She shoved past him and out into the hallway. "I don't want you to stay another minute . . . another second in this house," she said as she stalked toward his room. "I want you to get your clothes and your black candle and get out."

"Black candle? What are you talking about?" He grabbed her by the arm and whirled her around.

Oh, he was good. His features radiated only bewilderment and confusion. But she was finished being fooled by him. "Let go of me," she demanded.

He tightened his grip on her arm and his eyes narrowed. "Not until you tell me what the hell is going on."

The tears raced faster down her cheeks. "What's going on is that I found a black candle and an envelope with hair in the top of your closet. Tell me, Lucas, did you offer up me

and my daughter to Thanatos in the evenings when you re-
tired early?"

He dropped his hand from her then, his eyes radiating a
darkness that threatened to consume her. "Kathleen, I don't
know anything about a black candle and an envelope of hair.
And the only thing I know for sure about Thanatos is that
he's who we're fighting against."

She refused to be moved by his words. Lies, a voice
screamed in her head. He lied as magnificently as he made
love. "If you aren't out of here in the next fifteen minutes,
I'll call the police and have you physically removed."

"Kathleen . . ."

"Fifteen minutes, Lucas." She twirled around and walked
back to Gina's room, where she once again sat on the floor
next to her utterly immobile baby.

The trembling that had taken possession of her hands earlier, now took total possession of her entire body. She was
chilled to the bone despite the heat of the room.

Although her heart ached for Lucas, she couldn't deny the
horrifying facts of that black candle. She could tell herself
that Theresa was mistaken about seeing him at that party.
She could even convince herself that he had no idea what his
former lover, Belinda, was into. But she'd held that candle
in her hands, had seen the hair in the envelope with her eyes.
And Gina had slipped away when Kathleen had left her alone
with him.

She sensed rather than heard him in the doorway behind
her. She turned to see him standing there, his eyes beseech-
ing. He looked much like he had on the night she'd first met
him. Clad in a pair of black slacks and a white shirt, he held
his suitcase in one hand.

"Kathleen, I don't know how that candle got into my

253

closet. I don't know why Gina suddenly slipped away. We were working together and everything was fine. I went into my bedroom to find an old magic wand I was going to give her and before I found it I knew she was gone. Instantly I tried to get her back."

Nothing he said was going to change her mind, and he seemed to know that by simply gazing at her. He shifted his suitcase from one hand to the other. "I told you there would come a time when trusting me would be difficult, a time when you'd have to rely on your heart and not your head."

She looked at him for another long moment, then turned her back to him and stared at her daughter, who still slept the sleep of the damned.

"I love you, Kathleen." The words came softly. "And I would never do anything to hurt you or Gina."

"Get out," she said just as softly, not turning to look at him again.

There was a pregnant pause when she knew he remained in the doorway, felt his gaze on her back as if he stroked his fingers up her spine. Then the air displaced, and she knew he was gone.

A moment later she heard the front door open, then close. Never had she felt so alone in her life. She didn't have time to deal with the immense anguish and ache that filled her heart. She couldn't take the time to fall into a well of despair over Lucas's betrayal. She had to get Gina back. Somehow, someway, she had to figure out how to get Gina to wake up.

It was just after midnight when Gina drew a deep gasp and cried out.

Kathleen grabbed her, thrilled to find that her skin was

warming by the second. "I'm here, Gina. I'm right here," she said, soothing her as Gina began to cry.

"I was so afraid, Mommy. I was so scared that I wouldn't see you again." Gina clung to her and Kathleen rocked her back and forth until both of them had stopped crying.

"How about we go downstairs and have some milk and cookies. Then you can sleep with me for the rest of the night," Kathleen suggested.

"Okay," Gina agreed readily and together mother and child walked down the stairs toward the kitchen.

Thanatos threw back his head and roared with impotent rage. The child had eluded him yet again. She'd been so close . . . so close he'd been able to smell her strawberry shampoo, see the sparkling shine of her innocence.

But before he could lure her completely in, she'd escaped back into her body and away from him. Damn the little bitch and her bitch of a mother, too.

This child was the most important of them all. Without her, all his lifetimes of work would be for naught. He had to have her.

He stared out the large picture window before him, where the forest was deep and dark and shrouded in the cloak of night. As he watched, a deer appeared, a doe with soft brown eyes.

Sensing no danger, the doe drew closer to the house, foraging the grass beneath its feet. Such an innocent creature, like the children he called. He glared at the doe and watched as she lifted her head, eyes wide with terror. He grunted in satisfaction as the animal turned tail and disappeared.

He sank into a nearby chair, his thoughts returning to the problem of Gina. It was time to call a meeting of his most faithful, time to formulate a new plan. If Gina wouldn't come to him spiritually, then he'd have to make sure she came to him physically.

He smiled as he thought of the newest members of his group. They would serve him well. They would see that the child was brought to him and when she was, all the power of hell would be his.

He moved to his computer and logged on to the site he used to communicate with his apostles. Ah, the joy of modern technology. He threw back his head and laughed as he anticipated his sweet success.

Chapter Twenty-three

"Mommy?"

Kathleen fought through a thick blanket of fog, trying to focus on the voice that called to her.

"Mommy, wake up. I'm hungry."

Kathleen came awake with a start, surprised to find she'd slept at all through the long, endless night. Gina sat next to her in her bed, looking none the worse after her latest travel into the dark tunnel.

"I'm hungry. Will you make me some pancakes?"

"Sure, pancakes it is." Kathleen sat up, shoved her hair from her eyes and gazed at the nearby clock. Shock washed over her as she realized it was almost noon. She remembered eating cookies and drinking milk with Gina after she'd put away the groceries she'd bought what seemed like a lifetime ago. The two had finally crawled into bed about one. Kathleen had intended to spend the night keeping vigil over her daughter, but apparently exhaustion had won out.

"When did you wake up?" she asked Gina.

"Just a few minutes ago." Gina smiled. "And you were snoring."

"I wasn't," Kathleen protested.

"Oh yes you were," Gina said with a giggle. "Not real loud, but I could hear you." She made little snorting sounds. "Just like that." Her smile fell from her face. "Mommy? Where's Lucas? When I woke up I went downstairs and looked for him and he wasn't there. Then I went into his room and he's not there, either."

As Gina scampered off the bed, Kathleen rolled out as well. She grabbed her robe and pulled it on, trying to decide what to tell Gina about their missing houseguest.

She knew Gina had grown quite close to Lucas and the fact that he'd betrayed her daughter's love and trust as much as he had Kathleen's only deepened the hurt and anger she felt when she thought of him.

"Come on, let's go get some breakfast. After we eat I'll explain where Lucas is."

Thankfully, Gina seemed to forget about Lucas after breakfast. She stretched out on the sofa and began watching one of her Disney movies.

Kathleen cleaned up the kitchen, raced upstairs, and took the fastest shower of her life, then returned to the downstairs. She stood in the doorway of the living room for a long moment, watching her daughter watch TV.

Gina had been spending far too much time watching the boob tube in the past couple of weeks. Kathleen thought about taking her to the beach for the day, but knew it would be crowded.

Besides, she was reluctant to take her out in public at all. She hadn't forgotten the reason she had installed a security system on the house, couldn't forget that it was possible somebody might try to kidnap Gina.

It isn't fair, she thought as she walked back into the kitchen. Gina should be outside playing with friends. She should be going swimming and enjoying her summer. In less than a month school would start again. Then what?

Could she blithely send Gina off to school every day, never knowing if somebody might snatch her from the playground or if Gina would fall into a final coma?

No. If nothing changed between now and then, Kathleen would have to home school her daughter. She simply couldn't take the chance of pretending everything was normal in their lives when it wasn't.

She poured herself a fresh cup of coffee and moved to the window where storm clouds battled with the sun. If it rained, it would be a steam bath outside. This had definitely been a summer of weird weather patterns.

Lucas. His name reverberated in her head, echoed deep within her heart. If his goal had been to get at Gina, why had he so effectively seduced Kathleen?

If the visions of past lives she'd experienced had been manufactured by Lucas, why had she felt the truth of them so deeply. When she'd had those visions, she'd felt love for Lucas deep in her soul, had felt his love for her just as strongly. Had it all been lies and manipulation? The smoke and mirrors, the sleight-of-hand tricks of a master magician?

Magic. She'd felt it in his arms, in his kiss, and it had evoked in her the magic of true and lasting love. And now she felt more alone than she ever had in her life. Betrayed by the man she loved, afraid for the daughter she loved, her life was a mess and she was all alone.

She knew with a single phone call she wouldn't be alone.

She could call Bill, and he would be by her side in a minute. He would hold her and support her and love her. But she wouldn't do that. It wouldn't be fair to either of them. She would handle this on her own.

For a moment she marveled at the inner strength she had found over the last several weeks. She left the window and walked over to the cabinet where a notepad sat on the shiny, tiled surface.

It was the notepad where she had written Bill's directions to Whispering Pines. She stared at the directions, wondering if all the speculation about Sutton had been lies, too.

Had Lucas spoken of a faked death, science experiments gone awry, and the possibility of Sutton being tied to all the madness simply as a diversion? Was it possible that Lucas was Thanatos? Although her heart cried out in denial, she knew she couldn't afford not to think through every possibility.

"Mommy?"

She turned to see Gina standing in the doorway. "What, honey?"

"Where's Lucas?"

Kathleen crouched down and gestured for Gina to come into her arms. "Lucas had to go away," she said.

Gina's large green eyes held Kathleen's gaze. "When is he coming back?"

"Lucas isn't coming back, honey."

Gina stiffened, her eyes growing huge. "He has to come back," she said and tried to wiggle out of Kathleen's arms. "You have to get him back." She managed to squirm away from Kathleen.

"Honey . . ." Kathleen tried to pull her back into her arms, but Gina stiff-armed her away.

"You have to get him back right now." Her voice went up

an octave and she moaned, a deep moan of despair that raised the hairs on Kathleen's arms. Gina took two steps backward, her entire body taut with tension. "If you don't get him to come back, then I'm going to die."

Kathleen gasped as Gina turned and ran, moaning once again, an almost inhuman sound that turned Kathleen's blood icy cold. "Gina!" she cried, but the little girl didn't acknowledge her.

Kathleen ran after her, following her to her room, where Gina threw herself on her bed and sobbed as Kathleen had never heard her cry before.

"Gina, sweetheart. It's going to be all right," Kathleen said as she sat on the edge of the bed and stroked her daughter's back. Gina shook her head vehemently, then sat up.

"I'm going to be sick," she said and tumbled from the bed and into the bathroom where she wretched over and over again.

When she was finished, Kathleen cleaned her face and carried her back into the bedroom. She'd known Gina would be upset to learn that Lucas was gone, but there was no way she had anticipated this kind of violent reaction to the news.

Gina lay listlessly on the bed, her face devoid of all color and her eyes reflecting a fear that tore at Kathleen's heart.

"Lucas is the only one who can save me," she finally said. Tears slid from her eyes. "Mommy, please. Make him come back. I don't want to die."

Indecision ripped through Kathleen, along with a terrifying fear. Had she made a mistake in asking Lucas to leave? Or had he somehow brainwashed Gina into believing he was the only one who could save her? As Gina shot up from the bed and ran to the bathroom to be sick once again, Kathleen made up her mind.

It didn't much matter what the truth was where he was concerned. Gina's reaction to his absence was as threatening as anything else.

She would bring Lucas back, and if he helped Gina, all the better. But if he were Thanatos, she would go head-to-toe with him for Gina's well-being. She would see him dead before she allowed him to do her child any further harm.

It was nearly five o'clock when Kathleen sat on the train carrying her into the city. She'd managed to get hold of Theresa, who had agreed to come sit with Gina.

She told Theresa nothing of what had been happening, simply explained that she had no idea how long she might be gone.

She had driven to the nearest train station, knowing the best way to maneuver around Manhattan was in cabs, rather than a car. The address she'd seen on Lucas's bills in the shoebox was emblazoned on her brain, and it was to his Upper East Side penthouse that she was headed first.

She had no idea whether she was doing the right thing. She only knew that Gina hadn't calmed down until she'd agreed to try to get Lucas to come back.

The train was relatively empty. Most of the commuters would be heading out of the city at this time of the day. She frowned, trying to remember exactly what day of the week it was. Thursday? No, it was Friday. Amazing how such things hadn't mattered over the last few weeks. Nothing had mattered but keeping Gina safe.

If she found Lucas and he returned to their home, would she be bringing danger back to Gina or saving her? God help her, but she wished she knew the answer to that.

The train ride seemed to take an eternity, but finally she

was walking briskly toward the address she'd seen for Lucas. Her heart pounded so hard, she thought she might be on the verge of a stroke, but she knew it was only fear, anxiety and despair.

Just after six-thirty, she found the address. The Brickman Tower building was an attractive fifteen-story structure with a polished brass plaque bearing the name and address by the front door.

A security guard behind an elaborate desk greeted her in the small lobby. "May I help you?"

"I'm here to see Lucas Connelly," she replied.

The guard, an older man with a head full of beautiful gray hair shook his head. "I'm afraid Mr. Connelly isn't in."

"Are you sure?" she asked.

He must have heard the touch of desperation in her voice and he gave her a kindly smile. "I'm pretty sure."

"Could you buzz him or call him or whatever to be certain?"

He looked as if he were about to protest, then nodded and picked up a phone. He punched in a couple of numbers, then waited. After several moments he shrugged and hung up. "Sorry, there's no answer." He looked at her for a moment, then added. "He's been gone for some time. I think he must be on a trip or something."

"Thank you," Kathleen murmured, then left the building. If he hadn't come home, then where would he have gone? The club! Club Diablo. He had to be there. He had to be.

She stepped to the curb and hailed a cab, her heart pounding madly, her palms sweaty with apprehension. With each passing minute, her alarm grew.

What if Gina was right? What if Lucas truly was the only one who could save her? What if while she was desperately hunting for Lucas, Gina fell into a dreadful, final sleep?

She leaned forward in the seat. "Could you hurry, please?" she asked the taxi driver.

"Lady, I'm doing the best I can," the driver growled as they remained stopped in a traffic gnarl. "I can't see what's going on, but something up ahead has us bottle-necked." He leaned on the horn as if that would magically move them forward.

They sat unmoving for twenty agonizing minutes, then finally they were able to resume a slow crawl forward. By that point a scream was lodged in Kathleen's throat.

It was almost seven-thirty by the time the cab dropped her at Club Diablo. Unlike the last time she'd come, she heard no noise from the building as she approached the front door.

It was far too early for the place to be jumping, and sure enough, when she walked into the dimly lit place, there were only a few couples seated at the tables surrounding the dance floor.

"Is the manager in?" she asked a bored-looking bartender drying glasses behind the bar.

"Yeah, hang on." He set his towel on the counter and disappeared into what she assumed was the kitchen area. He appeared a moment later and gestured her onto a stool. "Have a seat. He'll be with you in just a few minutes. Can I get you something to drink?"

"No, thanks." She'd choke trying to swallow around the scream in her throat.

She didn't have to wait long before a short, squat man came out and introduced himself as the manager. "What can I do for you?" he asked.

"I'm looking for Lucas Connelly."

The little man laughed without humor. "I'd love to find

Lucas. Since he quit performing here, business has dropped in half."

"So you haven't seen him in the last day or so?"

"Nah, although if you find him, tell him I got his job here waiting for him."

Kathleen felt light-headed with disappointment. "What about Belinda? Do you have a waitress here named Belinda?"

"Used to. She took off on me the same time Lucas did. Sorry I can't help you. Is there anything else?"

She shook her head faintly and he started to leave, but she quickly called after him. "You don't happen to know where Belinda lives, do you?"

"Sorry, but I don't."

Night was falling and thunder echoed in the distance as she stepped out of the club. She leaned against the building, for the first time allowing herself the luxury of tears.

She didn't know where to go, didn't know how to find him. She knew he had no family, had no clue if he had friends with whom he could be staying. She couldn't even remember Belinda's last name.

A dull hopelessness was her only companion on the train back to the Hamptons. She had no idea how to find Lucas and worse, had no idea how to break the news to Gina.

It was just after ten-thirty when she pulled into her driveway, exhausted and defeated. A light drizzle hung in the air and lightning flashed intermittently, lighting the night sky to announce a responding boom of thunder.

The house was quiet as she entered. "Hello?" she called softly, wondering if maybe Gina was already asleep and Theresa was napping in the living room.

But in the living room the television wasn't on, and there was no sign of Theresa. Maybe they're playing a game in

Gina's room, she told herself as she hurried up the stairs, trying to ignore the frantic pounding of her heart.

"Gina?" she called as she hit the top of the stairs. She raced into Gina's bedroom, where the utter silence was deafening. The bed was neatly made, as it had been when Kathleen had left. No toys were scattered about, and there was no sign of Gina or Theresa.

"Gina? Theresa?" she cried and ran from room to room, but even as she frantically searched in each room, she knew with horrifying certainty that she was alone in the house.

Hurrying back downstairs and to the living room window, she peered outside, for the first time realizing Theresa's car wasn't parked at the curb as it had been when Kathleen had left.

Don't panic, she told herself. Maybe they went out for a quick ice cream run, or to rent a movie or to Theresa's house for something she'd forgotten to bring with her.

She picked up the phone and dialed Theresa's number. The phone in Theresa's apartment rang four times before Theresa's answering machine picked up. "Theresa, it's me," Kathleen said after the beep. "Where are you? I'm back now and you need to bring Gina home." She hung up, but stared at the receiver for a long moment, trying to fight the nauseating sense of panic that threatened to consume her.

You know how impulsive Theresa can be, she told herself. She could have taken Gina anywhere. But Theresa would never let anything bad happen to Gina. Theresa loved Gina like she was her own daughter.

Kathleen just needed to be calm, to be patient and wait. At any moment Theresa and Gina would pull up, laughing about an adventure they'd shared.

She moved to the living room window once again and stared out, watching for Theresa's car, watching as the storm intensified overhead, and praying that they would appear at any minute and everything would be just fine.

Chapter Twenty-four

Belinda had her instructions. She stood on the porch of the main building in the compound, watching the headlights of an approaching car.

It was late, almost midnight and she'd expected the child to be sleeping. But as the vehicle came to a halt in front of where Belinda stood, she saw the girl was still awake.

"He's waiting for you," she told the painfully skinny blonde who got out from the driver's side of the car.

The woman nodded and opened the door for the girl. "Come on, Gina. This nice lady is going to take you to your room for the night."

"And my mommy will be there?" Gina asked.

"Sure, later," the blonde replied and raced up the stairs and into the huge cabin.

Belinda eyed the little girl curiously. She was a pretty child, with her sharp green eyes and long dark hair. Belinda didn't know why Gina was so important, but her instructions were to take her to a room and keep her there until they were summoned.

"Hi, Gina. Come with me and I'll show you to your room."

"What's your name?" she asked, not moving from her position on the porch.

"Belinda. Now, come with me. It's very late." To her surprise, the child grabbed her hand and offered up a bright smile.

"It's way past my bedtime," Gina said as Belinda led her into the cabin and down a long hallway.

"Yes, I'm sure it is," Belinda agreed, unsettled by the warmth of the little hand in hers.

"Is it past your bedtime?" Gina asked.

"Yeah, sure." The bedroom where Belinda took her was a sterile room, with only a single bed, a straight-backed chair, a dresser, and a lamp. The bars on the window were not to keep anything out, but rather to keep unwilling guests in.

"Did you bring your pajamas?" Belinda asked, grateful when the child released her hand and walked over to the window.

"No, Aunt Theresa didn't tell me to. When is my mommy going to be here?" Gina turned from the window and looked at Belinda, her gaze holding no fear, only trust.

Belinda glanced away, not knowing why but unable to maintain eye contact. "Soon," she replied. "Look, why don't you take off your shoes and socks and go ahead and get into bed. When you wake up in the morning I'm sure your mommy will be here."

Gina sat on the bed and kicked off her shoes, then leaned over and pulled off first one sock, then the other. The socks were white, with pink lacy tops. Belinda wasn't sure why the sight of those childish socks bothered her.

When she was finished, she looked at Belinda. "Are you going to stay here with me until I go to sleep? My mommy always sits next to me until I fall asleep."

I'm not your mommy, Belinda wanted to scream, but her orders were to keep the child happy. "Okay, I'll sit right here," she said and pulled the chair next to the bed.

Gina nodded, lay down on the mattress and once again reached for Belinda's hand. Belinda fought the impulse to pull back from the warmth and innocence in the child's touch.

"Did your mommy used to sit with you before you'd fall asleep when you were younger?" Gina asked.

"I guess so." Belinda's head suddenly filled with memories of her childhood, memories of a time when it had been just her and her mother, before her mother had met and married the wicked pious stepfather.

"She used to like to brush your hair," Gina said softly. "You have the prettiest hair."

The words echoed in Belinda's head as she remembered sitting on her bed while her mother slowly combed out her tangles. "Oh, sweetheart, God blessed you with this mane. It's the red of the prettiest sunset He could create."

She could smell the scent of her mother, lavender and just a hint of vanilla. But more than anything, Belinda remembered the innocent child she had been before George Randolf Samuels had entered her life and violated her soul.

She'd been filled with such hope, such joy. The hope and joy of innocence, the same kind of innocence she saw in Gina's eyes.

Confusion swept through her and she tried to pull her

hand away from Gina, but the child held tight. "I'm going to die here," Gina said softly, her beautiful eyes so sad.

"Don't be ridiculous," Belinda scoffed. "Nobody is going to hurt you here." But the instant the words left her mouth, she recognized the lie.

She wasn't sure whether they intended to kill the child, but she knew with certainty that they intended to steal Gina's innocence, corrupt the goodness of her childish soul.

With an epiphany that stole her breath, Belinda recognized that Thanatos was cut of the same cloth as George Randolf Samuels.

And in Gina's eyes, Belinda saw herself. There had been nobody to save Belinda from the evil of her stepfather, nobody to save her from the darkness and point her toward the light.

Just as suddenly she realized she could not allow the darkness to possess this child who held her hand so tightly, so trustingly.

"Gina, put your shoes and socks on," she commanded urgently. "We've got to get you out of here."

Gina held her gaze for a long moment, then released Belinda's hand and did as she bid. Belinda moved to the window and stared out at the night. A storm was brewing in the distance, the lightning flashes briefly illuminating thick, ominous clouds.

She had no plan, knew that if she were caught she would die, but she felt as if she'd just awakened from a long sleep and was seeing the world for the first time in years. And for the first time in years she knew fear, but she was filled with the need to save this child. She knew that ultimately in saving Gina, she might be able to save herself.

All they had to do was get out of the cabin unseen. Then

271

they could get into Belinda's car and drive away from this evil place and from the man who'd wielded such power over Belinda.

Don't be a fool, a small voice whispered in the back of her head. The girl means nothing to you, and Thanatos will kill you if he catches you trying to leave with her.

She jumped as Gina's hand once again sought hers. She looked down at the girl and Gina smiled. "Thank you," Gina said and in the light shining from her eyes, Belinda found the strength to still that tiny voice.

"You must be very quiet," Belinda said as she opened the bedroom door. She peeked out of the room, looking first one way, then the other down the long hallway.

Seeing nobody, she gripped Gina's hand tightly and stepped out of the room. Together they walked side-by-side, slowly, quietly. Just a few more steps, Belinda thought, sweat trickling down the small of her back. Just a little bit farther and we'll be at the door and can escape.

"Going somewhere?" A familiar voice boomed from behind them.

A chill of horror swept through Belinda.

"Daddy!" Gina cried and breaking away from Belinda, she ran right into Thanatos's arms.

By midnight, Kathleen was one breath short of insane with frantic fear. She had left a dozen messages on Theresa's machine, but hadn't heard a word from her.

Where were they? What was happening to Gina? For what seemed like the hundredth time, Kathleen picked up the phone to call the police only to slam it down again.

How on earth could she explain everything that had been going on to the police? How could she tell them that she'd spent the evening hours hunting up a magician she thought was in league with Satan? Dear God, they would lock her up and throw away the key.

Besides, she continued to have faith that Theresa would never let any harm come to Gina. Theresa was Kathleen's friend, wasn't she?

She jumped and a small scream flew from her as the phone rang. She grabbed the receiver. "Theresa?"

"Kathleen, my love."

The deep, familiar voice washed over her in waves of shock. "Sutton," she gasped. She sank to the sofa, wondering if this phone call, his voice, was all a figment of her imagination, if she'd finally, truly gone mad. "Sutton," she repeated faintly.

"I know what a shock this is, my darling. But I'll explain everything. First, Gina is safe with me here at Whispering Pines. Theresa brought her to me. If you leave right away you can join us by dawn. Then we'll talk and I promise I'll explain everything to you. We're going to be all right, darling. We're all going to be just fine now."

Relief fluttered through her. Gina was okay. "I'll leave right now."

"Do you know how to get here?"

"Yes . . . yes, I have directions."

"And Kathleen, Lucas is here. He won't be able to hurt you or Gina again."

Now that the initial shock of hearing his voice had worn off, confusion swirled through her. "I don't understand . . . what is Lucas doing there? And how did Theresa get there?"

"Everything will be clear after we talk. Hurry, my love. We're waiting for you." Before she could ask anything more, he hung up.

She didn't give herself an opportunity to think, but instead grabbed her purse and her car keys and immediately left the house. She would have plenty of time to think on the five-hour drive to the cabin.

Sutton hung up the phone and smiled at Theresa. "You've done well."

She nodded, her gaze reflecting both a touch of fear and a healthy dose of desperation. "Will you heal me now? I did as you asked. I brought Gina here. Now will you use your power and heal me like you said you would?"

He walked closer to where she stood. He could smell the sickness on her, knew from what she'd told him that she'd been in denial for so long about her illness that no medicine could help her. Nor did he have the power to heal.

She eyed him like a lover hungry for his touch, but he knew what she hungered for was a jolt of Satan's power to take away her AIDS. She had chosen to betray her best friend in order to save herself.

He withdrew a small container from his pocket and handed it to her. "A gift from Satan. There are five pills in there. Take them all at once and you will be healed."

She clutched the bottle as if it were a morsel of bread given to a starving woman. "Thank you." She turned and left the room.

Sutton eyed the big man seated in the corner of the room. He was bald, with biker tattoos decorating both of his thick arms. "Dill, follow her and when she's dead take her out in the woods and bury her."

Dill Stickler rose with a nod and disappeared after Theresa. Sutton sank into a chair, a sweet rush of success filling him. Everything was neatly falling into place.

The pills he'd given Theresa were exceptionally strong animal tranquilizers. They would kill her. Dill would follow his instructions and bury her body where nobody would ever find it.

Dill had once killed a man for making the mistake of calling him "Dill Pickle." He'd been out of prison for a year when he found his way to Thanatos. Not only would he take care of Theresa's body, he'd already taken care of the bitch betrayer Belinda and that nosy reporter—with a little help from Thanatos, whose power ensured the man would never awake from his coma. And when the time came, Dill and Thanatos would take care of Lucas Connelly as well.

Sutton leaned back in the chair and smiled to himself. The magician had been an unexpected surprise. Dill had found him skulking around the perimeter of the property. The magician's powers hadn't been enough to save him from a blow to the back of the head. He was now chained to a bed in one of the guest rooms, awaiting his final demise.

Even Gina had cooperated. They'd shared a loving reunion, and he'd told her how important it was that she go into the dark tunnel, that the only way they could all be a happy family again was if she conquered her fear and walked through the tunnel alone. And she had done it just for him.

He'd captured her soul and placed it with the others. Now there was only one thing left to do, then he would own the future and his power would reign through eternity.

He waited only for Kathleen's arrival. He didn't need her to complete his mission, but he wanted to show her exactly what he'd managed to accomplish.

Interesting, that of all the human traits he'd lost in his transformation into Thanatos, pride was one of the last to go.

* * *

Rain pelted her windshield, but Kathleen refused to slow her speed in deference to the storm. She had to reach Gina. She understood none of what had happened, and in the four hours she'd been driving, nothing had become illuminated in her mind.

She didn't understand why Theresa would have taken Gina to Whispering Pines. She didn't understand why Sutton had faked his death. And she certainly didn't understand why Sutton and Lucas were together there.

She only knew a burning, aching desire to hold Gina in her arms, to assure herself that her daughter was safe and sound.

Finally, she had to slow her speed as the storm intensified and the curving road grew narrow and hilly with thick woods on either side.

Clutching the steering wheel tightly, wincing against the frequent intense lightning, she tried to ferret out the truth of her situation while she drove.

What reason would Sutton have to fake his death? Were he and Lucas partners in some sort of wild scheme? Whom, if anyone, in this mess could she trust?

She pulled over to the side of the road and came to a halt. Turning on the interior light, she reached for the notepad with Bill's directions.

She read them quickly, once, twice, then turned off the light and resumed driving, her thoughts drifting to the man she had married so long ago.

Sutton. She searched her heart to see if there was any love left there for the man. But she could find none, wondered if there had ever been any real love for him.

Before Lucas, she would have never questioned her feelings

for Sutton. But having experienced a depth of love and passion for Lucas, she recognized that she'd never felt anything remotely like that for her husband.

But she couldn't trust Lucas any more than she trusted Sutton. There were just too many unanswered questions. Instead, she prayed for the strength to depend solely on herself.

The storm grew stronger as she got closer. She slowed to a crawl as she looked for the turns and little-traveled roads Bill had indicated she must take.

The wind whipped around the car, and in the flash of the lightning the trees and bushes near the road looked like crazed beings intent on impeding her progress.

Her imagination began to play tricks on her. The storm had been sent by Thanatos in an attempt to keep her away from her baby.

What if she took the wrong road? It would be easy to get lost, driving endlessly on unmarked, narrow roads the size of cattle paths.

She looked at her watch, saw that it was nearly six. There was no sign of dawn in the sky. Here amid the thick vegetation she wondered if dawn ever occurred, or if she had somehow been cast into an endless night.

Despair was just about to claim her completely when through the slashing, driving rain she saw the sign tacked to a thick tree trunk in her headlights. WHISPERING PINES. NO TRESPASSING.

Adrenaline rushed through her as she made the narrow turn and traveled down a tree-lined lane. Gina, her heart cried. Hang on, honey. I'm almost there.

She broke out of the trees and into a huge clearing. It was just like she'd seen in the photos Sutton had of the place. Several outbuildings lined the perimeter of the area, but just ahead was the main compound, a low, long log structure with a porch.

Light flowed from every window, piercing the darkness of predawn. She parked in front of the porch and got out of the car, unsure what to expect.

Lightning flashed, nearly blinding her and when she looked at the building again she saw a massive bald man standing on the porch.

"Mrs. Marlowe?"

"Yes?" Who was this huge man and what was he doing here?

"If you'll follow me, I'll take you to meet your husband."

She hesitated only a moment, then walked up the stairs to where he stood waiting for her. "Where's my daughter?" she asked.

"Your husband will explain everything to you. Please, just come with me."

With her heart beating madly, she followed the big man into the house and down a long hallway. He opened a door and gestured her inside. "You can wait in here. He'll be with you soon."

Kathleen walked into the room and instantly turned to the big man, but he closed the door and she heard the click of a lock. "Hey, wait a minute." She banged on the door with her fists, but there was no reply.

She whirled around and eyed the bedroom. Stark, sterile. A bed, a dresser and a chair. And bars on the window. She walked over to the glass and wrapped her fingers around two of the cold steel bars.

If she was about to have a loving reunion with her husband and daughter, then why was she locked in a room without any means of escape?

Chapter Twenty-five

"Kathleen."

Lucas sat straight up on the bed, the clanging of the chain against the metal bed frame and the bite of steel around his wrist reminded him of where he was.

Kathleen was here. He felt her sweet essence in the air, knew her beloved presence in his heart. She was here, and he couldn't help her because he was tethered like an animal to the bed.

Since he'd been here he'd seen nobody but the bald bruiser who had smashed him over the head and rendered him unconscious in the woods.

When he'd come to he'd been in this room, held captive by a handcuff. Even if he managed to slip the handcuff, the locked door and barred window would keep him a prisoner. He had not attempted to night travel, not wanting to leave his physical body unprotected. He sensed great evil in this place.

Over the past twenty-four hours he'd been given food and water and had been allowed to use the bathroom, but that had all been accomplished with the barrel of a gun trained on him. He had a feeling the big bald man would love for him to screw up, that he would take joy in pulling the trigger and blowing Lucas's brains out.

Lucas couldn't allow that to happen, so he had been co-operative thus far. He had yet to meet the elusive Sutton or Thanatos. He had the feeling they were all waiting for something. The atmosphere in the cabin had been rife with anticipation.

And now he knew that something had arrived.

Kathleen.

He still didn't know what had happened the night that she had cast him out of her house. But he'd seen the pain in her eyes, pain mingled with deep mistrust. As he'd left, he'd been filled with heartache . . . and a growing sense of anger.

He had no idea how the black candle and the envelope of hair had appeared in his closet, although the obvious culprit was Theresa. She was the only one who had had access to the house the night that he and Kathleen had gone to see Keith Kelly in the hospital.

She was one of Kathleen's betrayers, although he had no idea whether Kathleen would ever realize that. At the moment he knew Kathleen regarded him as the enemy, and he had to figure out a way to change her mind before the darkness closed in around them. For Kathleen he would leave his physical body.

Kathleen. Kathleen. He closed his eyes and focused on her, needing to reach her and let her feel his love one last time.

* * *

Kathleen sat on the bed and leaned against the wall. She was exhausted by the long drive, and these endless moments of waiting only made her exhaustion worse.

She wanted to see Gina. She needed some answers from Sutton. But it would seem she would have to wait. She rubbed her eyes, which felt grainy and tired, and fought against an overwhelming desire to sleep.

She couldn't sleep. Not until she knew that Gina was safe. But Sutton wouldn't harm Gina, a little voice whispered inside her head. Sutton had adored Gina. He might not have been the perfect husband, but he'd been a doting father.

Yawning, she shook her head in an effort to stay awake. Gina, her heart cried. Where are you? Are you all right? Kathleen had promised her daughter a hundred times that she would keep her safe. Was it a promise she wouldn't be able to keep?

She felt the shadows of fatigue reaching out to claim her, tried desperately to fight against them, but the hours of driving, the hours of stress and worry all came together in a crashing instant and she succumbed to the shadows.

She smelled him before she saw him, the slightly wild, wonderfully familiar fragrance that was his alone. He appeared just inside the locked door, a vaporous chimera, a shimmering transparent phantasm.

Lucas. As she looked at him she forgot about her mistrust of him, forgot all the reasons why she'd made him leave her house. "Lucas," she whispered, knowing she wasn't speaking aloud, but communicating with him through thought and mind.

He moved toward her, his eyes filled with the gentleness of generations of love and Kathleen knew deep in her heart that their love had to be real, that they were truly souls who had been connected in each and every lifetime.

"Kathleen," he said softly, his low voice like a full-body caress. His eyes shone like mercury and as he slid closer to her she felt warmed. "Don't be afraid," he whispered. "I love you."

He shimmered brighter and brighter, then he shot through her, wrapping himself around her heart, illuminating all the dark corners of her soul.

She gasped with the exquisite pleasure that swept through her, the pleasure not only of physical lovemaking, but something deeper and more profound than that.

He was making love not only to her body, but to her mind and her soul. He wove himself into the very fabric of her heart and she felt a complete fulfillment when he finally separated from her.

"Remember, I love you Kathleen. Remember to use your heart, not your head. Follow your heart for Gina's sake . . . for our sake."

As quickly as he'd appeared, he was gone, taking with him his sweet warmth and leaving her with the awful feeling of abandonment.

She awoke with a start, unsure if what she'd just experienced had really happened, or if it had only been a figment of her imagination, or a wishful dream of love by a woman who'd been manipulated and betrayed by the man she loved.

Before she could get it straight in her head, the door to her room opened and Sutton walked in.

"Kathleen!" He grabbed her hand and pulled her up and into his arms, hugging her more tightly than he ever had in his life. "Oh, my precious wife. I feared I would never see you again, that they would never allow me to be with you again."

She held herself rigid in his arms, refusing to be moved by anything he might say or do. It had been Kathleen who had comforted their daughter and listened to her cries when she'd been told that her daddy was dead. It had been Kathleen who had tried to be both mother and father to the little girl who'd mourned his death.

"Where's Gina?" she asked as he dropped his arms from around her.

"She's fine. She's sleeping like a baby. And now that you're here we'll be a happy family once again."

Kathleen stepped away from him and eyed him curiously. He'd always been a handsome, distinguished-looking man and almost a year of "death" hadn't changed him much. He looked a bit thinner, but his hair was still dark, sprinkled with silver at the temples, and he still had the weak chin she knew was a genetic curse from looking at pictures of his ancestors.

"Are you going to tell me exactly what's going on?" she asked. His eyes. They were different. His green eyes had always been rather soft and fuzzy looking, as if focused on internal thoughts rather than the outside world. Now, they radiated a brittle intensity she found oddly disconcerting.

"I can't tell you what's going on, but I can show you. Come . . ." He held out his hand toward her, his eyes shining with an excitement she'd never seen before.

Tentatively, she placed her hand in his. He led her out of the room and down the long hallway. "You haven't been here before, have you?" he asked as they walked. "My grandfather built this place," he continued, not giving her a chance to reply. "He was a man of great vision, as was my father. They spent hundreds of thousands of dollars transforming this seemingly innocuous building into a marvel of science."

As they walked, Kathleen was vaguely aware of a murmur of voices coming from the various rooms they passed. Who were these people? What did they have to do with Sutton? Why were they here in his family's cabin?

He led her through a large living area, decorated like a typical hunting lodge. Brown leather furniture and oversized end tables filled the room, along with the stuffed heads of various wildlife that hung on the walls.

On the far side of the room, he opened a door that led to a staircase, which appeared to descend into the very bowels of hell.

She hesitated on the top stair, unsure whether she wanted to see what might be in the basement. Instead she turned to look at him. "Why did you make me believe you were dead? How could you do that to me . . . to Gina?"

"I had to. They made me," he replied.

"Who made you?"

"The government. Come on, let me show you what I've been doing, the marvels that my research has uncovered." He gestured for her to precede him down the stairs.

The narrow stairway was flanked on both sides by rock walls, and it seemed to go on forever. But when they reached the bottom, the rustic look disappeared. Carpeted flooring appeared underfoot and brilliant lights shone from overhead. He pointed her into a doorway on the right, and she turned and gasped in surprise.

White tiled walls and stainless-steel counters greeted her, along with machines and instruments she couldn't begin to understand. A laboratory.

"Beautiful, isn't it?" Sutton said, his voice filled with obvious pride. "My grandfather did some of his best research work here, as did my father, and as have I."

"What kind of research?" she asked, intrigued despite the ball of fear that pressed against the back of her throat.

Sutton reached out and took her by the shoulders, his eyes boring into hers. "I found the human soul, Kathleen. Not only did I find it, I've managed to isolate it."

"What are you talking about, Sutton? I don't understand."

"It was part of a government project, a secret project funded by the military. Somehow, word leaked out and the government, fearing for my life and the success of the project, made me fake my own death."

"But I saw what was left of your car. I saw what was left of you." She looked at him searchingly.

He sighed impatiently. "The FBI set it all up. The body remains were that of a man who was dead before they put him in the car. He was my height, my bone structure, and they put my ring and watch on him before they pushed the car over the cliff."

He dropped his hands from her shoulders. "We knew somebody was after me. Someone wanted to steal my notes and gain possession of the knowledge. That man is Lucas Connelly. He's a rogue agent working for whatever country will pay him the highest fee. When he couldn't make it as a magician, he turned to a more lucrative field."

"No," she whispered. Was it possible? Had Lucas's real interest in her and Gina been to steal scientific knowledge? Had he entered their lives, offered his help, seduced both her and her daughter just to get information about where Sutton might be?

"It's true. The name of the project was Thanatos." He stopped talking at the sound of footsteps approaching.

The big man who had greeted Kathleen on the porch when she'd arrived entered the lab with Lucas in tow. "Ah good,

285

so we're all here together at last." Sutton clapped his hands. He smiled thinly at Lucas. "I was just explaining to Kathleen that this is a scientific project you've been trying to steal."

Although Lucas said nothing, she thought she saw the denial in his eyes. She also spied a thick, long piece of wood leaning up against one of the counters. It could be used as a bat.

But who would she hit? Lucas? Sutton? She didn't know whom to trust, knew it was possible she couldn't trust either one. She simply didn't have the answers she needed to make a plan to escape. She didn't even know where Gina was.

"And you said the project is named Thanatos?" she asked.

"There is no project named Thanatos, only the man who sits at the right hand of Satan has that name," Lucas said, his eyes glowing with a strange, silvery light.

Sutton laughed. "A second-rate magician who obviously has a flair for the dramatic."

"The children? What did you do to the children?" Kathleen asked.

"They are safe. They are all safe. Come and let me show you." Sutton took her by the arm, then turned to where the bald man stood next to Lucas. "Come, Mr. Magic, come see what genius can accomplish."

He pointed to a counter, where what appeared to be two large water-dispensing machines sat. But instead of water, the two bottles held something else. One appeared to contain little twinkling lights that darted around the enclosure like fireflies. The other one had what appeared to be black flying bugs.

Sutton placed his hand on top of the one containing the black buglike things. "My grandfather discovered the secret of how to isolate the soul from the body. And he spent most of his lifetime attempting to capture the blackest souls he could find. My father followed in his footsteps, and this is the result of their work."

"What is it?" Kathleen asked, feeling a deep revulsion as she looked into the container.

"Souls, Kathleen. Evil souls. Hitler's soul is here, along with Mussolini's, Ted Bundy and a sundry of others, one blacker than the next."

"And in that one?" She pointed to the container of sparkling brightness.

"Ah, the souls of innocence. The souls of the children. Gina is here now with the others."

Kathleen stared at him in horror. "How could you do this?"

"I have done nothing to harm them," Sutton assured her. "The atmosphere in the container is perfectly balanced to keep them safe until they can once again be reunited with their bodies."

"But why? Why would you do such a thing?" she asked.

"Imagine the ramifications, Kathleen. Show a little visionary thinking," Sutton said, his eyes gleaming with a light that made him look half insane. "If we recognize evil in a soul, we can simply remove that soul from the body."

"Or fill the bodies of innocent children with evil souls," Lucas said.

"Shut up, magic man. You don't know what you're talking about," Sutton spat. He turned back to Kathleen. "We can banish evil from the earth."

"Or fill the earth with evil. Think, Kathleen. These people celebrated each harvest of a child's soul. They fouled a church with their dark celebration," Lucas said, his eyes now completely silver.

"Shut him up," Sutton raged. The bald man raised a fist and smashed it into Lucas's mouth. Kathleen cried out as she saw the blood from his split lip fly from him. She grabbed the piece of wood she'd seen earlier and wielded it like a bat.

"Kathleen," Sutton said softly. "Put that down. You don't want to do anything crazy."

"What you've done is crazy," she exclaimed.

"I did it for my country . . . for my science," Sutton replied.

He did it for himself. The voice was Lucas's but it didn't come from his mouth, it came from someplace inside her head.

Sutton took a step toward her, but she held the bat at the ready and he stopped in his tracks. "Kathleen, do you really believe I could ever do anything to harm Gina? My own flesh and blood?"

She was the final sacrifice to Satan, the voice whispered. *He will unleash the horrors of evil onto the earth, and it will be the beginning of the end.*

Kathleen felt as if she were going mad. She knew she wasn't thinking clearly. "Where is Theresa?" she asked.

Sutton frowned. "I'm afraid Theresa passed away earlier this evening. You knew she was in the advance stages of AIDS."

"Oh, no . . ." Grief pierced her, and the bat suddenly grew too heavy. But as if sensing her weakness, Sutton took another step toward her and she gripped it tighter. "Don't come any closer, Sutton," she warned. "I don't want to hurt you. I don't want to hurt anyone. I just . . . I need some answers. Then I want to get Gina and go."

"All right," he replied. "Just don't do anything foolish."

"What happened to Keith Kelly? Did you have something to do with him getting beat up?"

"Not me," Sutton protested. "But I can't vouch for the people who have been protecting me. This project is far too valuable, and I'm afraid they have been overly zealous in defending me. Now, put down that bat."

His eyes had never appeared so green. She felt herself falling into their depths. Visions exploded in her head, visions of her and Gina and Sutton together, sweet visions of laughter and joy, of family and love.

"We can have that again, Kathleen. Just put the bat down and let me finish my task here. Then we'll be the family we were before all this began."

It was what Kathleen had always dreamed of . . . home and hearth and family, but the visions were false. It had never been that way for them. Instead, it had been that way with Lucas. Lucas had brought laughter and joy and love.

Her head spun dizzily, and she wished the voices would all just shut up and let her think.

Break the container with the children's souls. It was Lucas's voice that filled her head once again.

"Kathleen, don't," Sutton said, as if he, too, had heard Lucas's command. "I told you that the atmosphere in the container is what's keeping the souls alive. If you break it they will die."

Break it! Lucas's voice was stronger, louder in her head.

"You'll destroy them!" Sutton roared. "Can't you see? He hates you. He wants you to pay for all the lifetimes where you betrayed him. He wants you to destroy yourself, destroy your daughter. If you break the container all of them will die, including Gina."

Kathleen looked at Lucas, the silver shine of his eyes other-

289

worldly. Could it be true? Was Lucas finally avenging life-times of pain and heartache? He had spoken of his pain, that it was always she who abandoned him and left him bereft. Was he manipulating her with his need for revenge? Dear God, she didn't know what to think. She didn't know who to believe.

Think with your heart, not your head.

Her heart. Not her head. Her heart. Not her head.

With a scream, Kathleen raised the bat and smashed the container with the children's souls. For a moment it was as if the world stood still. The glass shattered into a million pieces and to Kathleen it seemed as if everything happened in slow motion.

The bright lights clustered together for a moment, then separated, shooting through the room as Sutton bellowed in rage. One particular light shot through Kathleen and she gasped, recognizing the soul as her daughter's.

It pierced her heart, filling her with love, and she sobbed with the joy and beauty of her child's soul. Gina, she cried. *My sweet baby.* Then it left her and disappeared with the others.

"You fool!" Sutton screamed. He advanced toward her, but before he could reach her she swung the bat again, this time crashing into the container filled with the black buglike crea-tures.

Thunder crashed and boomed. The screech of banshees filled the room along with the stench of rotten flesh and virulent evil.

The black souls clustered and spun in a tight circle. The circle of the souls grew larger and began to move. The air in the laboratory darkened and lightning sizzled and sparked all around.

Sutton backed away from the swirling mass of inhumanity at the same time the bald man turned and raced up the basement stairs.

"What's happening?" Kathleen cried as Lucas grabbed her by the arm and began to pull her toward the stairs.

"They have no place to go. The children's souls have returned to their bodies and now the evil ones have nowhere to go. Come on, let's go find Gina and get the hell out of here."

He pulled her toward the stairs, but before they could start their ascent, Sutton screamed, an inhuman scream of sheer terror.

They watched in horror as the circle of souls surrounded Sutton, screeching and shrieking, they circled him faster and faster, spinning so fast it was like a black cloud swallowing Sutton whole. Above the screeching and shrieking, they heard Sutton howling. The circle of souls got smaller and smaller and smaller until there was nothing left of Sutton and no more cloud of souls.

Thunder boomed through the house and an ominous crackle of wood beams spurred them into action. They raced up the stairs and discovered that the roof of the cabin was on fire, apparently struck by lightning.

The air was thick with black smoke and the roar of flames out of control. Kathleen was vaguely aware of other people running past them to escape. "Get out," Lucas said, trying to shove her in the direction of the door. "I'll find Gina."

"No, I'll help." There was no way Kathleen was leaving this place without her baby. Together, choking on smoke, aware that at any moment the roof could come down, they ran from room to room, frantically calling Gina's name.

Intense heat seared them and the smoke made breathing

painful, but neither would give up the search for Gina.

Kathleen pictured Gina locked in a room like the one Kathleen herself had been held in. She wouldn't be able to escape through the barred window. She would die of smoke inhalation or worse.

"Gina!" The scream ripped from her burning throat over and over again.

"She's here," Lucas said and banged on a locked door. "Gina, can you hear me?" he yelled through the door.

"I hear you," a faint voice replied.

"Stand back from the door, honey." Lucas slammed his body, shoulder first, into the door. Again and again, he punished himself against the wood until it sprung open with a snap.

Gina ran into his arms. He picked her up and together he and Kathleen ran for the exit. They exploded out of the burning house and into a dawn breathtakingly beautiful.

There was no hint of the storm they'd believed had raged outside while they struggled in the basement, no aftermath of the storm Kathleen had driven through to get here.

Lucas pulled her to him and they hugged, Gina between them. Kathleen began to weep, unable to staunch the emotions she'd kept in check for too long. "Shhh," he said gently. "It's all over. You're safe now and you and Gina don't have to be afraid anymore."

They all turned to look as the cabin's roof caved in, shooting flames skyward and transforming the entire building into a complete inferno. They could hear the sirens of local fire engines approaching.

"Come on," Lucas said. "Let's get out of here."

Chapter Twenty-six

Kathleen's car was where she had left it, and she was grateful that she'd been in such a hurry to get inside the cabin and find Gina that she'd left the keys in the ignition.

Lucas drove and for the first hour of the trip, Kathleen held Gina in her lap. Safety rules be damned. She needed to hold her daughter close, feel the steady beating of Gina's heart against her own.

They drove in silence, as if too weary, too overwhelmed to speak. She stroked Gina's hair, surprised to discover that already the entire ordeal was beginning to feel like a horrible nightmare.

"That wasn't my daddy," Gina said, finally breaking the silence. "He looked like my daddy, but he wasn't really him." She looked up at Kathleen, her green eyes far too somber, far too wise for her age. "He fooled me for a little while. He fooled me and made me go through the tunnel. But then I knew he was a bad man and my daddy is dead."

She yawned. "A pretty lady named Belinda tried to help me get away, but they caught us." She yawned again. "Can I get in the backseat now? I think I want to go to sleep."

Although Kathleen was reluctant to let her go, she knew the best way to help Gina was not to hold too tight. She helped her into the backseat, where Gina fell asleep almost instantly.

"He intended to release the black souls into the children, didn't he?" she said softly.

Lucas nodded. "It would have been the beginning of the Apocalypse. Evil would have reigned on earth and everything good would have been lost." He turned his head and smiled at her, his eyes holding a weariness that was almost tangible. "But you foiled his plan."

She nodded and stared out at the blue skies overhead. "Is it really over?"

"Yes, it's really over."

She looked at him once again. Even with a split lower lip and a face covered with soot, he looked beautiful to her. "How can you be so sure?"

"I just know."

"Like you just knew Gina's name and where we lived? Like you just knew we were in trouble and needed your help?"

"Yeah, something like that." He stared out the window and continued. "I thought the strange powers I sensed growing inside me were in preparation for a final confrontation, a battle between myself and Thanatos for the souls. But you were the one who had to fight Thanatos."

"I couldn't have done it without you. Together we were strong. Together we made the power we needed to destroy Thanatos. I might not have made the right choice without you." She sighed. "I can't believe that Theresa is gone." A piercing grief swept through her as she thought of the woman who had been her friend for so many years. Why hadn't Theresa come to her? Talked to her about her illness? Her heart ached with an emptiness where a friendship had been.

"I should have guessed that she was dreadfully ill. She looked so horrible the last couple of times I saw her." Kathleen blinked back tears of regret and sadness for her childhood friend—the woman who had ultimately betrayed her. But that hadn't been the Theresa she knew, she told herself. That had been the actions of a sick, desperate woman.

"He promised to cure her. He promised if she did as he asked and brought Gina to him, he would make her well again."

She swiped a tear that had escaped from her eye. "But he lied."

"He was a master of lies and deceit."

"Saints become sinners and sinners become saints."

He looked at her curiously. "What do you mean?"

"Theresa betrayed us and tried to embrace the darkness and you heard what Gina said: It seems that Belinda rejected the darkness and at the last minute tried to embrace the light."

"I saw Belinda as we were trying to find Gina. She got out of the house alive," he said. "She tried to save Gina, but I don't think we'll ever see her again."

They fell silent. The smooth hum of the tires of the car combined with her exhaustion and Kathleen fell into a deep sleep.

It wasn't until the car came to a halt that she awakened, shocked to see they were parked in her driveway.

Lucas carried a still-sleeping Gina upstairs and put her in her bed, then joined Kathleen out in the hallway. "You look done in," she said. "Why don't you take a shower and get into bed."

He nodded. "That sounds like a wonderful idea," he agreed. "And we'll talk after I nap for a little while."

"All right." She watched as he disappeared into the guest bath. What would happen now between them? The danger was over and for the first time she was faced with what she hoped would be a very mundane, normal kind of life. And she desperately wanted Lucas to be a part of that life.

When she heard the sound of his shower water turning on, she went into the master bathroom and turned on the water for a shower of her own.

She would have loved to join him in his shower, to feel the warmth of his clean, naked body against hers, to see the shine of love in his eyes.

But what she'd seen in his eyes just before he'd turned to go into the guest bathroom was distance—as if he had one foot in her life, but already had the other foot out.

He was just tired, she tried to tell herself as she climbed in beneath a hot spray of water. Surely they hadn't gone through all this together, survived everything they had just to part ways and tumble through another lifetime in an attempt to get it right.

However, if there was one thing she'd learned over the past twenty-four hours, it was to take nothing for granted. There was nothing she could do now but wait to see if they were destined to be together in this lifetime.

Rosalyn Kelly sat by her husband's hospital bed, trying to think of yet another new prayer, one that might finally be heard. She'd said every prayer she'd ever learned when Sharon had been stricken by the mysterious illness, and now she prayed for her husband's soul as well.

The battering he'd taken was still evident on his face. One eye was blackened and swollen, and his skin was mottled with bruises. The pristine sheet covered the rest of his wounds, wounds the doctor assured her would heal and fade with time. What wasn't certain was when—or if—he would finally find his way out of the coma that had claimed him.

She alternated her time between the two hospital rooms. When she sat beside Sharon, she sang childish songs and spoke of springtime and bunnies and ballet lessons. When she was with Keith, she read him articles from the newspaper and whispered of lovemaking and Sunday morning brunches and all the things she knew he enjoyed.

It never entered her mind to give up hope, to lose faith. Hope and faith were all that were left to her and she knew once those were lost, then she would curl up and die.

She now had two lights on in the house at all times, the little pink lamp in Sharon's bedroom and the desk light in Keith's office.

"As soon as you get well, we'll take Sharon and go to the mountains," she said to her sleeping husband. "We'll go to that little place where we spent our honeymoon. Remember the cabins and how the chipmunks would come right up to us and eat peanuts out of our hands?"

"Nearly bit my finger off."

For a moment she thought she'd fantasized him speaking. He hadn't moved. His eyes were still closed and she wondered if perhaps she was finally losing her mind.

"What did you say, dear?" she asked, trying to remain as calm as possible.

"I said one of those damned chipmunks nearly bit my

finger off." His eyes opened and he tried to smile, but it quickly transformed into a grimace.

"Keith. Oh, Keith." Tears sprang to her eyes and she fought the impulse to throw herself against him.

"Don't cry, sweetheart." His voice sounded rusty, and he was obviously in pain.

"Let me ring for the nurse," she said, swiping the tears that had fallen.

"No . . . wait . . . ." He stopped her before she could push the button. "You have to do something right now."

"What?"

"Go to Sharon."

"I just came from her room a little while ago." She wished she had something better to tell him, but knew the truth would hurt whether she told him now or later. "Keith, honey, there's been no change with Sharon."

He struggled to sit up, obviously growing agitated. "Go to her now, Rosalyn. Run. Run to Sharon . . . hurry!"

Something in his voice, the urgency, the certainty, made her twirl on her heels and run. She raced down the hallway to the elevator that would carry her up to where Sharon's room was located.

When the elevator seemed to be taking too long, she took the stairs two at a time, driven by the need to do as Keith said. She flew into Sharon's doorway and halted. Nurses whose bodies hid Sharon from her sight surrounded the bed.

Dear God, had she died? Had the coma deepened into death? Rosalyn released a deep, wrenching sob, the sound of which drew one of the nurses' attention.

She turned and smiled. "Ah, here's mama now. We were just going to call for you." She stepped aside and gestured Rosalyn closer to the bed.

There sat Sharon. She smiled at Rosalyn, that beautiful childish smile Rosalyn hadn't seen for an eternity. "Hi, Mommy. I'm hungry."

"Sharon. My baby, Sharon." Rosalyn reached out and gathered her daughter in her arms and cried with the joy of miracles.

Kathleen stood at the French doors and watched Gina and Lisa play in the garden. They were having a tea party, and half of Gina's dolls and stuffed animals had been invited.

It was a gorgeous afternoon. The horrid heat that had marked the summer until now was gone, and there wasn't a storm cloud anywhere in the sky.

Had that awful heat been part of Thanatos's hold on the earth? She'd had all afternoon to think about what had happened at the cabin the night before. In her heart, she knew that what she'd faced had been evil.

Sutton had been the embodiment of evil. He'd spoken of his father and his grandfather before him, and she thought perhaps they had in their lifetimes attempted to bring about the Apocalypse just as Sutton—Thanatos—had done in this lifetime.

She also believed that Sutton had been devoted to Gina because he had known at her birth that she would be his ultimate sacrifice.

She turned from the window and squealed in surprise as she saw Lucas standing in the doorway of the living room. "Sorry, I didn't mean to startle you," he said with a smile.

"It's all right. I'm probably going to be a little jumpy for several days."

"Thanks for the clean clothes." He entered the room and sat on the sofa.

She nodded. While he had slept she'd taken his clothes and thrown them into the washer and dryer, then had hung them on his bedroom door. "You look better," she said as she sat next to him.

He touched the split in his lower lip. "I guess I'll be one of the walking wounded for a couple of days."

She smiled. "It gives you a decidedly rakish look." Her smile fell and she gazed at him intently. "What happens now, Lucas?"

He leaned back against the sofa cushion and swiped a hand through his rich, dark hair. "I'm thinking maybe it's time I put my magic hat and wand away. I miss being a carpenter, working with my hands. What about you? What are you going to do?"

She knew then that he saw their futures separately and an ache awakened in her heart. "I'm going to sell this place." She hadn't realized she'd reached that decision until the words came out of her mouth.

"Maybe I'll buy a cute fixer-upper and hire me a carpenter to help with the work." She knew her heart was in her eyes for him to see.

He frowned and abruptly stood. He raked a hand through his hair once again. "Kathleen." Her name was a protest on his lips.

"What?" She stood and faced him. "I love you, Lucas."

He winced, as if her words caused him enormous pain. When he looked at her again his eyes were as dark and tortured as she'd ever seen them.

"You fell in love with a magician, a man with powers who had come to save your daughter. But I'm no longer that same man. The powers are gone, Kathleen. I can't help you anymore."

"Help me? I don't want you to help me, Lucas." She placed a hand on his arm, felt the warmth of him through the fabric of his shirt sleeve. "Sutton helped me. Bill helped me. They both took care of me as if I were an imbecile who couldn't be trusted to make any decisions, live my own life. I'm a different person than I was. I don't want you to help me, I want you to love me."

He stepped away from her, as if he couldn't stand her touch. "I just think it's best if I go. You and Gina will be all right." He started for the doorway but halted when she called his name.

"The power you had, Lucas, was the power that grew through our love for each other. It was a gift from Heaven to help us fight Thanatos, but more importantly it was a gift to us so that we would finally get things right in this lifetime together."

"It's over, Kathleen. It's done." His voice sounded weary, resigned.

"Lucas, don't you see? If you leave now, nothing changes. The gift of the powers means nothing. It's you walking away. You told me that the reason we keep tumbling through lifetime after lifetime is because we never got it right, because I always rejected you. This isn't me rejecting you, this is you leaving me."

Tears dampened her lashes and she swiped at them impatiently. "Maybe our past lives were ruined because you were too afraid to fight for me, because you were afraid to fight for us. Maybe it was never me at all who ruined things for us. Maybe it's been you all along."

"Goodbye, Kathleen," he said softly, then turned and strode away. A moment later she heard the sound of the front door opening, then closing.

That sound echoed in every chamber of her heart and opened the floodgates of her tears. Lucas, her heart cried out. *Lucas, I love you.*

She allowed herself her tears only for a moment, not wanting to be watery-eyed if Gina should come inside. The house resonated with an emptiness that hadn't been there since Lucas had arrived.

She went to the French doors and once again looked out at the two little girls playing make-believe. Was that what she and Lucas had been doing? Playing make-believe? Had their love been something manufactured by the danger that had surrounded them?

No. There was nothing resembling pretend in her heart. Lucas was in every part of her and would remain there for a very long time to come.

She jumped as the phone rang. Maybe it was him. Maybe he was calling to tell her he had been a fool and he was on his way back to her and to Gina where he belonged.

She grabbed up the phone. "Lucas?"

"Kathleen?"

She instantly recognized the feminine voice. "Hi, Rosalyn. How's Keith?"

"It's a miracle." The woman's voice bubbled with life. "He woke up this morning and so did Sharon. They both just opened their eyes and there they were."

"Oh, Rosalyn, I'm so happy for them . . . for you." A bittersweet joy rushed through Kathleen.

"We're a family again, Kathleen. It's truly a miracle."

The two women spoke for another few minutes, then hung up. Kathleen's heart was filled with joy for Keith and Rosalyn and Sharon. They were a family again.

However, her happiness for them simply deepened her

own heartache. She'd hoped that she and Lucas and Gina would be a family. But it would seem that once again in this lifetime it had gone all wrong.

Lucas had intended to walk to the bus stop that would take him to the train station, but he found himself on the beach where he had come on the night he'd thought about leaving Kathleen and Gina.

He sat down on the soft sand and stared out at the water as the sun set behind him. Leaving Kathleen had been the most difficult thing he'd ever done, but surely it had been the right thing.

His powers were gone and he was once again just a second-rate magician with parents who had come to tragic ends. He'd made the decision a year ago when his father died that he would never marry, that he would live his life alone. But at that time he hadn't anticipated meeting Kathleen; he hadn't anticipated loving Kathleen.

Kathleen, who had rejected him lifetime after lifetime. Kathleen, who had wrapped him around her heart, then cast him aside. He waited for the anger that always accompanied such thoughts.

It was the anger that frightened him. He remembered now the killing rage that had come upon him in Sutton's office, a rage directed at her for lifetimes of pain.

Maybe it was never me who ruined things for us. Maybe it was you all along. If you leave now then nothing changes. The gift of the powers means nothing. Her words played and re-played in his mind as the night began to usurp the last of the day's light.

Where was the anger, the fury? He loved her too much to

stay and take a chance that one day his feelings would rage out of control and he would hurt her.

Just as Thanatos physically attacked you with a sand storm right here in this spot, he mentally attacked you by filling you with anger directed at the woman you love.

He stood and brushed off the seat of his pants. Was it possible? Was it possible that the anger had never been a real emotion of his own, but rather another tool in the battle between good and evil?

Had Kathleen been right? Was he the one who had to act differently in this lifetime to stop their endless pain?

Stars began to appear overhead, blanketing the dark sky with their brilliant twinkling. They had flown among the stars, and their spirits had made love in the Heavens. She had filled him up as he had never been filled before and he had turned his back on her and run.

"Fool," he muttered. If he walked away from Kathleen and Gina, Thanatos would get the last laugh. He would have successfully destroyed the love that was destined to be, a love that Lucas now realized he didn't want to live without.

"Thanatos," he yelled and waited to see what happened.

Nothing.

No boom of thunder, no spark of lightning. No sand storm, no visions, nothing happened. Thanatos was dead, carried to the underworld by angry, black souls.

And Lucas was alive and in charge of his own destiny. All he had to do was decide whether that destiny was with Kathleen . . . or without her.

"I had fun today, Mommy," Gina said as Kathleen tucked her into bed. "Lisa is my bestest friend."

"I'm glad, honey." Kathleen smoothed Gina's dark hair

from her face and thought of how close she'd come to losing her forever. "Are you going to be able to sleep okay?"

Gina nodded. "I'm not afraid anymore. The bad man and the tunnel are gone, and I don't think they'll ever come back." She frowned. "Is Lucas coming back?"

The question pierced through Kathleen's heart. "I don't think so, honey."

"I loved him," Gina said softly.

"I know, sweetheart. So did I."

"He would have made a good daddy."

Tears pressed precariously at Kathleen's eyes. "I know, but we'll be okay without him, won't we?"

Gina nodded, then reached up and hugged Kathleen around the neck. "I love you, Mommy."

"I love you, too." She got up from the bed. "Now, get a good night's sleep and tomorrow we'll spend the day at the beach."

"Oh boy!" Gina dutifully closed her eyes. "I'm sleeping already."

Kathleen laughed, then left the bedroom and went back downstairs. It was too early for bed, but she had no desire to watch television. She wandered around the living room, mentally choosing the items she'd take when they moved. Most of the furniture she decided she would sell in an auction. There was very little from this place she wanted as a reminder in a new life.

A new life. She would buy a cozy little house that felt like a home and fill it with comfortable furniture that portrayed warmth. She'd go back to her teaching job, and Gina would get on with her normal childhood. They'd be fine.

It would only be in the dark hours of a lonely night that she would allow herself to think of what might have been with Lucas. It would only be in the dark hours of a lonely night that she might allow herself to cry for him.

The doorbell rang and she hurried to answer. He looked much like he had that first night he'd appeared on her doorstep. Dark and mysterious and wonderfully handsome, the sight of him made her heart leap to life.

"Hello, my name is Lucas Connelly and I'm here to apply for the job as a carpenter."

"Lucas." She threw herself into his arms and he wrapped her up in a near crushing full-body hug. She leaned her head back to look at him and his mouth found hers, kissing her with a hungry abandon that sent waves of love rippling through her.

"You came back," she said breathlessly when the kiss ended.

"I refuse to do this all again in another lifetime," he said with a gentle teasing tone. "I'd prefer we get it right once and for all."

"Why did you leave? What were you afraid of?" She looked at him searchingly as they walked over to the sofa.

They sat side-by-side and he took one of her hands in his. "Every time I got a vision or had a dream about a past life, I became filled with rage. That night that I was in Sutton's office alone, I felt the blackest, most horrible wrath toward you that I could ever feel. It scared me. I didn't want to take a chance of hurting you or Gina."

"Then what brought you back?"

He smiled, and for the first time she saw that his eyes were a warm chocolate brown with tiny gold flecks. "I think Thanatos sent that anger to me and now that he's gone for good, so is my rage."

He stood and pulled her back up into his arms. "I want

you, Kathleen. I want to marry you and I want the three of us to be a family. I love you and Gina with all my heart, all my soul, but you have to understand it will never be the same."

"What do you mean?" she asked.

"We'll never make love in the Heavens again. I've lost the power to astral project, I've lost the power to get inside you."

"You are inside me, Lucas." She took his hand and placed it over her heart. "You're right here, inside me. And each time you hold me in your arms, every time you make love to me, I feel as if I'm in Heaven. Don't you see, Lucas, you don't need any magical powers to win my heart. You already own it. We have the strongest magic anyone could possess; we have the magic of love."

"I love you," he said with a groan and once again his lips covered hers in a kiss that sparked with magic, that tingled with love and that promised a lifetime together.

In this lifetime they had finally gotten it right.

KATHLEEN NANCE
THE WARRIOR

Callie Gabriel, a fiercely independent vegetarian chef, manages her own restaurant and stars in a cooking show with a devoted following. Though she knows men only lead to heartache, she can't help wanting to break through Armond Marceux's veneer of casual elegance to the primal desires that lurk beneath.

Armond returns from an undercover FBI assignment a broken man, his memories stolen by the criminal he sought to bring in. His mind can't remember Callie or their night of wild lovemaking, but his body can never forget the feel of her curves against him. And even though Callie insists she doesn't need him, Armond needs her—for she is the key to stirring not only his memories, but also his passions.

___52417-1 $5.99 US/$6.99 CAN

THE TRICKSTER

KATHLEEN NANCE

Long after she's given up on his return, Matthew Mark Hennessy strolls back into Joy Taylor's life, bolder than Hermes when he stole Apollo's cattle. But Joy is no longer the girl who had so easily trusted him with her heart. An aspiring chef, she has no intention of being distracted by the fireworks the magician sparks in her. But with a kiss silkier than her custard cream, he melts away her defenses. And she knows the master showman has performed the greatest trick of all: setting her heart afire.

Mark has traveled to Louisiana to uncover the truth, not to rekindle an old passion. But Joy sets him sizzling. It is not her cooking that has him salivating, but the sway of her hips. And though magicians never divulge their secrets, Joy tempts him to confide his innermost desires. In a flash Mark realizes their passion is no illusion, but the magic of true love.

More Than Magic
Kathleen Nance

Darius is as beautiful, as mesmerizing, as dangerous as a man can be. His dark, star-kissed eyes promise exquisite joys, yet it is common knowledge he has no intention of taking a wife. Ever. Sex and sensuality will never ensnare Darius, for he is their master. But magic can. Knowledge of his true name will give a mortal woman power over the arrogant djinni, and an age-old enemy has carefully baited the trap. Alluring yet innocent, Isis Montgomery will snare his attention, and the spell she's been given will bind him to her. But who can control a force that is even more than magic?

___52299-3 $5.99 US/$6.99 CAN

Midnight Kisses

KIMBERLY RAYE

Get Ready for . . . The Time of Your Life!

Smooth, sensual, fantastic skin that begs to be tasted—Josephine Farrington just re-invented it. The new plastic is great for making lifelike toys, but she has a better idea: making a man. Tired of the pushy jerks that court her, Josie can now design the bronze-skinned, hard-muscled exterior of a robo-hunk that can fulfill all her deepest fantasies. And she knows just the man to build the body.

Matthew Taylor never had trouble erecting anything, and the handsome scientist knows that Josie's robot is something he can create. But the beautiful biochemist deserves better than the cold devotion of a machine; she needs the fiery embrace of a real man. In an instant, Matt knows his course: by day he vows to build her model of masculine perfection—by night he swears to be it.

___52361-2 $5.99 US/$6.99 CAN